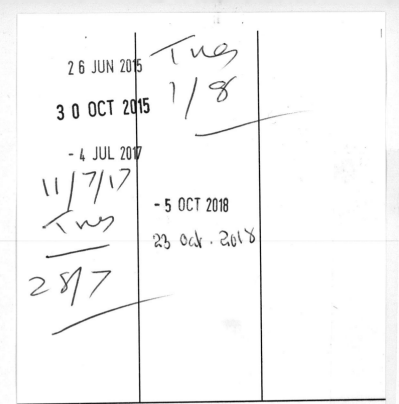

SET ME FREE

Daniela Sacerdoti

BLACK & WHITE PUBLISHING

First published 2015
by Black & White Publishing Ltd
29 Ocean Drive, Edinburgh EH6 6JL

1 3 5 7 9 10 8 6 4 2   15 16 17 18

ISBN: 978 1 84502 951 7

ALBA | CHRUTHACHAIL

A CIP catalogue record for this book is available from the British Library.

An Eala Bhàn (The White Swan) by Donald MacDonald of Coruna courtesy of
Comann Eachdraidh Uibhist a Tuath (North Uist Historical Society).

Typeset by Iolaire Typesetting, Newtonmore
Printed and bound by Nørhaven, Denmark

In memory of Bill Walker, much loved and never forgotten.

And in memory of Fraser Christison:
Now you've seen
The whole of the moon.

Recipes from *Set Me Free*
are available to download free at
danielasacerdoti.co.uk
and
danielasacerdoti.com

ACKNOWLEDGEMENTS

This book was written through dark times, and I'm so thankful to the people who kept me going, who rooted for me and made me laugh even in the worst moments. Thank you Ross, Beth, Irene, Francesca, Edo, Alessandra, Alison Green, Joan and to my mum: I don't know where I'd be without you all. And to the others who understood and kept me afloat: thank you; you know who you are. Also, thanks to the team around my writing, everyone at Black & White and Campbell Brown in particular for understanding a writer's ups and downs. To my editors, Kristen, Karyn and the beautiful, warm, wonderful Janne, whose hard work means that my books can now be read in twelve languages. Thank you to Acair for allowing me to reproduce 'The White Swan', a poem that has always inspired me.

Thank you to my new agent Ariella Feiner, and I raise a glass to my former agent Charlotte Robertson, who's moved on to great things – thank you, from the bottom of my heart, to you both.

A special thank you to Ivana Fornera, Rosa Frison and Flavia Spinello for helping me give you the best versions of Margherita's traditional recipes.

My musical thank yous are a bit short this time – while working on this book I only listened to *Hebrides*, a beautiful composition by Donald Shaw that makes me dream of wind and sea and frees my spirit. So thank you, Donald.

Thank you, thank you, thank you to my readers and to

the bloggers all over the world for loving Glen Avich and its people. I'm so glad I can take you there with me and I'm so grateful for your support of my storytelling

Finally, most of all, thank you to my husband Ross and to my little boys, Sorley and Luca, my sky and my sun: it's all for you – *all* of it, down to every breath I take. And Sorley, sorry, but as fun as it sounded, I haven't been able to weave an abduction by aliens into this Glen Avich book – maybe the next?

Daniela

An Eala Bhàn (The White Swan)
By Donald MacDonald of Coruna

Sad I consider my condition
With my heart engaged with sorrow
From the very time that I left
The high bens of the mist
The little glens of dalliance
Of the lochans, the bays and the forelands
And the white swan dwelling there
Whom I daily pursue

Maggie, don't be sad
Love, if I should die
Who among men
Endures eternally?
We are all only on a journey
Like flowers in the deserted cattle fold
That the year's wind and rain will bring down
And that the sun cannot raise

All the ground around me
Is like hail in the heavens
With the shells exploding
I am blinded by smoke
My ears are deafened
By the roar of the cannon
But despite the savagery of the moment
My thoughts are on the girl called MacLeod

Crouched in the trenches
My mind is fixed on you, love
In sleep I dream of you
I am not fated to survive
My spirit is filled
With a surfeit of longing
And my hair once so auburn
Is now almost white

Good night to you, love
In your warm, sweet-smelling bed
May you have peaceful sleep and afterwards
May you waken healthy and in good spirits
I am here in the cold trench
With the clamour of death in my ears
With no hope of returning victorious
The ocean is too wide to swim.

Courtesy of Comann Eachdraidh Uibhist a Tuath (North Uist Historical Society).

PROLOGUE

The boy who didn't come home

1916, Glen Avich

I was eighteen when I went to war. Many of us came from Glen Avich: men, and boys too. Mothers and girlfriends and wives and sisters and daughters cried as we went. We didn't dwell on the fact that some of us would not make it back; we knew, but we just didn't think about it. I, for one, would certainly return. I was so young I felt immortal, immune to the laws that rule the rest of humanity.

The journey from Glen Avich to Edinburgh, where we would be put on trains and sent south, and then further on towards the battlefields of Europe, seemed endless. Most of us had only ever gone as far as the next village, on foot or by bicycle. We stuck together, us Glen Avich men, pretending to be unfazed by our destiny unfolding, pretending that war didn't frighten us. We were given boots; they were heavy to walk in, they seemed indestructible. Little did we know how flimsy those boots would turn out to be after endless walks in the mud and snow, how sore and bloody our feet would become and how cold they would get as the ice seeped through our flesh and turned it blue. Little did we know about the gas that tears your lungs, about the shrapnel that tears your flesh, about how it feels to see grown men cry and call for their mothers. We knew nothing of all that, yet.

1

We stood in a little cluster, surrounded by men and boys from all over Scotland, some speaking English, some Gaelic. Women and children were there, too, accompanying their husbands, fathers, sons. Promise and hope hung in the air. We would all be back victorious, the propaganda promised us. The war would be short, and we'd be fighting for the greater good. A quick campaign, and we would be back home, crowned in glory.

But some of us knew that nothing comes without time and toil; some of us suspected that there would be a higher price to pay than we'd been told. It was a thought in the back of our minds, an omen of much pain to come.

When the trains took off, the women and children waved and cried at the edge of the tracks. It was goodbye to Scotland. But of course I would be back, of course I would not die. I would see it through. Barbed wire and mines and gas and trench fever, they would not stop me from making it back. Nothing could stop me from going home.

We saw foreign faces and heard foreign languages as we travelled south; it was the first time I had been among people who were not my own. Soon I would meet the enemies, and the rifles we'd been given would be used to injure and kill them. I'd only ever killed animals to be put on our table, and I wondered what it would be like to look into the eyes of a dying man, knowing that I'd been carrying the scythe that ended him.

I lay awake at night listening to the rattling carriages, trying to dispel the images of fallen men from my head: men who would die at my hands. We all would kill, and some of us would be killed. Was the die cast for each of us? Was it already decided, who would make it back and who would be buried under a foreign sky? Around my neck there was a little chain with a medal of St Christopher, the patron saint of journeys; my mother had given it to me the night before I left. I held the chain in my hand as I lay awake, and wondered if St Christopher knew who would drown and who would be saved.

So we went to a place that was cold, so cold, and there were no peat fires to keep us warm; a place where men and boys were shredded into pieces or gassed or lay fevered in muddy trenches. The threads of destiny were woven for each and every one of us, for the ones who would make it home, and for the ones who would never see Glen Avich again.

1

Miracle

Margherita

"I know I should make the best of a bad situation," my husband said a summer evening of three years ago, a few days after I'd told him I was pregnant, when our baby was barely a speck inside me. "But I can't help how I feel."

As I sat at the kitchen table in front of him, I found it impossible to wrap my head around the fact that he'd called our baby a *bad situation*. I rested a hand on my still-flat stomach, in an unconscious gesture of protection, and didn't say anything, not then. I knew that if I opened my mouth at that moment I would not be able to control what came out and the conversation would turn into an argument in a matter of seconds.

After we adopted our daughter, Lara, Ash didn't want another child. But this baby had come along, unexpected like a bloom in winter, and there was nothing I could do – nothing I *would* do – to change that. I thought he would come round. I was sure he would. I was sure that as he saw my belly growing, as this baby slowly became a reality and not just two pink lines on a stick, he would accept him – or her. And then certainly he would grow to love this baby we'd made, whether he'd come to us by chance or by choice. Or by miracle, like I thought.

"It's all that comes with having a baby," he continued. "The sleepless nights, and our lives being turned upside down, and all that hard work. I'm forty-five, Margherita. I don't want all that any more."

"We *never* had it, Ash. We never had a baby before, so we don't really know how it's going to be," I managed to say, too overwhelmed with disappointment to articulate more. I could have screamed, *This is your baby! And you are a selfish, selfish bastard!* Looking back, I wish I had. Oh, how I wish I had, instead of sitting there in shock, half-mute. But I didn't know what was to come next; I still hoped that this was just fear talking and he would accept this baby in time.

I was wrong.

"Look," said Ash. "I see my colleagues with new babies. They come to work on three hours' sleep and their performance is affected. Everyone can see that."

"That's inconvenient," I muttered, thinking how it would feel to slap his face.

"Oh, Margherita, it's easy for you to be sarcastic, but we rely on this job. You aren't working. I've been carrying this family for years."

I took the stab in silence once again. I had left my job when we adopted Lara. Before she entered our lives, I had been a pastry chef and I worked long hours, often into the night. Once Lara arrived, a six-year-old with a traumatic past, she needed me so much – she needed stability more than anything. She clung to me with all her might – she wouldn't let me out of her sight, and every separation, even the smallest one, was overwhelming for her. Getting her used to her new school, to her new surroundings, to her new friends was a feat, and it took time and energy and an infinite amount of patience. Ash was never there; one of us had to be a consistent presence in her life. As much I loved being a stay-at-home mum, I missed my job and I resented being spoken to in those terms, as if somehow I didn't pull my weight. I bit my tongue, feeling that all my good intentions of not turning this into an argument were dissolving quickly. I wondered how long it would be before I exploded.

"Anyway. That's not the point. I see Steven and Bea and their sons. They have no time for themselves, their house is always a tip, they never go on a decent holiday because they're always broke."

Steven, Ash's brother, wasn't a happy man for sure, but it had nothing to do with the upheaval of having two little boys close together, I thought. He was simply one of those people unable to be happy, for some reason, and I'd long realised that Ash was the same. If that had something to do with having a controlling, hyper-critical mother – my not-so-dear mother-in-law – who'd suffocated them both all their lives, I can't tell. All I knew was that Ash and Steven were always unsatisfied, always squirming in their skins, as if they weren't that fond of the people around them, and themselves as well. I'd always felt protective of Ash because of this. I'd hoped he'd learn to love himself as much as I loved him, but it never happened.

Ash was forever seeking *something*, forever needing more – more success, a bigger house, a bigger car – and for this he'd work all hours of the day. I would have preferred fewer things, less status and more of his presence. He worked for a big insurance company with branches all over the world and he was climbing the ladder as quickly as he could. He just couldn't stop. Whenever he was doing family things with us he was restless, as if there was always somewhere else he'd rather be, and always checking phone and e-mail like a major deal would come along any minute and he would miss it if he ever relaxed.

That was Ash. And I used to love him.

I know it's a cliché, but I loved him from the moment I saw him, desperate to impress, with his floppy blond hair falling on his face. We were playing golf, of all things. I loathe golf: the dress code especially drives me up the wall – what's with the tartan trousers and the caps? But I was there for my sister Anna, who for some strange reason loves golf, and all other sports too. As for me, I'm hopeless when it comes to pretty much anything resembling exercise.

Anyway, I was twenty-five and nowhere near ready to settle down; Ash was ten years older and looking for someone. We were opposite in nearly every way, even in looks: I was small and Mediterranean, with my parents' Italian skin and dark-brown hair. He was tall and blond and thoroughly English. He was restless, I was peaceful; he was tense, I was serene. I think that in me he found peace; and in him I found a sense of purpose, of resolve, that was alien to me.

My dad always said I was the sun in my own solar system, self-sufficient and independent. Love took me by surprise. It ambushed me. I fell in love with Ash. I never thought I could love anyone as much as I loved him.

And now there we were, years later, discussing a baby that was all I'd prayed for and that for him was somehow an inconvenience.

My eyes searched his face. "I don't understand. Why is this so terrible? I know you didn't want any more children, but it's happened, and why can't we just get on with it and be happy?"

"Happy? Margherita, I'm forty-five. When this child is ten years old, I'll be fifty-five. When he's twenty—"

8

"Yes, I can do the maths," I said quietly. "A lot of people have children later in life. Especially men . . ."

"This was going to be our time to have some fun, Margherita. Go on holidays. See a bit of the world . . . What exactly can you do with a baby in tow?"

I couldn't quite take in the absurdity of what he was saying. Going on holidays? Having fun? We barely saw him. When he had a rare break from work, he went on golfing trips with his brother. When exactly was going to be our family time?

"Well, Ash, what do you want me to do? There were two of us when this happened," I said, gesturing to my belly. My jeans would soon be too tight, my breasts full and tender. "I didn't plan this, Ash. You know that. We thought it was impossible . . ."

"I know you didn't plan it. It was stupid of us not to take precautions. We should have done." He rubbed his forehead with his fingers and looked at me. I noticed with dismay that his clear blue eyes were hard, harder than I'd ever seen them. He was saying he didn't blame me, but his eyes told a different story.

"We didn't take any precautions for years, and it never happened," I said in a low voice. "We'd taken every test under the sun. Nobody knew why we weren't conceiving. This was a complete surprise." In spite of the circumstances, a little bubble of delight at my good luck burst inside my heart.

"Well, we don't have to just go with whatever happens," he said, his tone even, sensible all of a sudden. "We can make choices."

I felt cold.

"What choices?" I asked, hoping with all my being that he didn't mean what I thought he meant.

He looked down, as if he were ashamed to say it.

"There are other options, Margherita."

He saw my horrified face, and again he looked away. Suddenly my husband's familiar face looked that of an enemy's.

"Look, I'm sorry if that sounded harsh—"

I stood up and ran out of the room. The discussion was over. He didn't follow, like part of me hoped he would. He didn't run after me to say he didn't mean it, that it was okay, that we would raise this child together. All that followed was silence, as often happened with Ash. Silence. Like he never had enough time, enough energy to spare words for me.

Once upstairs in our bedroom, I stood in front of the window and breathed deeply to try to calm my pounding heart.

There are moments in life when a veil seems to drop from before your eyes and you can see things for what they are, not for what you'd always perceived them to be. A moment of clarity, of deeper understanding. This was one of them.

As I stood in my bedroom I looked around me. I considered how my husband had shaped everything I saw, from the right postcode to the expensive furniture, the two cars in the garage, the electronic gadgets I didn't even know how to use. And I realised there was no sign of me, of the real me, in this place I called my home.

On a warm evening of three years ago, when my son had barely started inside me, I saw how my life had fallen away from me and how it had been moulded around somebody else's needs and desires; I saw it as clearly as the waning moon that hung in the sky before me, yellow and bright in the twilight sky.

But the moment ended, and the clarity subsided, and habit took over again.

I lay sleepless for hours, wondering if when he spoke about choices, he really meant what I'd thought he meant – something I couldn't even put in words, something I couldn't even fully think about, only skirt around its terrible, terrible edges.

I wondered how Ash could think that this baby would make us broke. Or how having another child would suddenly mean him having to be at home more, as if having Lara ever kept him at home anyway. I would look after the baby, just like I looked after Lara, during his absences. It shouldn't have been this way, of course, but I didn't have a choice.

Yes, the discussion was over, and it would never take place again.

There were no other options for me.

A hairline crack had started in the love I felt for Ash – one of those fractures that are nearly invisible when they appear but have the potential to shatter and destroy all.

"Of course he'll come round," Anna reassured me as we sat in her conservatory with a cup of tea. Her home was only a few minutes from mine, somewhere so leafy and tranquil you would forget it was London. Relentless, freezing rain was falling from the pewter sky and flogging the glass. There were toys strewn everywhere around us in happy chaos. I loved my sister's home, messy, cheery, with friends dropping in for a chat and children on play dates with my youngest nephew. Anna had two boys: Pietro was eleven, Lara's age, and was already taller than me, and little Marco was only two.

"I hope so," I said, trying to convince myself. Maybe when he saw the first scan, or maybe when we found out the gender, or maybe when we bought the cot and he saw it up in the spare room that would become the nursery. Of course, sooner or later he'd have to come round. He would not be able to help loving this baby. Then maybe the cruel words he'd said to me two months before would just be a memory.

But a memory that would never fade.

"It's his baby. And he loves you," Anna said. "He will come round. He has to. I have all faith in him," she added, sounding somehow less convincing. I looked into Anna's face and I realised she was feeding me a kind lie. She was aware, just like me, that there was a chance Ash would never come round, never accept this baby. We both knew Ash well. We knew the secret side of him – his potential for coldness, for selfishness. For just not loving enough, or not loving at all. Maybe it was the defence mechanism of a child who hadn't been much loved himself, but whatever Ash's childhood traumas at the hands of his mother, this baby needed a father.

I took a sip of my tea, hoping it would stay down. I was now nearly three months gone. The morning sickness had been terrible, but I was too happy to care. I now had a tiny bump, small and tight. There was no way I could still wear my normal clothes any more, so I was wearing soft trousers with an elastic band at the waist and a white empire-line top. I felt beautiful – I kept looking at my profile in the mirror, marvelling at the changes in my body, marvelling at the roundness, the softness of it. My sister became enormous during her pregnancies – no offence to Anna – and I suspected the same would happen to me. Once I told her that if I ever wanted to jump out of a plane I could use her maternity bra as a parachute – she laughed until she got the hiccups. I was looking forward to my bump growing and I wanted to enjoy every minute of it.

"The three-month scan is next week. He's trying to wriggle out of it."

Anna's eyes widened. "What? What on earth is his excuse? OK, I understand he's not over the moon about all this, but it's his baby! He has to be there!"

"Well, he hasn't plainly said he doesn't want to go, not as such . . . but he's sort of saying he has a lot on, that the next few weeks are going to be very busy, that he'll try and be there but he's not sure he'll manage and blah blah blah . . . which could be true, I suppose."

"Right." Anna slammed the cup down on the coffee table so hard that some tea spilled out of it. She wasn't looking at me. She was trying to hide her anger, but I *knew*. "So he can't spare two hours for his pregnant wife. He must be really very *busy*." She spat the word.

"He is very busy. I know that. But I want him there. I need him there."

"He *must* be there!" Anna snapped.

When she's angry, my sister sounds like my mum; the hint of an Italian accent comes out and she starts gesturing wildly. The women in my family are very hot-tempered – I seemed to have skipped the temper gene, being quite easy-going most of the time. But when I get angry, I get *really* angry.

"When I see him I'll give him a piece of mind, I can tell you."

"Please don't. Honestly. Things are complicated enough at the moment."

"Someone has to give him a reality check, Margherita! He can't possibly think that his behaviour is normal! Or justifiable! How long have you been married? Ten years now? This is how he treats his wife of ten years, pregnant with her first baby? The guy needs to take a long, hard look at himself!"

Ash had clearly gone down in my sister's estimation. He didn't even have a name now. He was *the guy*. Short for *the guy who is rejecting his own baby*.

"I know. But please don't go in all guns blazing now. Don't go in at all, actually. I'll deal with it myself."

"How?"

"I don't know."

"I don't recognise you, Margherita. Why aren't you reading him the riot act? What's all this . . . submissiveness?"

"It's not submissiveness. You don't understand."

"What do you mean? I don't understand what?"

"I want him to decide for himself, Anna!" I snapped. "I need him to see for himself that he should come to the scan. Not because I shout at him, or you do, or because it's the decent thing to do. I need him to *want* to be there."

Anna sighed. "I see what you mean." A pause. "But he still needs a kick up his backside."

"I know." I looked out to the rain soaking my sister's garden, bouncing on Marco's slide and drenching abandoned toys.

It was all so different from the way I'd imagined my first pregnancy would be. In my mind, I'd have had two perfect children before I was thirty and Ash would adore them both. We'd have the ideal family. Back then, twenty-five and newly married, I was still to learn that you didn't order a family from a catalogue, picture-perfect and ready-made. The reality was something else entirely.

My reality has been years of infertility, a million tests, a difficult journey to become adoptive parents. And then Lara arrived, and that was when, all of a sudden, reality was better

14

than my dream, better than any ad-worthy family and perfect babies. Because after the years I'd spent trying to create a child that would not materialise, we'd found Lara, and Lara had found us. A child who needed a family and a family who needed a child. She came to us like a blessing. How could I ever wish for anything to be different? We'd chosen each other, and having Lara was, with all its difficulties and challenges, perfect.

I would have loved to adopt again, but Ash didn't want any more children. He simply said he was happy with his little family, that he didn't need anything else. And I went along with it without regrets or recriminations, because Lara filled me up. There would be no more trying to get pregnant, and no more long and convoluted adoption journeys. Just us: Lara, Ash and me.

And then, the two pink lines. Followed by another six tests, each with two perfect lines shining nearly fuchsia in their little windows.

My sister squeezed my hand. "Listen. If Ash doesn't come to the scan, I'll be there. You know that, don't you?"

I forced a smile. "Yes. Thank you."

"I don't know how long I can keep my mouth shut, though."

"That makes two of us."

Ash had to cancel some all-important meeting, but he came.

I was strangely calm as they spread a blob of slimy jelly on me and put the cold hand of the ultrasound arm on my stomach. And there it was, tiny and alien-like, with a huge head and minuscule arms and legs. A little fish swimming inside me. A human being growing inside me.

It was hard to believe, and still it was true.

I couldn't speak. I just stared at the screen and I couldn't stop smiling. I had to stop myself from reaching out and laying my fingers on the screen, in a strange impulse to feel those little hands. I turned towards Ash, and what I saw astonished me. He was smiling too. He was entranced, gazing at the screen.

He had sort of . . . thawed. I couldn't believe it as he began bantering with the sonographer, asking for three copies of the scan, to give his parents and my mum. He kept smiling as we walked out, clutching our baby's very first photograph.

"So. What do you think? Boy or girl?" he asked, squeezing my hand.

"I don't know. I don't even have a hunch. Really, I have no idea."

"I think it's another girl. A sister for Lara."

"Maybe. Who knows."

"Are you okay?" he asked as we were about to get into the car.

I slipped into the passenger's seat. "I think so."

Was I okay? I felt a bit wobbly. All of a sudden, before I realised what was happening, I burst into tears.

"Margherita, what's wrong?" Ash said, taking hold of my hand again.

"It's the hormones, I'm a bit emotional." Which was true. Honestly, pregnancy books could not warn you enough about how weepy you could get. I was moved to tears by just about everything.

But what was making me cry then wasn't the turbulent hormones, it was *relief*. Relief and joy, because for the first time my husband had shown something that wasn't regret and annoyance towards our baby. And he knew that. He knew why I was in tears.

"Margherita . . ." he began.

For a moment, I was afraid. Was he going to say something terrible again? Had I misunderstood his joy at seeing the baby on the scan? I held my breath.

"I just wanted to say . . . I'm sorry. For the way I reacted when you told me about this baby. To see her on the screen . . ." *Her?* I thought. What if it was a he? "I don't know. It just felt . . . right. I've been an idiot. I'm sorry."

For a while Ash was more attentive, and miraculously less busy, which was a first since I'd known him. He was home more, and he began to actually talk about the baby, to acknowledge its presence. We discussed little things, like what colour we'd paint the nursery, or if we should buy a cot or a Moses basket, what would be more comfortable for her. I noticed that he was always calling the baby *she*, and although there was a little pinprick of fear there – would he be disappointed if it was a boy? – I thought it was sweet. I didn't mind the gender and, unlike Ash, I didn't even have hunches. I just wanted the baby to be here, healthy and happy.

By the end of the third month, the sickness hadn't gone away at all and I was constantly exhausted. It was wonderful to be able to lean on Ash and not experience it by myself. I think it was the first time since we got together that I had been so dependent on him – me, usually so self-sufficient. Too independent at times, I suppose.

Meanwhile, Lara was going through a difficult time. Being eleven is hard enough – on the brink of a new era, and a tumultuous one – but with Lara's background, it was even harder. As my bump grew, she grew quiet, anxious. She followed me around everywhere like a puppy scared of being abandoned. On top of all her fears and worries, now she was afraid I'd love this baby more because it was 'mine'. She never said as much, but I knew. I could feel it in the words unspoken between us, in the way she looked at me when she thought I couldn't see her. That could never happen, of course – I would love the new baby just as much as I did her, but to love anyone more than I loved my Lara? That was impossible.

When she came into our world, Lara was withdrawn, full of grief for her earlier experiences. But she was brimming with strength and courage as well, a little fighter and a lover of life. I fell under her spell, this little creature who had changed many homes already, who was desperately looking for something to hang on to, something safe that would not change and sift through her fingers. I, for my part, was looking for someone to shower with all the love I had inside me and had nowhere to go.

Her real name was Laura, like my baby sister, but she asked to be called Lara, and she was so convinced, so forceful about it – as if she were renaming herself – that we went with it. Our social worker, Kirsty, wasn't keen on the name change and I could see why: so much of our sense of self is woven into the name we are given at birth.

"Unless there are safety issues, we prefer it if the adopted parents don't change the child's name. It can cause further trauma and loss of identity," she said. Kirsty had been a real ally in our quest for a child, at our side every step of the way, even if her workload was impossible and her job highly stressful. She'd trusted us all along, and we trusted her.

"I can imagine," I explained. "I would hate to have my name changed like that, all of a sudden. But it came from her; we didn't have a say in it. She didn't ask us to call her Lara. She *told* us to."

When she was interviewed by Kirsty, Lara made her point. "I am Lara Ward," she said, tapping a little foot on the floor in the perpetual motion of a six-year-old child.

"Is that a nickname you like, Lara?"

"It's not a nickname. It's my name. And this is my mum and dad. Their names are Margherita and Ashley Ward. And my gran makes cakes. She is from Italy, where there's a lot of sun. I'm going to learn to make cakes and open a shop and call it Lara's Bakery and Sweets." I was so touched; my mum and dad had a bakery in Hertfordshire called Scotti's (my family name) Bakery and Sweets. Lara had given herself a history; she had rewritten herself as part of our family already.

The next day Ash ordered a little wooden kitchen from a catalogue, and he painted Lara's Bakery and Sweets on it in big blue clumsy letters. Lara loved it and played with it for hours. He'd do little things like this, in the past. Not any more.

Reassuring Lara and nurturing her during my pregnancy took a lot of work, a lot of energy, a lot of time. I wanted to speak to her openly about her fears, but I didn't know how to broach the subject. Words seemed so clumsy in the delicate universe that was Lara, and words could be comets, bringers of doom.

I decided that there was no need to put her worries – and my reassurances – into words. I decided that the only way was to show her how strong my love for her was and always would be, and how she was my daughter through and through, whether I'd carried her or not.

Just before my four-month scan I took her for a day out, just the two of us. We went shopping, and then to the Tate gallery, a place she'd been enchanted with since the first time we'd taken her there. We stopped in front of one of her favourite paintings, *Mother and Child* by Sir William Rothenstein. She always stopped in front of it, contemplating the domestic scene full of quiet happiness. It portrays a mother sitting by a sunny window and holding her small son up in the air, a smile of contentment on both their faces. In the background there is a stone fireplace, a hearth – a safe, warm place that mother and child call home. The scene speaks of quiet domesticity and love.

"That's you and the baby," Lara said thoughtfully, without looking at me.

A heartbeat.

"That's me and you," I said.

"I didn't know you when I was that small." She was matter-of-fact about it, like it was an undeniable, if painful, reality.

My mind wrestled for a moment with the best words I could use to reassure her. I felt that it was a pivotal moment, one where the words said would be remembered and stored away. The truth came out in all its simplicity.

"But I've known you all my life. You were always in my dreams."

She slipped her hand in mine and stepped a little closer to me.

2

Leo

Margherita

At the four-month scan we found out I was carrying a boy. I was overjoyed, not because it was a boy as such – I would have loved a girl too – but because now I *knew* him. I felt like finally this little dream I was carrying inside me was real, a small human being in the making. We chose his name: Leo, after my father. I was in love already.

But for some reason only he knew, Ash started drifting away from us again. The babymoon was over. It happened slowly, over a few weeks. More meetings, more trips away, silence creeping between us like ivy up a wall. I had no energy to challenge him, to question him. I needed him as my belly grew bigger and I stepped into uncharted land – but he just wasn't there any more. The last five months were so hard, but something in me was resolute and focused. This baby was all that mattered, and my little Lara. I would be strong for them, no matter what.

"I don't know what's happening to him. I don't know why he's changed," I said to Anna. We were sitting at her kitchen table, Marco playing at our feet. "He seemed to have accepted it, he even seemed happy about it . . . oh, who is that? Is it for me?" Marco was handing me his toy phone.

"Yes! For Ziarita!" That was his nickname for me. *Zia*

meant 'auntie' in Italian, so *Zia* Margherita had become Ziarita, which never failed to make me melt inside. He was the only person in the world allowed to shorten my name.

"Hello? Is that Marco?"

"It sure is!" He threw his little chubby hands up in the air. Marco and Pietro had a hint of an American accent because their dad was from Colorado.

"Maybe it's just a phase," Anna offered.

"Maybe."

I agonised over Ash's change, but I couldn't bring myself to ask him what was wrong. I was too frightened to hear that what was really wrong for him was that he'd gone back to square one, and once again he didn't want this baby.

"Maybe he's nervous, that's all," she said unconvincingly. I could see she didn't believe what she was saying. "Marco, sit beside Ziarita, not *on* her. There, good boy. No room to sit on her lap any more. Paul was terrified when Pietro came along. You know, about becoming a father. But he was always there for us."

"Paul is a good man."

"And Ash isn't?" she said, and looked up to study my face.

Anna and I were very close – we had been all our lives – and I knew very well she had never been sure about Ash. She often said we were like two different species. I'd always known that, always, but it never worried me before. I was too in love to even suspect it could one day be an issue. His reaction to my pregnancy had completely thrown me – but I seemed to be the only one who was surprised. Anna certainly wasn't.

"Of course he is. You know that. It's just that he's never been like this."

"He wasn't that keen on adopting Lara, I seem to remember."

I felt my stomach churning. I didn't want to remember that. I'd wanted to forget how he'd resisted the process, how often I'd suspected he was only going along with it because of me. I'd been too hungry for motherhood to acknowledge it, to even admit it to myself. That stung. And it stung even more because it was true.

"I remember you telling me many times that he wasn't convinced about the adoption at all," she continued. "You seem to have removed this from your memory. Like you've pressed the delete button on it. Look, I'm sorry . . ." she said, seeing my face crumple. "I don't want to upset you."

"Ziarita? Look!" Marco had wiggled down from his little seat and was handing me a Spiderman costume.

"Oh, that's a fancy costume! Shall we put it on?" I busied myself slipping it on him, trying to hide my disquiet.

Anna was right. Ash had dragged his feet about adopting, although I didn't like remembering that. He eventually came round and embraced the idea, but right at the beginning he'd had his doubts.

"Better head back," I said, fighting back tears, and I rose to go.

Anna looked hurt. "Look, I'm sorry. Come on, stay for a little longer. Another slice of cake?" She gestured to the chocolate delight on the table.

With the amount of cake I was eating every day – it was the only thing that settled my stomach – I feared I wouldn't be able to move by the time I got to the end. I hadn't been very slim before either. Thankfully my sister dragged me on interminable walks – she walked, I waddled – to keep me trim. Although *trim* was the last thing you would have said about me right now. My bump sat comfortably on my small frame, making me look like a little Russian doll. My hair was shiny and thick and my skin was glowing, though: overall, pregnancy seemed to be kind on my looks.

"Come on, you're eating for two," Anna insisted.

"For five, more like." I sank my spoon back into chocolate heaven with only a hint of guilt.

Finally, the time had come. Come and gone. I was ten days late, fit to burst and completely fed up.

One night in April Lara and I were reading *The Hobbit* together, cosying up on the armchair in her room – I took up all the space, and she had to perch on the armrest – when I felt like a huge hand was squeezing my insides. A thin film of sweat settled on my forehead, and I knew.

Ash was in Liverpool on business, so I called Anna at once. She arrived in ten minutes flat, which was quite remarkable because her house was twenty minutes away by car. I'd rather not think *how* she managed that with her tiny Mini Cooper. We left Lara with my next-door neighbour, a kindly woman who had worked as a childminder and had a house full of children day in and day out, and off we went.

After hours of howling, kneeling on the floor and leaning on the hospital bed while contractions came thick and fast – I had long said goodbye to any remains of my dignity – Ash arrived. At last. He was white-faced and still in a suit and tie, more than a bit frayed around the edges. He went from white to green as I screamed and grunted and did all the unbecoming things that women do when they squeeze a human being out of their bellies. I cried a lot, mainly because it was all so painful and I'd never felt such agony before, but also because I was so completely overwhelmed by it all. It was just too . . . *enormous* an experience. My body was an alien thing, contracting and expanding and turning itself inside out. My birth plan had gone straight out of the window and I begged the midwife for an epidural – she smiled cheerfully and said it was too late. At that moment, I hated her with all my might. I briefly contemplated shaking her until she had no choice but to call the anaesthetist, but I couldn't sit up straight so I abandoned the idea. I cried some more, I screamed some more, I cursed some more, and someone, somewhere, said the head was out, and then the whole baby was. His cries filled the room, and it was finished.

I had done it.

They weighed him and wrapped him in a little blanket, and then they gave him to me. I cried some more – from happiness. He was perfect. He was Leo, with his little face and a mop of fine blond hair, and his little chubby fists and his scent – how I had dreamed of breathing in the scent of a baby of mine, a baby I had brought into this world! He was screaming, and he would not settle. I couldn't blame him: the birth, and the bright lights, and being whisked away to be weighed, and people talking all around – it had been quite a lot for him. His screams were surprisingly loud, somewhere between a kitten meowing and a siren. When he was in my arms, I held him in a haze of happiness, whispering soothing words, smiling like I would never stop smiling ever again.

"So what's his name?" the midwife asked.

"Leo," I said, and my father's name enfolded him like a blessing.

It seemed impossible that Ash would not fall for Leo too, and I turned to him in trust, and love, and gratefulness for having given me the gift of a son. I was expecting the same rapture painted all over his face.

I couldn't believe my eyes. Instead of shining with happiness, he was frowning as poor Leo cried. And then, as his eyes met mine briefly, he decided to put on his martyr face. His expression said it all: *I never wanted this child, but I'll do well by him, as it is my duty.*

At that moment, as I held Leo and slowly, slowly soothed him with my presence, my scent, my whispered words, I felt a part of my love for Ash leave me, painfully, inevitably. Like losing blood, I was losing love, pouring out of my heart and dissolving in the air between us. We sat in silence. All of a sudden, my husband seemed a stranger to me, and I wished he'd go and leave me alone with my son.

One night, not long after we'd come home from hospital, Lara came to sit beside me as I nursed Leo. She touched his head with infinite gentleness. Around him, Lara was like this little instinctive animal, geared to protect and nurture. After all my fears about how she'd take his birth, I was immensely relieved.

"I can't remember who I lived with when I was a baby," she whispered.

"You lived with several foster families, my love, until you went to Uncle Peter and Aunt Beth, who loved you very much." Peter and Beth were an older couple who had fostered Lara for two years after it was decided she couldn't go back to her father and that an adoptive family was needed. The social workers had done everything they could not to separate her and her dad, after Lara's mother's traumatic death when she was two. During those two years with Peter and Beth they looked for a suitable family until they found us. An older child with a difficult history can be hard to place, as opposed to babies and toddlers, who usually find a family relatively quickly.

"Yes, but I don't know who looked after me when I was a baby."

"Well, it was your mother for a while. And then other kind people ... Do you want me to ask Kirsty for their names? Would that help?"

She shrugged. "No point."

I was flooded with regret, the pointless, useless regret that it hadn't been me looking after her since the beginning. Because it felt that way, it felt like she'd been with us forever, that she was mine. Although she'd only been with us five years, it felt like that there could never have been a time in which we simply didn't know each other.

"They certainly did a good job, your foster parents. Look how lovely you are, how clever and smart and pretty."

Leo had stopped suckling and had fallen asleep at my breast. Lara rested a hand on his sleeping form, bundled up in blankets. "I'm happy Leo is here," she whispered.

"Yes. Lara and Leo. They sound good together, don't they?"

"Yes," she said with a little smile, but I could see the ever-present spark of sadness in her eyes.

3

A house of straw

Margherita

Leo was now two. I delighted in him, and so did Lara. She was fiercely protective of her little brother and showered him with love. Ash mainly ignored both of them.

To everyone else, my husband was a model father, coping with his daughter's issues and a demanding job. Behind closed doors, it was a different matter. Things weren't going well between us at all. He was distant, both in body and in soul, and I waned under his indifference, like my world was slowly being drained of colour.

Love was leaving us both, slowly and silently, and I hurt, I hurt.

And then Lara's father died suddenly. Among his belongings they found a picture of Lara's mum with Lara in her arms – it was the first photograph of Lara's mum I'd ever seen. Apparently her father had destroyed them all when she'd died.

When she saw the photograph, Lara said nothing.

"You have her eyes, Lara. Beautiful blue eyes," I said, my heart in my throat as I studied her solemn face.

"I know why she died."

"You do?"

"She killed herself. With pills."

I was speechless. Those words, so much bigger and darker than any child that age should contemplate. "Nobody knows for sure," I whispered. Which was true. Lara's mother had had a history of drug addiction, and it was unclear if she'd overdosed or if she'd decided she couldn't keep on living.

"I know she did."

"How do you know?"

"My dad told me. He said she left us because she didn't care and she didn't love me. That's why he burnt her photographs."

"That is not true. Your dad was talking nonsense. Your mum was a vulnerable person, Lara, but I am so sure she loved you. Really, I am."

"Why?"

"Because it's impossible not to love you. But she was ill, and it all got too much for her . . ." I felt compassion for that strange woman who'd had so much darkness inside her that she had ended her own life, though she had unleashed a chain of consequences that had damaged her daughter so much.

"She left me. What mother does that? I mean, you wouldn't leave Leo, would you?"

"No. And I wouldn't leave you."

"But she did."

"We don't know what went through her mind. You should forgive—"

"I can't forgive my mother," she interrupted, her words sharp and cold, and I was silenced by her rage. "I don't want to."

I reached out for her, but she'd taken a step back.

"If I keep being angry at her, I won't miss her as much," she explained, her mouth in a hard line, her eyes steely.

What else was there to say?

29

After that, she became very withdrawn again, just like she was when she'd arrived. She was so quiet we hardly ever heard her voice. What worried me the most was that the portions on her plate became smaller and smaller, and so did she. She was like a fawn, all long, slim limbs and huge eyes, beautiful and fragile. I took to mixing cream into her mashed potatoes, breaking an egg into her soup, baking brownies with extra butter, anything to give her some extra calories.

All throughout, Ash had no words for her, no time to help her.

He took her shopping a couple of times and she came back laden with bags of clothes, which she barely looked at. I tried to explain to Ash that she didn't need money spent on her, she needed tenderness. But it was like he didn't hear me.

I was at a loss. An American friend of mine, Sheridan, was a child counsellor. She agreed to see Lara privately. After a few months of sessions, Lara was speaking more, eating more and smiling again. Sheridan had a final chat with me. She said that Lara had been grieving, not so much for her father but for her mother. It had been the picture that triggered her distress more than the news of her father's death. And that was understandable, with all Lara had been through. With the way her dad used to be with her.

With the violence.

With each of Sheridan's words I felt I was sinker deeper into an icy pool. Ash and I didn't know about any violence; nobody had told us about it, not Lara herself, not the social workers. There was nothing in her dossier.

I phoned Kirsty and told her what Lara had confessed to Sheridan. Kirsty was silent for a moment.

"We knew that Lara had been terribly neglected by her

father, but we never saw signs of violence, and that is why this wasn't in her dossier."

"How could you not know, Kirsty?"

"It happens more often than you think: that nobody knows, not other members of the family, social workers, teachers. Violence can be very, very hard to spot; often bruises are hidden and there are no evident injuries."

At that point, I cried.

Bruises and injuries.

On my child's body. That little body I had nourished, looked after, washed and dressed with such love and devotion, somebody else had *hurt*. I was full of rage, a rage I could have never imagined I had the potential to feel.

I could not imagine anyone raising their hand to my daughter. I could not bear to think how she must have felt. A helpless, vulnerable child hurt by the person who should have loved her most.

A year passed and Lara seemed to improve. She kept the picture of her mum in her diary, and many times I'd seen her looking at it, studying it as if she could somehow get her back, bring her back to life, be reunited with her.

I could feel her heartbreak, I could feel the fury she carried inside her and had nowhere to go, a fury that must have been a thousand times stronger than mine. It was bound to spill out of her sooner or later, unstoppable, like a black flood. My heart bled for my daughter, and I held my breath, knowing in my bones that a storm was on the way.

And it came. One weekend, to my surprise, Ash decided to take the children for Sunday lunch at their grandparents' house, which was a very rare occurrence. Apparently, Harriet had *summoned* them. *Them*, not me. It was generally advisable for the two of us to avoid each other. My mother-in-law always thought her son had married down. After all, I was a daughter of humble bakers, Italian immigrants. It's a wonder they came to our wedding – in all photographs we took that day, Harriet looked like she was drinking curdled milk.

Later that day, Ash came home livid. He dropped Lara and Leo at the house without a word, ignoring my questions, and went for a drive. Lara looked mutinous and mortified at the same time, a tangle of emotions that I was left to deal with, and Leo was very pale and very quiet. I settled Leo in front of CBeebies so that Lara and I could talk.

"What happened?" I asked as she leaned on the kitchen island, her body language tense and unsettled.

"Well, Grandma was sort of horrible in general. She asked me if they teach us manners where I come from."

I gasped. The bitch!

"I couldn't think of a smart remark fast enough, but Leo said, 'Lara comes from England, like me,' and gave her a look, you know that look he does when he's mad at you? It was funny."

"Did you say anything?" I asked, fearing the answer.

"No. But then Leo toppled the gravy boat and there was gravy everywhere. Apparently that was an expensive linen tablecloth." She rolled her eyes.

"The perfect choice for when you have a three-year-old at your table!"

"Exactly. Leo was mortified, he was bright red and I thought he would cry. Dad shouted at him and then at that point he *did* cry. Grandma said he deserved a good spanking, and I couldn't help it, Mum, I tried, but I was so angry. I don't want anyone to hit Leo . . ."

Like her father did to her, I thought, and my heart broke.

"Lara, I understand you wanted to defend him. I really do. I would feel the same if that woman ever tried to lay a hand on Leo."

"You don't know what I did." She looked down. I felt my blood run cold.

"What did you do?"

"I threw the gravy boat at her."

"Oh, Lara." I rubbed my forehead. There was no excuse for that.

"It didn't hit her. It landed on the floor and it shattered. It was horrible. She said nothing like that ever happened at her table. That I was crazy and probably my parents were crazy, too, and—"

"Okay. Okay. We have established she's a complete . . . witch, but Lara, seriously, you don't throw stuff at people!" I said, aware of how lame my reprimand sounded. Of course she knew that.

"I swear I couldn't help it, Mum." Her eyes were shiny and she was wringing her hands, the way she did when she was upset. My heart went out to her, but I steeled myself.

"Lara, you need to try to control yourself! You'll get into a huge amount of trouble."

"I know, I'm sorry," she said, and I could hear tears in her voice. One moment later she began to sob, lifting herself up on a stool and taking her face in her hands. I wrapped an arm around her shoulder.

"Look. I am sorry you had to go through this. I knew it wasn't going to end well, but I couldn't say no, they are

33

your grandparents . . . There won't be a next time. I promise."

"No. I'm never going back. Never!"

"Oh, Lara," I said, and held her tight. Thank God the gravy boat hadn't actually hit Harriet, I thought. And then an uncomfortable notion made its way into my mind. Gravy spread everywhere on her perfect floors . . . the vision was actually quite satisfying.

No. I couldn't in any way condone Lara's act. Even if Harriet was cruel and obnoxious and just horrific.

Big brown stains on her linen tablecloth . . .

I had to admit it. In my deepest heart, though I would never, never say this to Lara or anyone else, I thought that the woman had it coming. It was Lara I worried about, not Harriet's feelings. She had pushed Lara's buttons to the point she couldn't take it any more, and although Lara's reaction was in no way acceptable, for once Harriet hadn't been able to get away with her cruelty.

But Lara was never to know I thought that.

"I know what I did was terrible. And I felt sorry for Dad, anyway," she said. She'd taken off her glasses and was drying her tears.

"You did?"

"Yes. Grandma was horrible to him, too, bossing him around like he was a child. She was talking about gardening, and how they had their garden landscaped, and Dad said we needed to do that too. She laughed – her laugh is weird, isn't it? All *hi hi hi* like only dogs can hear it."

My mouth curled up in spite of me, and then I felt terrible about it. "Lara, this is serious!"

"I know! Anyway, she said to Dad, 'You'll never be able to afford that, the way you are going.'"

34

I couldn't help laughing openly this time. The way Lara imitated Harriet's clipped tone was so accurate. "Is that an insult? That we can't afford a landscaper? What planet do they live on?"

Lara shrugged. "You know the way Dad gets with his mother. Trying to please, trying to impress them . . ."

I was speechless at how precisely Lara had read the situation and understood the dynamics of Ash's family. She'd never articulated her grasp of her father's relationship with his mother as clearly as that before.

"He started going on about all that he'd been doing, and how the company thought he was all that, and Grandma just went to the kitchen like she wasn't interested and Grandpa just sat there stony-faced. It was sad."

It was. But I had no energy left to be sorry for Ash.

I just wondered why our family, a family that could have been so loving, so close if only we'd allowed ourselves to be, was imploding slowly. And the epicentre of this destruction lay not in my troubled, fragile daughter, but in my husband, the man I'd loved for so long, and so deeply.

That night Ash sat in the living room drinking glass after glass of some fancy wine he kept for show – which was out of character, because he seldom drank. I was worried after what his mother had said to him, and I hovered around him. Harriet was toxic. She had a destructive effect on Ash, and the sad thing was that he still looked for her approval. But he never got it.

"You okay?"

"As okay as I can be. I don't understand Lara. I don't know her any more."

"She's going through a rough patch."

"She threw a piece of crockery at my mother, Margherita!"

"Keep your voice down!" Lara and Leo were in bed, and Lara was a very troubled sleeper at the best of times. There was no way I could have her stumbling in on our conversation. "I know that's unacceptable—"

"Really? Is it? Because I didn't see you being particularly angry at her . . ."

"She's grounded for two weeks. I took her laptop and her phone away—"

"She's out of control, Margherita!"

"Tomorrow I'm going to speak to Lara about seeing Sheridan again."

"Like that's going to help."

My heart sank. Why did he have such little faith in our daughter?

"She'll get better, Ash. I'm sure of that. Your mother wanted to spank Leo, and you know what Lara has been through with her dad."

"It's not an excuse."

"No, it's not. What she did is just . . . terrible. I'm not looking for excuses for her. I'm just explaining—"

"Leo's behaviour was appalling too."

"He toppled something, Ash. He's three years old. What do you expect?"

"He was hyper!"

"He was excited! He doesn't get to go out with you often. He was beside himself with happiness! He wanted to go dressed as Batman because you love the Batman films, for God's sake! Try and understand!"

"And who understands *me*, huh? You always take their side, Margherita."

"What is this? A competition between you and the children? You are a grown man!" I snapped.

I'd always known that since Lara had come along, and then Leo, Ash felt like he didn't have my full attention any more. But he had never spelled it out as clearly as that, as if I'd been taking sides. As if he and the children were on two different sides, instead of being a unit. A family.

"Look, Ash. I'm sorry it didn't go well with your mum."

"You can say that again."

"Yeah, well, it would have been easier if I'd been there, but your mum didn't invite me!"

"Can't she have some time alone with her son and her grandchildren?"

"Of course. I mean, everyone involved had a great time!"

Immediately, I felt guilty. With all his faults, Ash couldn't help his mum's unpleasantness, and I knew he'd tried, without success, to smooth things over between her and me. She was unconquerable.

"Anyway. You didn't let me finish. My mum says she never wants Lara in her house again."

And now she didn't want to see Lara either.

He wasn't looking at me. He couldn't. Silent rage filled me, and I had to be quiet for a moment. Good riddance, I thought finally.

"If my daughter is not welcome there, then I am not welcome either." Of course I wasn't welcome, I'd never been. "And Leo. I won't have your mum poisoning him against his sister and me!"

"Margherita. My dad phoned me. He had a message for me from my mother . . ." he said quietly.

"What else, now?"

37

"That she won't speak to me until I've left you."

Wide and black, the chasm between us kept getting deeper.

"And what did you say?"

"I said nothing."

How could she? How could she put such a choice in front of Ash? How could he be forced to choose between his wife and children, and his parents?

I felt sick, and I had run out of words.

"We shouldn't have had children," he said. "Our life would be so much better now if we hadn't."

I blinked, letting his words sink in.

The pain in my heart was almost physical as I realised the full extent of what he'd just said, and all my limbs started to shake. I stood up slowly, taking a step away from him as if suddenly I couldn't breathe the same air as him. "You should be ashamed of yourself," I murmured.

"I am," he said. He was wallowing in self-pity now. "But I can't help how I feel."

A sense of déjà vu floated in my mind. The conversation we'd had when I'd found out I was pregnant with Leo. *I know I need to make the best of a bad situation, but I can't help how I feel.*

Nothing had changed. Things had only got worse.

"That's true. You can't," I said calmly.

He must have sensed a change in my tone, because he looked up. "Margherita—"

"Check yourself into some hotel, or go stay with Steven, because I don't want you here tonight."

"Listen—"

"No. I won't listen, Ash. I want you out of my sight."

I turned around; I turned my back to him. I went upstairs with a sense of inevitability, of finality in every step I took.

Every step took me further away from him, not only in body but also in heart and soul. I stood on the landing for a while, holding the banister to try to stop the shaking in my hands, until I heard the front door opening and then closing again. He was gone. I took a breath. It felt like I'd been holding it throughout our argument.

I checked on Lara. She was sleeping, thankfully, exhausted after her troubled day, and then I slipped into Leo's room. He lay sprawled across the bed, clutching Pingu, his favourite toy, one little leg out of the duvet. I covered him with his blue and green duvet, tucking both him and Pingu in, and then I sat on the armchair, to guard him through the night. I watched the fluorescent stars glued on his ceiling, a mini Milky Way inside his room, and listened to his breathing until I fell asleep too – a light sleep that brought no respite, full of anxious dreams.

When I awoke, still on Leo's armchair, the world looked different. There was no going back for me. The hairline crack, the fault line that had opened between us when Leo was born, had turned into an abyss. I knew then that Ash could make no reparation, that even if we stayed together, the bond between us was forever broken.

The following night Ash came home pretending nothing had happened. The week went by in silence while we avoided each other's company, until the weekend arrived. Ash was getting ready to go and play golf with his brother, and Lara and Leo were at my sister's.

There was a strange atmosphere in the house. Electric, like the air before a storm. And I was at the centre of it. I hurried about with a million things to do, finishing nothing. I couldn't find peace, so I decided to cook – my default mode when I'm anxious. Cooking and baking focused me: the act of lining up all the ingredients and mixing them together in a miraculous alchemy, to create something beautiful and nourishing out of nothing, was like meditation. Making bread was one of my favourite stress-busters: I loved seeing the yeast bubble up in warm water and the dough coming together and rising as if it were something alive. Sinking my hands into it was therapeutic.

I was busy working the dough when Ash walked into the kitchen. There had been a lot of silence between us, but in the last couple of days we'd been speaking again, although not more than was strictly necessary.

"Maggie, have you seen my Pringle jumper? The yellow one? I must be off in twenty minutes."

Now, I can't stand it when people call me Maggie. It's a lovely name, it really is, but it's not *my* name. I had told Ash many times that I didn't like my name shortened like that, and after years of marriage he still hadn't got the message. I bit my tongue.

"I haven't seen it, no." The dough took a beating.

"Right. Never mind, I'll wear a polo shirt. Thanks," he said, and stepped out.

I stopped pounding the dough and straightened myself.

"Ash."

"Yes?" He peeped through the door. "I'm late," he said, tapping his expensive Omega watch, the one he had tweeted about and Facebooked about so that everyone would know he could afford it.

The words came out by themselves. "We need a break. *I* need a break."

There was a silence. For a moment he looked bewildered.

"What?"

"I need a break. From you."

His eyes widened some more; then his features rearranged themselves into his pious, martyred look. "Well, if you want to destroy this family—"

In a moment, and before I knew what I was doing, I'd thrown the ball of dough at him. It hit him on the shoulder and fell to the floor, bits of it strewn on his T-shirt.

"What did you do that for! You are deranged!"

"*I* am destroying the family? *I* am?" I shouted back. The dough was on the floor, and everything was ruined, and tears began to fall from my eyes. They weren't tears of sadness yet – those would come later – just fury.

"Well, it's you who needs a break. Not me. Not even when my mother said I had to leave you! And we wonder why Lara can't control her temper! You are throwing stuff at me! You are mental!"

"Do you love them, Ash?" I said quietly.

"What? What are you talking about?"

"Do you love our children?"

"Of course I do. I do. Oh, I see what this is about. God, are you still thinking about what I said that night? I thought it was finished, but no, you have to drag it up. I was drunk. Do you understand? Drunk. I think you do, because I've seen you and your sister having a good time before. You don't say stupid things when you're drunk?"

"I don't say that I wish my children weren't here!"

I banged my sticky hands on the granite, and it hurt, but I didn't care.

"For God's sake, Margherita. You don't realise how hard it is for me."

"For *you*?"

41

"Yes. For me. The children adore you, both of them. You're like this little unit, the three of you, and I'm left out." He spread his arms. "Lara is so difficult, and Leo doesn't even like me. I'm always working, trying to earn a living. My parents hate you—"

"Your parents hate me for no good reason except they think I'm not good enough for you or for them! Lara is difficult because her birth mum died and her father beat her up, Ash! What do you want us to do? Return her, like damaged goods? What do you want me to do? Go and beg your mother to finally accept me?"

The bitterness of those words made the back of my throat burn.

"You turned Leo against me—"

"How can you say that! How can you say it's my fault if you and Leo have no relationship to speak of! Leo is a clever little boy and he knows how you've always felt about him. He tries to catch your attention, he tries to impress you, to make you happy . . . just like you do with your mother, can't you see?"

But Ash wasn't listening any more. "You put him up to it, Margherita. Your precious little boy, he can't have anyone else but you! You put him up to hating his father." His mouth was twisted in a bitter curve, his eyes cold. Where was my husband? Because this man wasn't him. Couldn't be him.

We just kept shouting, both of us. We threw accusations at each other until we ran out of steam and were both drained. The air was acidic with resentment. He leaned on the wall; I leaned on the kitchen island, just like Lara had after the argument at her grandma's. I was too angry to cry, but I knew the tears would come soon; I could feel them gathering in the coldness of my heart.

"We can't go on like this, Ash," I said softly. "Can't you see? Can't you see how we need a break?"

"Fine." He sounded defeated. "Fine."

"You need to go now. I can't take any more of this," I whispered.

He must have seen something on my face, something that spoke of heartbreak, because he opened his mouth to reply, and then he closed it again.

He went upstairs without another word, and I waited in the kitchen until he came back, a suitcase by his side and a rucksack on his back.

His eyes met mine briefly. "I'm off then."

I almost felt sorry for him. "Yes. Your mother will be relieved."

"I suppose she will be, yes."

Suddenly it was all very civilised. No more shouting, no more recriminations, no more accusations. The quiet death of love. Or maybe the ugliest part was still to come, if we found we weren't able to move on from all this. If we were faced with the reality of it all, its inevitability.

"I'm sorry, Maggie," he said, and he looked devastated, truly devastated. Gone was the angry man, the patronising, fake-pious husband who made a big show of being lumbered with a troublesome family. For a moment he looked a bit like a little boy; and for a moment, for the briefest of instants, I contemplated asking him to stay. In that split second I wanted to start again, to forget the past and be the unit we used to be, that we'd been for years. I wanted my husband back.

But the moment passed.

"My name is not Maggie," I said quietly, and turned around before he saw my tears.

43

4

Aftermath

Margherita

I sat there, stunned and trembling. Suddenly, the house seemed enormous. Empty. There was dough everywhere and everything was broken, everything was ruined. I needed to speak to someone. I needed to speak to my mum. I dialled the number of her coffee shop with shaking hands.

"Hello, La Piazza?"

"Mum?"

"Margherita? Are you okay?"

She'd heard the distress in my voice. For a moment I couldn't speak.

"I've been better, I suppose. Mum, Ash just left . . ." I began, wearily gathering crumbs from the table. It all seemed so futile. So pointless. Cleaning up the kitchen, cleaning up the house, cleaning up the wreckage of my marriage.

"He left you?"

"I asked him to leave." Tears began to break my voice.

"Oh Margherita, I'm sorry."

She didn't sound surprised. "She smells us and knows what we're thinking," Anna had said once. It sounded weird, but it was true.

"You're not surprised, are you?"

"Not really."

"You knew it would happen. You knew . . ."

"I'm not blind, Margherita. Even being away up here, it's not hard to guess. I had my doubts about Ash, and so did your dad, but you always had our support, you know that, don't you? It's not like I wished this on you, *tesoro mio*. Please believe that."

"I know you didn't. And I know that you and dad never thought that Ash was right for me, and here I am—"

"Margherita, there's no point in looking back right now . . ."

"You and Dad stayed together until the end."

"Some people do, and some don't. It's just the way it is. You and Ash made a wonderful child together. Something very, very good came from your love for him. And anyway, we're talking like you've filed for divorce! This is just a temporary separation . . . maybe it's just a blip . . ."

I had to take a breath before I answered. "I don't know. I don't know if it is. Some things he said . . . I don't know. Maybe. I hope so."

"I just hope that whatever happens, you'll be happier than you've been in the last few years, because I know that things have been very hard for you."

I was too choked to reply.

"Why don't I come down for a couple of weeks?" she said, and I was so happy she'd offered. I didn't want to ask because I knew she was under so much pressure running a busy coffee shop.

"That would be wonderful. Thank you, Mum."

"I'll speak to Michael and see what we can arrange for cover, okay? Don't worry about a thing. I'll come down soon."

When I put the phone down, the house didn't seem so empty any more.

45

That night, at dinner, the children didn't notice their dad wasn't there. He was hardly ever with us in the evenings anyway. But I felt Lara's eyes on me, studying me. She was no doubt wondering why I was so pale and why my eyes were rimmed with red. She was quiet during dinner, and later she stood in the bathroom doorway as I bathed Leo.

"Are you okay, Mum?"

"Yes. Don't worry. We'll speak in a little while, after I put this young man to bed." I began lathering my son's dark hair with no-tears shampoo.

"Okay," she said in a small voice.

"Nothing to worry about," I called as she walked away, but my tone denied my words.

Later, after Leo's bedtime stories, it was time to share a cup of chamomile tea on Lara's bed. It was a little ritual we'd started when she began having trouble sleeping, and it had become precious to both of us. The tea and honey helped her sleep better, but it was having some time together, alone and in peace, that made the difference for both of us. She probably felt it was a terribly uncool thing to do for a teenager and would have died if her friends knew, but they didn't need to – when it was just the two of us, she could still be my little girl.

Tonight, though, there would be no peace. I had to tell her about her father and me. I hesitated in front of her room and rested my forehead on the bright-yellow wooden plaque with her name painted on it. I braced myself and knocked at the door.

"Hey." She was on her bed, writing in her journal. Since she'd read Anne Frank's diary a couple of years ago she'd taken to writing to "Kitty", just like Anne had done. There was

46

a little pile of books on her bedside table, as always, topped by her yellow iPod.

"What are you reading?"

"*Jane Eyre*. It's brilliant. It's part of next year's curriculum, but Mrs Akerele gave me the reading list and I'd thought I'd start it now."

"That's good," I said, resting her steaming mug on her bedside table. She sat up cross-legged, her back against the pillows. Her dark-golden hair was up in a bun and blue-rimmed glasses framed her face. A spattering of yellow flower stickers decorated the wall behind her, still unchanged since she'd first arrived. I'd offered to refresh it for her many times, to make the decor a bit more suitable for a fourteen-year-old, but she always refused. I think her old room made her feel safe.

"Mum, what's wrong? Is it me? Is it me upsetting you?"

"No, of course not, sweetheart." Another painful breath. "Something happened between your dad and me today. We decided to take a little break from each other."

I felt so guilty. With all the upheaval she'd experienced in her life, I couldn't believe we were going to unsettle her again. When we'd adopted her, we never, never thought it would come to this. I hadn't, anyway.

"You are separating," she said matter-of-factly, and stirred her chamomile, gently blowing to cool it down.

"I'm sorry."

"I knew it would happen. I mean, I'm not blind."

The same thing my mum had said. It seemed like the people around me could see my life more clearly than I could.

"I suppose we didn't hide it very well."

"He's never here. When he is, you don't talk, apart from

47

what you really need to say to each other, like stuff about the house or us or things to do. You don't even look at each other sometimes," she said.

To hear it spelled out – the reality of it, and the fact that our daughter had been so aware of it all along – hit me hard.

"What happened at Grandma's . . . well, that was bound to make things worse."

"I'm sorry," I repeated, too choked to say anything else. "We tried. We just don't seem to get on, we don't agree on anything. We just . . ." I shook my head, unable to say any more.

"I think it's also because of me. Because of . . . you know, the way I've been. The way I get angry."

"No, no, Lara! It's not like that at all!" I exclaimed, putting my mug down. "Oh, please don't think it's your fault. None of this is your fault. Your dad hates seeing you upset. He finds it hard to see you going through this." I would never, never tell her what he'd really said. "It's not because of you or Leo. It's us, it's Dad and I. We just don't understand each other. We haven't understood each other for a long time now."

"I think that if we hadn't come along maybe you'd still be together," she said, and I saw her scrutinising my face, like she was frightened of what I would say and at the same time desperate for reassurance. The thing was, from Ash's point of view she was probably right. If the children hadn't opened this deep, deep fracture between us we would still be together, Ash unthreatened in his selfish little world of work and golf and fancy watches, in his never-ending, never-to-be satisfied quest to impress his parents and make them proud of him. He'd still have me all for himself, exclusively his. Lara's words echoed Ash's, in a way; they certainly echoed his thoughts.

48

I looked into her eyes, and told her the truth. I told her *my* truth, not Ash's.

"I don't even want to *think* about you and Leo not being in my life."

I saw her relaxing a little at my reply, and I stroked her face, tucking a wavy strand of hair behind her ear.

"I'm sorry you're upset, Mum."

"I'm sorry too."

"We'll be fine."

I smiled a little. It should have been me comforting her; instead *she* was trying to reassure *me*. "Yes. We will be."

My mum came to London and worked her magic on all of us. She was such a positive, loving, cheerful person; it was impossible not to be happier around her. But when she left, things started going downhill again. Ash barely saw the children, and he'd started phoning less and less. Every time he did, we fought. Lara kept having night terrors and she seemed to explode for no reason. Her anger was never directed towards Leo or me, but she seemed to be falling out with all her friends. She got a few warnings in school – they were shocked, because Lara had always been a model pupil. I'd explained to them about her background and I'd told them that Lara's dad and I had just separated, but there was only so many allowances they could make for her rages.

One morning I got a call from Lara's school, summoning me. I knew it would happen, sooner or later, but I was horrified all the same.

They said that Lara had shouted at Mrs Akerele, her English teacher, in the middle of a lesson, that she'd gone into a complete rage in front of the whole class and would not calm down. They'd sent her to the head teacher's office, but she was so distraught that she'd ended up in the nurse's room with a cup of sugary tea. A million thoughts raced in my mind – and of those thoughts, the one that screamed the loudest was that I'd *failed* her. I'd seen this coming, and I'd done nothing.

But what could I have done?

How easy, how *automatic*, even, it is for mothers to take the weight of the world on their shoulders, to feel responsible for every little piece of their children's world. As if we were omnipotent, as if somehow we should know how to shield them from everything, and we should do that all the time. And if anything goes wrong, it is our fault – we should have predicted it, we should have stopped it, we should have done *something*.

I was flustered, my thoughts scattered like leaves to the wind as I ran up the school's steps. I stopped for a moment and breathed as deeply as I could – three shaky breaths that didn't quite clear my mind.

The first thing I saw when I walked into the head teacher's office was Lara's back in a chair. She looked very small.

Mr Kearns rose with a greeting I didn't really hear and he offered me a seat. Lara kept looking down.

I sat beside my daughter and I touched her shoulder. She turned towards me – she was very pale and looked shocked, as if she couldn't quite believe what she'd just done. Her eyes were red behind her glasses; in her hands there was a mug that said Little Miss Smiley. For some reason, I found the combination of my daughter's face and the cheery mug terribly sad. I wanted to hug her, but I was worried it would not be appropriate, so I just held her hand as we sat and waited for Mr Kearns to speak.

"Mrs Ward, like I said to you on the phone, Lara's behaviour was unacceptable. Mrs Akerele is shaken and upset, as you can imagine. She said she feared Lara would hit her."

My eyes widened. I looked at Lara, who in turn was gazing down at her black ballerinas. "Now, this is a bit much. I mean, she lost her temper, and that's bad, but to say Lara was going to hit her is outrageous!"

"Well, we were surprised ourselves. Mrs Akerele and Lara have always had a good relationship, haven't you? She's been teaching you for two years now, and with all the extra work you took on . . ."

Mrs Akerele, a young, vibrant woman, had always encouraged Lara's passion for language, and she had involved her in a few projects with more advanced classes. They seemed to have a great relationship, which made the incident all the more baffling.

"What happened, Lara?"

She swallowed. She looked very young and very scared. "She said she was going. She's moving away."

"That's why you shouted? You were upset that she's moving away?"

She shuffled in her seat. I noticed that her eyelashes were still wet. "Sam and Mosi were acting up. For a change." She rolled her eyes. "Mrs Akerele said she was glad she was moving on, so she wouldn't need to put up with all that any more. I . . ." Her voice trailed away.

"What went through your mind, Lara?" I encouraged. I had a lump in my throat.

"That it's not fair."

"What's not fair, that Mrs Akerele is going?" Mr Kearns intervened.

"That someone ups and goes like that and leaves us because she doesn't care enough."

My heart swelled for my daughter.

"Oh, Lara . . ."

Mr Kearns cleared his throat. "Shouting at a teacher is not acceptable, Lara. But I understand you were upset, and you have never been in trouble before. Usually for something like this I would look to suspend a student for a day, Mrs Ward . . ." I nodded, ashamed, and out of the corner of my eye I saw Lara's head drop further. "But I spoke to Mrs Akerele and she agrees that what we'll look for at this time is simply an apology. We'll move on. There will be no consequences. Now, should this behaviour present itself again . . ." – he glanced at me again, and I could sense a private conversation, without Lara present, was to follow – "I won't be able to be so lenient."

I nodded once more. He knew about Lara's background and he was taking her circumstances into consideration, though of course he couldn't have been aware of what we ourselves had just recently found out.

"Will you apologise, Lara?" I said, clutching my bag, eager to get out of that office, out of that school, and to be alone with my daughter. There was no doubt in my mind that she would.

"Yes. I'm sorry," she whispered, still looking at her shoes.

"Lara, just for you to know," Mr Kearns said as we were about to leave his office, "Mrs Akerele is leaving here because her husband took a job in Devon. Her decision has nothing to do with you or with your class. She always enjoyed working with you."

Lara nodded again, like a sad marionette. I just wanted to hug her. "Is it okay if I take her home?" I didn't want her to have to face her classmates again, not today.

"Of course. And Mrs Ward?" I turned around and once again met Mr Kearns' eyes. He wasn't long for retirement, the pictures of his granddaughters hanging on the wall underneath official-looking diplomas and pupils' achievements. He had a mellow way that I'd always liked, but I still felt somehow on trial, as guilty as my daughter. Like I was a young girl again. "Don't worry. It'll all be sorted," he said. "Just give me a call in the next few days and we can have a good chat."

I was touched, but there was no way I would not worry. In fact, I was pretty much terrified.

I decided to wait for Lara to open up, instead of jumping in there with a row or requests for an explanation. She was contrite. In the car, she was quiet for a bit, listening to her iPod. Then she removed her earphones and I saw her shuffling, like she was getting ready to tell me something. I held my breath.

"Mum?"

"Yes?"

"What Mrs Akerele said about hitting her—"

"I know, I know. Nonsense," I interrupted, and I clutched the steering wheel, feeling the tension rise in my body once again.

"I nearly did."

I was stunned into silence.

My Lara. My Lara and her demons.

"Nearly, but you didn't," I said firmly. Inside, I was drowning. What was happening to my daughter?

"No," she whispered. And then she read my mind. "I don't know what's happening to me. I get so angry and I can't stop."

"Whatever is happening, we'll sort it together. You don't need to worry."

A short silence followed, while I tried to hide how upset I was. How exactly could we sort it? Could something like this be *sorted*? I was so frightened for Lara, but I could never, never show it. If only I could slay all her demons for her – if only I could protect her from everything, even from what had already happened to her but wasn't there to prevent.

I slipped on my sunglasses and switched the radio on.

"Is it time to get Leo from nursery already?" Lara asked, and I knew why she was so keen to see him. Leo always seemed to comfort her, to pacify her.

"Yes. We'll go straight there."

She was glued to her brother and me for the rest of the afternoon and evening, never letting either of us out of her sight. I wasn't surprised when later on, as I went to check on Leo just after midnight, I found her in his bed, sleeping beside him. Leo had his small arm around her waist, keeping her close.

The incident with Mrs Akerele was just the beginning. Lara's unhappiness and distress had come to a head. Her outbursts were sudden and explosive, and always followed by intense shame and upset. She was never hungry, and she couldn't sleep at night either.

"Maybe you could go back to Sheridan."

"I don't want to."

"Perhaps talking about it, talking it all out, would help."

"It wouldn't change anything. It happened," she shrugged. "I don't want to talk to a stranger about that stuff."

"Sheridan is not a stranger. You spoke to her before."

She wrung her hands. "I don't want to, Mum. Please don't make me."

"No, my love, of course not. I won't make you. We'll find another way. We'll see this through, okay?"

"Okay," she said, and she slipped her earphones back on.

Lara needed help. And I did too, because apart from loving her and listening to her and being there for her, I didn't know what else to do. I was spreading myself so thin I was see-through. I was trying to be everywhere, to be everything to everybody. I went to bed at night with barely the energy to pull the blankets over me, and that's when Lara's nightmares would start, and I was up again. I was exhausted physically and mentally.

I missed my mum. I missed her wisdom, her practical help, her advice. I missed her good humour and her ability to see the best in every situation. The phone just wasn't enough. And I desperately, desperately needed a change of scene, the chance to *breathe*.

That night, during our little chamomile ritual, I decided to speak to Lara and test the waters about going to Glen Avich for the summer.

"Lara, I was thinking," I began carefully, "maybe it would be nice to go and see Nonna—"

"Yes!"

I laughed. "You didn't need much convincing, there!"

"I *want* to go, Mum. I want to go away from here and not see anybody from my school this summer. No one. I could start packing now!" she said, and it was lovely to see the enthusiasm in her eyes again. Since the incident with Mrs Akerele, she'd been so low.

"Fine. But honestly, Lara, if the summer is too long, well, we'll only stay a couple of weeks . . ."

She shook her head. "No, please! Let's go for the whole

summer! I want away from here, I really do." She shrugged and looked into her mug. "I'm fed up with everything."

"I know. I'm fed up, too. You wouldn't see your dad for six weeks though, do you understand that?"

"It's not like I see him much anyway." She shrugged. But I could see the hurt behind her indifference. I couldn't bring myself to say that maybe she could spend half of the time with him, or even just a week or two – not out of selfishness, but because I was genuinely worried she would end up distressed, or rejected.

"But do *you* want me to come?" she said in a small voice, looking down. I'd just asked her if it was okay for us to go, but it wasn't quite enough for her. She always looked for reassurance, she always feared being unwanted. And every time she needed to know how loved she was, every single time she needed me to tell her, if it was once or ten times or a hundred, I would do that. I would always be the safety net for my little trapeze girl, walking on a tightrope of self-doubt and past hurt.

"I'm not going anywhere without you." I took the mug from her hands and dared to wrap my arms around her, breathing in her fresh, clean scent of young girl and cherry shampoo. Hugs had become rare between us: she'd outgrown them, so fast, so soon. Only yesterday she'd been my baby, falling asleep in my arms and running to me for cuddles all the time . . . She was slipping away from me, and still, she needed me so much.

"And after the summer?" she asked in a small voice. "What's going to happen?"

"You don't need to worry about a thing, Lara. Whatever happens, both Dad and I love you so much and we'll always be there for you."

"But Dad is *not* there for me. He doesn't care about Leo either."

"Of course he does . . . he just doesn't know how to show it. I think he never had much love when he was growing up . . ." I was furious at myself for feeling the tears gather in my throat again.

Ash. My Ash, and all our history, all the years we had together.

My Ash, mine no more.

"I know. I know unloved when I see it," Lara said in one of those moments of insight where she was fourteen going on forty. "Oh, Mum, don't cry . . ."

"I'm fine. Really, I'm okay. Everything will be fine. Promise me you won't worry about anything," I said. She took off her glasses and rested them on her bedside table. Without them she looked younger, with her thin face and big blue eyes. She looked just like her birth mother in the picture I'd seen, with bones like a bird's and wavy, dark-blond hair.

"I promise. Goodnight, Mum."

"Goodnight, sweetheart."

I turned around to glance at her one last time. By the sliver of light that came from the corridor I could see her hair fanned on the pillow, her small body curled under the blankets like a blossom waiting to unfurl. I hoped she would sleep through, the same hope I had every night, though I knew it was unlikely. I was so relieved she had agreed to go to Glen Avich; we would all get away from this house where there had been so much conflict, so much heartache, at least for a while. Once again I thanked in my heart whatever or whoever it was that had brought her to me – God, or the universe, or fate. If karma existed, I thought I must have done something very, very good in my previous life to deserve my children.

Before going to bed I went to check on Leo. Every time I went to see him through the night I found him tangled with the duvet and never actually under it. His little, dense body was relaxed like a sleeping puppy, and his hair smelled of puppy too, I often thought, especially when he slept: warm, tender, not quite fully human yet. A man cub. *My* man cub.

"Night, baby," I whispered in his ear and leaned over to kiss him. I tucked him in; I knew he was going to wriggle out of the blankets once more, but I did it anyway. He turned over and slipped his thumb into his mouth. I knew he was too old for it, but hey, who was there to see? And with all the upheaval we had ahead of us, he needed all the reassurance he could get.

5

Dawn

Margherita

The next day, with Lara in school and Leo in nursery, I sat at the kitchen table, ready to make two phone calls. The first one was the hardest.

"Oh, Margherita." Ash said my name like a sigh. Like a chore.

Was this really my husband? Was this really the man I'd loved so much? This man who sounded like he felt nothing for me any more?

Nobody, nobody in the world had the ability to make me feel as cold as he did.

"I just wanted to let you know I'm taking the children on holiday," I said. "We'll go to my mum's for the summer."

A pause. "To Scotland?"

"Yes."

"Are you sure it's a good idea to uproot Lara for so long? With her state of mind . . ."

"It's hardly uprooting. It's just for the six weeks."

"Look, nobody wants you to go so far away." Oh, how he loved patronising me.

"Maybe I want my family around me, Ash. Have you thought of that?"

"Your sister is here, and you spend a lot of time with her, certainly more than you do with me."

"Now you're jealous of my sister? You're never around, Ash. Who else should I spend time with?" It was starting again, and I hated myself for letting him get to me. "I just want to see Mum, Ash, that's all."

"At the expense of your daughter?"

"I'm taking her on holiday to Scotland, not to a labour camp! And I notice you didn't even mention Leo."

"This again." A deep sigh. "Leo is always at the top of my priorities."

"You hide it well," I said, recalling all the times he'd let Leo down, all the times he'd shown his indifference, openly and unashamedly: like when he missed his first Nativity play in nursery; like when he left him at a party for an extra hour because he had something urgent to do. Once, Leo had drawn our family: there was me, him and Lara as stick people under a tree dotted with apples, and far away, in a corner, was Daddy. Leo was extending a spindly arm to him, but Daddy's arms were at his sides. I left the drawing on the kitchen table, hoping that he'd see it and maybe do something about Leo's feelings, but he never showed signs of having seen it. This made it all the more heartbreaking: that Leo *knew*. He could feel with a child's instinct that his father had somehow rejected him.

I dreaded the day he'd be old enough to ask me why, and I would have no answer.

"Talking to you is just impossible, Margherita. All you do is throw accusations at me."

"Well, all you need to know is that we're going to see my mum and Lara will be fine. You're welcome to come and see them if you want."

A pause. "I'll be very busy, workwise . . ."

Of course. Of course.

"Bye, Ash."

"Right. Fine. Bye."

I put the phone down and I felt empty. I hoped that the second call would restore me a bit, but first I needed coffee. I made myself a cappuccino and sat at the table once again. I dialled the number for La Piazza. It rang a few times and I began to feel apprehensive – would it be okay to go to Glen Avich for so long? Had I made a mistake to assume she would have us? Oh God, I should have asked her first, before telling Lara and Ash . . .

But my doubts melted as soon as I heard her voice. That was my mum, my ally and best friend through thick and thin. She would not let me fall.

"Hi, it's me," I said, stirring my cappuccino, hoping it would keep me going after the sleepless night.

"Margherita! What's wrong? You sound stressed."

"Yes, well, I am. Oh, it's Ash, it's a million things, really. But mainly . . . Lara is having some trouble in school. She needs a change of scene. *I* need a change of scene. So I was thinking—"

"Of course! Nothing would make me happier."

I smiled. "You guessed! I was going to ask you if I could come up."

"Please do. Please, please do." The joy in her voice was like a balm for my aching heart. "It would be such a treat to have you up. How long are you coming for? Why not the whole summer?"

"I was hoping so. But what about Michael?"

"What about him?" she said, and I could hear the fondness in her voice.

"Will he be okay with us being there for so long?"

"Of course! He'll love having you around. You know his daughter and his grandchildren are in Canada, and he misses them a lot. Honestly, he'll be delighted to have you."

"Thank you, Mum," I said tearily. The strife of the recent months was really getting to me – I was crying more often than ever in my life, even more than when I was going through fertility treatment.

"No need to thank me. I'm so glad also because I won't be seeing either of your sisters. Laura is working all summer and Anna—"

"Yes, she told me. She's going to Colorado to see Paul's family. I'll miss her."

"So, will I be expecting you tomorrow?" she said hopefully.

I couldn't help laughing, even between my tears. "Tomorrow? I haven't even packed yet!"

"Sorry. It's never too soon . . . I can't wait to see you. The day after, then?"

I smiled again. "Schools break up next week down here. I'll be there next Saturday."

"Okay, then. I'm so sorry this is happening to you . . . but I'm so glad to have you up for so long! I'll get the cottage ready and everything sorted for you."

The cottage was a miniature two-room building at the bottom of their garden. They were once stables, but my mum and Michael had had them done up for us and for Michael's daughter to come and visit.

"Thank you. Really."

"Are Lara and Leo happy to come up?"

"Lara jumped at the chance. She wants to leave her friends . . . her *so-called* friends behind. They have been *vile* to her, after she started having trouble. Especially Polly and Tanya,

62

you know, the girls who were supposed to be her best friends? The ones she'd been in class with since Reception."

"Vile indeed! Girls can be so cruel. And is she eating okay?"

"We're up and down with that too. She's so small, like a bird."

"We can work on that," my mum said, and I imagined her rubbing her hands in glee. She loves nothing more than feeding people, and she has passed on her love of food to my sisters and me. Laura is tall and slender and she seems to stay that way even if she works as a chef; Anna eats like a horse but sweats all the calories off with her love of sport; and I happily accumulate them on my five-foot-two frame. You only live once, after all.

"I hope Lara will relax a bit, up there. She's not sleeping well. She never did, but recently it's got worse. I think she should see someone. I really do."

"I think the summer in Glen Avich will do her a world of good. And you too. And after that, you can decide what to do about Lara."

"Yes. Leo doesn't know yet. I'll speak to him later, but he's so young, I'll just tell him we're going to see Nonna and he'll be happy. Six weeks is a long time to be away from his dad, but he never really sees him anyway."

"Is Ash still coming round every weekend?"

"No. Something always comes up. It's been every two weeks for a little while, now it's if and when. He wasn't involved at all with Lara's school either. It's so sad to see, you know . . . Every time Ash is around Leo follows him like a little shadow. He tries to catch his attention and never quite manages."

"Well, he'll get plenty of attention here; we'll give him a really good time, I promise. There are quite a few kids his age in Glen Avich and there's a really good play park just across the road from our house, he'll have plenty of little friends to play with."

"That's good," I said in a shaky voice, and took a sip of my cappuccino. The caffeine was slowly waking me up after the sleepless night.

"Margherita?"

"Yes?"

"You told me something happened at Lara's school, but never the details . . ."

I swallowed the coffee through the lump in my throat. "She shouted at her English teacher. Apparently she was about to hit her." It was horrifying to say it aloud.

"*Lara?*"

"Yes."

"My poor little girl . . ."

"Yes. She's been through a lot."

"I meant *you*," my mum said. "Don't worry, *tesoro*. We'll sort things out, okay?"

"Okay," I whispered, feeling like a little girl for real. And a lost one, at that. I was a thirty-eight-year-old mother of two, but I wanted my mum.

6

Roots

Lara

Dear Kitty,

I can safely say that things have been a bit rubbish recently. I'm not sure what's up with me, but I can't sleep. I get these night terrors, they're called, and this makes me grumpy during the day. Extremely grumpy. As in, shouting-at-people grumpy. I get so angry, and I don't even know why. I ended up screaming at Mrs Akerele and it was horrible. I have no idea what comes over me. Maybe in a way I know myself what's wrong with me, it's that it feels like I'm boiling inside, and every once in a while it spills over. I was always able to keep it locked inside me, but it's coming out and I can't stop it. It's scary.

In less freaky but still distressing news, I think Ian likes Polly. It's okay because I don't fancy Ian any more. I'm over that kind of thing now. Nobody wants to hang out with me in school anyway. Since the incident with Mrs Akerele, Polly and Tanya have been avoiding me. Polly's mum said to Tanya's mum that I'm not the best influence on their daughters. Tanya told me when I asked her why they're not sitting with me at lunch any more. It's okay because I've sort of lost my appetite, so I just avoid the cafeteria altogether. I eat on my own on the bench by the football pitch, how pathetic is that? Or I don't eat at all. Everyone thinks I'm a freak. It feels like they're right, because there's something wrong with me, but I'm not sure what. Even Mrs Akerele doesn't look into my eyes now. She sort of looks away. I apologised, but she's shell-shocked. I can't blame her.

On the other hand, Polly was always mean. I can't believe she was ever my best friend. She always said that me wearing glasses and having my head stuck in a book most of the time meant nobody was ever going to like me, as in no *boys* were ever going to like me, and I used to believe she said those things for my own good. What was I thinking? She believes she knows everything, and she speaks in a funny way. Her voice goes up at the end of every sentence, like she puts question marks everywhere. She's ridiculously pretty. While everyone else is straightening their hair, she has what she calls a *bedhead*, all messed up but *on purpose*. My hair is messed up full stop. She even looks good in her school uniform, and that's not easy because we have to wear these enormous blazers at all times and we're not allowed miniskirts. She *still* looks great. So Ian is going to ask her out, obviously. It hasn't happened yet, but I'm sure it will, especially now that I'm way off his radar. I did say to Polly that I fancied Ian and I hoped that would make him off limits, but of course it didn't. I should have known.

Anyway, I'm not even thinking about Ian any more. He looks at me like he feels sorry for me, which makes me feel so ashamed. I wish nobody knew about the Mrs Akerele thing, but it happened in the middle of class and people spread the word. Everyone loves a good story and Lara freaking out at the teacher was the story of the day. "Nobody was expecting you to flip," Tanya said to me like it was all a lot of fun. She said it with one of her smiles, you know the ones where she opens her mouth and you can see all her teeth.

It gets worse. Somebody, I'm not sure who, put pictures of me on Tumblr with funny speech balloons like "I'm mental" and "Watch, she'll stab you" and it went viral. Everyone in the school saw it. I cried. I showed my mum and she said she was going to strangle the whole lot of them – if I hadn't been adopted, I'd say that my temper is genetic.

So yes, I can safely say things are rubbish.

To top everything off nicely, Dad has gone AWOL. When he first left, he came back every week, then every two weeks. Now we barely see him, and when we do, they argue all the time. My mum cries a lot.

I don't think my dad likes me much, especially since what happened with Grandma, which is rotten because he's my dad and it feels like he's giving up on me. So anyway, the long and short of it (like Nonna says) is that we are going to Scotland. Which is just as well because nobody in school wants to be seen with me. Especially not after those pics. Not that I'll be missing out on much. If we stayed it would be a case of going to the shops practically every day – or going to the *mall*, like Polly says because she wants to sound American. I would have to *oooh* and *aaah* while Polly and Tanya and the others try on clothes I'm too skinny and self-conscious to wear – in their book, skinny is good, but I'm not the right kind of skinny, apparently – and stand there while they take selfies. Just *kill me*. If I stayed in London, I'd rather be at home with a book and hide away all summer, but my mum wouldn't let me anyway, and also I don't want her to think I'm sad again like I was when my dad died and I saw a picture of my real mum, and then I was so low for weeks they sent me to Sheridan to "talk things out". So I'm not going to do that again.

Going to Glen Avich: a win–win situation. I love Nonna, AND I love Glen Avich (though it's really cold there, like ridiculously cold). I was there only once for a few days, but it was amazing.

We all thought Nonna was crazy when she decided to leave London and move to the back of beyond with this guy called Michael, to open a coffee shop. In the Highlands of Scotland, which sounds so romantic but it's really *very far away*. We couldn't even pronounce the name of the place – Glen Avich, that strange *ch* sound that Scots make at the back of their throats. I practised because I like to do things properly, and now I can say it: Glen AviCH. The sky is so dramatic there, you feel like you're in a novel. *Bride of Shadows* by Megumi Henderson, my favourite book of all time, is set in Scotland. Coincidence? I think not. I think it's a sign.

B of S is the story of a girl born in a magical clan who falls in love with a boy from a rival clan, Damien, and it's just the Most. Amazing. Book. Ever. Written. Mrs Akerele says that it's commercial fiction and I should be focusing on the classics, but she doesn't understand what that story means to me. She says that Megumi Henderson is not a very skilled writer but "she spins a good yarn". I think Megumi is the best writer of all time, and Emily Brontë the second best (narrowly). I want to be a writer and I want to be skilled and *also* "spin a good yarn". Mrs Akerele says she thinks I do have talent, but I should stick to writing what I know and stay away from vampires and werewolves. I say I'll write whatever I want and what I don't know I can make up, and I don't really like stories of vampires but I love werewolves and I can put whatever creatures I want in my stories. She said that if I'm wilful I'll never get anywhere and I should listen to advice. I *want* to listen, but I think I can only listen when it comes to other stuff. When it comes to books I'll do my own thing.

But I digress. I was talking about Scotland. I intend to spend a lot of time with my mum, my nonna and my brother, and also read a lot and do a lot of wandering. I love wandering, just walking without a destination, listening to music on my iPod. I'm off social media all summer, that's for sure. Otherwise I would have to put up with a Tumblr-ful of Polly's pouting selfies and that's more than I could bear. Also, more crappy pictures of me might crop up. And I don't think I can take it.

Anyway.

Things to do this summer:

1) Sort out my hair once and for all. I don't really have a plan on that one, though; it seems to get frizzy whatever I do.

2) Put on weight in the right places. That won't be hard because Nonna is forever feeding us.

3) Re-read all the Bride of Shadows books and highlight all the best bits, then copy them in my diary.

4) Try contact lenses again and absolutely DO NOT GAG if the optician puts his fingers on my eyeballs to slip them in (SHUDDER). I'm fed up with looking like Velma from *Scooby Doo* with my glasses, though Mum says it's not true, that they make me look very cute. But she always thinks I'm cute so I can't really rely on her opinion.

5) Try not to get angry.

7

New moon

Margherita

We drove through countryside that grew wilder and wilder, until daylight faded and a sliver of moon rose in the clear sky. We went from the motorways and the houses and shopping centres to the silence of the moors and mountains, up and up through winding roads. I had the strange feeling of making a passage to another world entirely, a world where nature was stronger than anywhere I'd ever lived before. I was taking my children to a place that had nothing familiar to us, somewhere new and alien, and it was daunting and scary and exciting, like coming back to life.

The sky was immense, and it was very dark, with the occasional lights like reflected stars in a sea of black. All of a sudden, we were cold. I stopped at a petrol station to bundle Leo in a blanket, and bought myself a cup of hot tea. As I was about to get back in the car, I stood alone for a moment and took a deep breath. A fresh wind blew in my hair and it felt as if it was purifying me, blowing away all that was old and no longer fruitful from my mind and soul. I looked at my little green Corsa fondly. All that was home to me was bundled in the back of my car. I gazed at them once more: Leo was asleep again, a bundle of tenderness snuggled in his new blanket. Lara looked so pretty in her oversized hoodie and jeans, her eyes closed as she listened to her iPod. Yes, all I needed was there. In the glovebox I had one of my most prized possessions: a battered notebook where my grandmother had copied her family recipes. She was my mother's mother and I was called after her, Margherita, though everyone called her Ghita. The recipes were traditional cakes and biscuits from Castelmonte, our home village in the Italian region of Piedmont, at the feet of the Italian Alps. My grandparents – Giovanni and Ghita Scotti – emigrated to England in the fifties, just after the war, and never went back. Anna, Laura and I had been to Castelmonte many times as children but had only been back a couple of times as adults, now that the family home had been sold and ties with Italy were more and more frayed. I hadn't baked from the notebook for a long time, and I felt the urge to do so again.

It was past midnight as we drove by the loch shore, its waters still and dark, and through the village with its empty streets to my mum's cottage. Above, the moon watched over us. Leo was fast asleep when we arrived, but Lara sat up straight, watching out of the car window. All the lights were on in my mum's cottage and she came out as soon as we parked at the side of the street. I stepped out into the sweet-smelling air and my mum held me close. "*Tesoro mio*," she said over and over again, and although we were so far away from everything I knew, in a world of wind and moors and purple hills, it felt like home. For the first time, alongside the sorrow and fear there was a little spark of excitement. When I'd left London, I'd wanted to get a break from myself, in a way, as well as Ash, but there was no new Margherita to replace the one I needed to leave behind.

I watched my mum gather Leo in one arm and wrap her

other around Lara's shoulder, clutching them both to her chest. And as I stood there in the semi-darkness in front of my mum's house, having carried the whole family safely over to this new reality, my perception shifted. A terrible weight fell off my shoulders then.

In spite of all my worries and fears and regrets, I felt safe.

In spite of all the uncertainty, I thought that maybe I would be just fine, the three of us would be just fine.

I smiled, and it was a genuine smile, not the pretend ones I'd had to put on in the last few weeks, while lying to everyone that I was all right, that I was coping great with the upheaval in my life and I had everything under control.

At that moment, Leo's penguin slipped out of my hands as I tried to hold on to my bag, my jacket and a few bits and pieces, and fell on the pavement. I was about to pick it up when someone came from behind and did it for me. I hadn't heard him approaching, so I jumped slightly. I turned around to see a man wearing a dark jacket and jeans, his eyes framed by silver-rimmed glasses, the light of the lamp post reflected in them. I had the strange feeling of having seen him somewhere before, but I couldn't remember where.

"Thank you," I said, and he nodded briefly.

"Come on, Margherita," my mum called, and I walked away. I don't know why I turned around just once more before I stepped inside the house, just to see the strange and yet familiar man walk away.

Michael was waiting for us in the living room, with a wide smile and his arms open.

"I'm sorry to fall on you like a ton of bricks . . ." I began.

"I don't want to hear any of that," he said in his lilting

72

accent, putting both his hands up. He had a booming, deep voice and he rolled his r's – he was like a huge, friendly bear. "It's an absolute pleasure to have you and the children." He gave me a warm, tight hug.

I was touched. My sisters and I had been astounded when my mum announced she was remarrying, and Laura had been firmly against it. It seemed impossible, when Mum and my dad had been so in love, so close for over thirty years. But Michael had won us over by making my mum happy again, and by being so kind to us every time we met. There was an easy charm about him, and a zest for life, an optimism that shone through him and over everything around him. Also, Michael was a chef, like me and Laura – which, I suppose, helped him fit seamlessly into our family. If you want to win over a Scotti, cook for them, feed them beautiful food and they'll be yours forever.

"Let me go and get your luggage from the car," Michael said, and made his way outside. My mum and I exchanged a glance. She smiled as if to say *I told you it would be fine,* and I found myself smiling back.

We settled Leo on the sofa, snug in a nest of blankets, and Lara and I sat down for a cup of tea and walnut cake before going to bed. Lara's head slipped on my shoulder as she ate. She was exhausted.

"How much you've grown in such a short space of time!" Mum said to her, squeezing her hand. "And your hair!" She stroked Lara's head softly.

"My hair is frizzy," Lara said sleepily.

"Your hair is gorgeous. Come, I'll show you the cottage. You won't recognise it!"

We walked across the courtyard and my mum opened the

door for us to walk through the threshold. As she switched the light on, my heart swelled. I couldn't believe how lovely the place was – it had only been an empty shell when we last visited.

They had left the bricks on show on the walls and on the rounded ceiling; it made the place look like a miniature castle but at the same time cosy and warm. Against the left wall there was a fireplace with a sweet-smelling peat fire smouldering away, its mantelpiece decorated with tiny yellow fairy lights. Right in the centre of the room was a wooden double bed covered in a creamy duvet, and just beside it was a little blue toddler's bed for Leo. Michael had carried in our luggage, and it sat on the floor in front of a huge antique wardrobe carved with flowers and blooms.

"What do you think?" My mum was beaming. I was momentarily speechless.

"Oh, Mum," I said. "I can't believe this! It's just . . . perfect," I sighed, rocking Leo gently. He felt warm and heavy in my arms, sleeping deeply like only children can.

"I knew you'd like it. Come, across here there's Lara's room . . ."

"My room!" Lara exclaimed, suddenly awake, and ran through. As I settled Leo in his bed, I heard Lara cooing. I followed her through and just had to join in. My mum had assembled the perfect room for her personality. The walls were turquoise, with an old-fashioned cast-iron fireplace lit with tiny dragonfly fairy lights. Behind her bed hung a fabric drapery decorated with hummingbirds and flowers in every shade of turquoise and blue. An antique wardrobe sat against the wall opposite the bed. And then Lara spotted the *pièce de résistance*: an antique writing cabinet with little drawers and shelves to keep her stationery in, and even an ink and pen holder.

Lara went from corner to corner, taking it all in, her eyes wide.

"Do you like it?" my mum asked.

"It's *amazing*!" she said, and threw herself on her bed, only to get up again and sit at her writing cabinet. "Just awesome. It's like you read my mind for the room of my dreams. Thank you, Nonna," she said, and ran and hugged her tight.

"There's a bathroom, too," she said, holding Lara. "In case you were wondering if you had to walk across the courtyard in the middle of the night! Look."

The bathroom was tiny but perfectly formed, and I already saw myself soaking in a hot bath.

"I can't thank you enough, Mum." It was my turn to hug her.

"You don't need to thank me at all."

I was too wound up to sleep. Leo was snoring softly like a baby seal snorts under water, and I lay in my bed under the creamy duvet, watching the embers smoulder red in the gloom. I just couldn't switch off. In the small hours of the morning I gave up and went to check on Lara.

She was fast asleep, curled up in her turquoise bed. It was the first time in weeks she hadn't woken up through the night, and I was surprised, especially considering that we were in an entirely new place. I noticed with a smile that she had already sorted her books in the bookshelves and that her pens and Kitty were sitting on the writing cabinet.

I went back into my room and sat at the window. A few stars still shone in the morning sky, but a sea of grey edged with pink meant night was turning into day. I took in the silhouette of the pine-covered mountains and the patches of purple heather and the million shades of brown and green on the hills. It looked so wild, so raw, compared with the manicured London suburbs I lived in. On impulse, I grabbed my phone.

We are in Glen Avich, I typed. I was about to tap the little message icon, but I hesitated for a moment. And then, before I could stop myself, I sent the text to Ash. He replied at once.

Good to know.

He must have been awake, waiting to hear from us.

All of a sudden I felt tears pressing behind my eyes again. Some ties, even if worn and constricting and infused with bitterness, are very difficult to break – maybe impossible. Not without severing parts of yourself with them, anyway.

8

The weight of years

Torcuil

My heart always soars when I return from Edinburgh to Glen Avich. The sight of my family home, Ramsay Hall – of the deer in the fields and the tree house on one of the oak trees beside the stables – is enough to make me smile, even today. Even when I know that a cold, empty house awaits me. Mrs Gordon, my housekeeper, handed in her resignation just last week, and she was the one who kept things going. I suppose it would be easier for me not to come back to Ramsay Hall at all except during the holidays, and just stay over in my flat in Edinburgh. But I don't seem to be able to stay away from Glen Avich.

I *try*. I make my plans for the weekend with my Edinburgh friends, and then, after work on the Friday, I get restless. It's like I have some sort of inner compass that always points north. It always leads me here with a magnetic force I can't quite control. It's Ramsay Hall that calls me, our family's residence for many generations, and my *home*. Before anything else, this mansion and its fields and woods is home to me like no other place can ever be. I used to lecture in medieval history in London, but I just couldn't settle so far away from Glen Avich. I managed to find a post at Edinburgh University, which took me closer. But still not close enough.

Anyway, my housekeeper. She'd worked at Ramsay Hall for the best part of thirty years, since I was a child. When my dad died and my mum moved to Perth, Mrs Gordon remained. She kept living at Ramsay Hall while I was in London and only came back for the holidays, but she moved back to the village after a few years, saying that Ramsay Hall had become too lonely, too spooky for her. I could hardly blame her; living in such a huge mansion on my own didn't exactly appeal to me either. For a few years we followed the same routine: every Thursday and Friday she'd get the place ready for me, cleaning the living areas, shopping for groceries and seeing that Dougie, the local handyman, did the odd jobs that needed done. This meant that when I came back on a Friday night I'd find the place (relatively) warm and food in the cupboards. But last year Mrs Gordon had a midlife crisis at the ripe age of sixty-three, and took up ballroom dancing with another local gentleman, Mr McNally from the Post Office. She swore that their relationship was based on their mutual love of dancing and was not romantic at all – actually, Mr McNally had a lady friend he'd met on a cruise, and he was hoping to move to Shropshire to be with her soon. But he and Mrs Gordon were forever taking time off to go to dancing tournaments and rehearsing in the ballroom here at Ramsay Hall, in spite of the freezing temperatures, until finally the passion they'd been denying for so long bloomed in all its sequinned glory. Mr McNally wrote to the Shropshire lady; Mrs Gordon left her last steak pie in my fridge, hung up her apron and donned a feather boa. Together they're going to tango to Blackpool, the heart of ballroom dancing.

I thought I would manage fine on my own, but this was only last week and already I miss her terribly. I'm too busy and too disorganised, and Ramsay Hall is just overwhelming, it needs so much work. I've asked Fiona, who works at the stables, to kick the boiler for me every Friday morning – it's the only way to get the heating going, but you have to know *where* to kick it – so at least I don't freeze every weekend. It has to be done in the summer too; Ramsay Hall has its own microclimate, a constant winter. The heat of the sun can't get through the thick stone walls, and the only way to heat the mansion is from the inside.

Anyway, this week Fiona is away, and I forgot to ask my cousin Inary to come and sort the heating, so the house will be a *fridge*. I also haven't had time to get the groceries, because I had an enormous backlog of paperwork to do and hand in to the office before I left. I can't remember what's in my cupboards, but I vaguely recall a jar of pesto and some stock cubes – that's pretty much all.

It's nearly midnight now as I drive into Glen Avich, and there's nowhere open except the petrol station, but I don't fancy a mummified sausage roll and a tin of beans. Visions of the steak pies and lasagne that Mrs Gordon used to leave in my fridge float in front of my eyes. I decide to stop at the Golden Palace, the first – and only – Chinese takeaway in the village. It opens late on a Friday to cater for those coming out of the pub. As I walk back to my car with a parcel of Singapore noodles, spring rolls and prawn crackers, a lovely sound makes me turn around, the voice of a woman resounding a few doors down from the Golden Palace.

"*Tesoro mio!*"

The little scene, illuminated by the light of a lamp post, makes me stand and watch for a moment. An elderly lady is standing a few steps from me, in front of a green car, beaming like she's just seen the most beautiful sunrise. She takes a younger woman in her arms, repeating *tesoro mio*, and then she leans down to recover something – someone – from the car. It's a little dark-haired boy in blue pyjamas, covered with a plaid blanket. She holds him and closes her eyes for a moment, caressing his head. Next, a young girl steps out of the car and the lady holds her too in a three-way hug. I'm entranced by this display of family love. Suddenly, the younger woman turns towards me for a moment and the lamp post illuminates her – I stop in my tracks. She has big, dark eyes and long, dark hair framing her face, and there's something about her that makes me think of sunshine, even in the middle of the night and in the north of Scotland. All of a sudden I'm embarrassed – staring at this woman, standing and watching such an intimate scene that belongs to them only. And then, as she balances her bag and her jacket, something falls from her hands. It's a little stuffed toy – a penguin. She turns her back as she tries to retrieve it and I step forward to help, picking it up and dusting it off before handing it to her.

"Thank you," she smiles, and her eyes meet mine. They are soft, brown, shaded with long black eyelashes and circled with tiredness.

"Come on in, Margherita," the older woman calls, rocking the little boy from side to side. I recognise her now: it's Debora, from the coffee shop – I've been there once with Inary. I say hello, but she doesn't seem to hear me or recognise me. I walk away from the little family scene, somehow reluctantly. I feel stranded, as strange as it might sound. I can't help thinking that I'm going home to an empty house.

Ramsay Hall stands dark and lonely tonight. I make my way to the back and unlock the door. Theo and Dolinda, my cats, slip in beside me. They rub themselves against my legs as I step over the pile of post, dotted with little muddy cat prints, and let my rucksack fall to the mat.

"Hello, cats. How have you been?" They seem in great form. Since Mrs Gordon has gone and there's no more food to be had around the house during the week, they've moved their territory to around the stables. There, Fiona leaves them bowls of food and plates of milk to top up the mice and birds they hunt. Theo and Dolinda pretend to be domesticated, with their purring and their little collars – but they are panthers in disguise. Honestly, there is not a mouse to be seen around here, in spite of all the nooks and crannies where they could hide.

As I step into the kitchen, a wall of cold hits me. The place is freezing. Why, oh why did I forget to ask someone, anyone, to turn on the heating? Now it'll be hours before the temperature goes above zero. I go through the post quickly and one letter jumps out to me. Punches me in the face, more like. It's from my mother. Perth is an hour away but might as well be on another planet, because my mother never phones and visits barely once a year: she keeps in touch with me with letters, proper letters, on creamy paper with her name embossed in a corner. *Lady Fiona Ramsay.* Just seeing it written down knots up my stomach – this is the effect my mother has on my brother and me, and has had since we were children.

Torcuil, (no wasting time with Dears, then)
My friend Helena has been in touch. She said the last time she was at the stables she noticed that the grounds are getting wilder and wilder. I hope you realise how distressing this is for your sister and me. We trusted you to look after the estate, and

you're simply not doing that. Between you and Angus things are just going to pot – this is her being informal – *I implore you, for my sake and your sister's and yours* – I can just hear her stressing that word the way she does, like she's speaking to a halfwit – *get it sorted.*

I sigh in frustration.

She trusts me to look after the estate with no money to hire people to do it and no time to do it myself. My brother Angus is away playing his violin all over the world and his wife's health is getting worse every day, so they can't help. It's just me, trying to keep Ramsay Hall from crumbling.

This letter will be kindling for the fire – and I'm vaguely angry at myself for still letting my mother make me feel inadequate, like a child, at thirty-six years of age; for always, always letting her get to me.

I can't deal with this right now anyway. I have stuff to do. *A lot* to do, I consider as I plug in the kettle and unwrap my rather sad takeaway for one. I have to mark a million essays before I go back to Edinburgh, and I have to find a housekeeper who actually stays and works instead of going off to dance the marimba with a retired postman, bless her.

But although my mother is horrible – that's not an opinion really, more a fact – she's right about Ramsay Hall needing to be looked after. Gravity seems to be stronger around it. It looks as though it's endlessly falling to pieces, even if we seem to be doing repairs day in and day out. Suddenly I'm exhausted and not hungry any more. I'm fed up, sitting in the cold eating even colder noodles.

I leave my dinner unfinished and go straight to bed, trying to forget everything and to manage some sleep. The night seems so wide and windy, so lonely. I close the curtains to the world, I shiver my way under the duvet and, finally, I close my eyes.

A word comes back to me: *Margherita*. The name of the dark-eyed woman. Her eyes looked a bit like Stoirin's eyes, my horse – huge and with impossibly long eyelashes. Such a beautiful name. It must be Italian for Margaret . . .

I'm sinking into sleep, and then I feel my hair stand on end and my skin ripple with static. Here we go, I think, and sure enough, something thumps my bed gently: once, twice. I know it's not the cats.

"Yes, I'm back!" I whisper to the darkness around me. All that's left at Ramsay Hall are cats, horses and restless spirits. And me.

9

Somewhere to be

Margherita

And so there we were, on a clear, chilly morning in Scotland. It was like waking up in a different world. I was exhausted from the sleepless night, but my mum's espresso – so thick that you could have cut it with a knife – managed to wake me.

As we walked through the streets of Glen Avich for an exploratory wander, it still felt surreal. The village looked so different from everything I knew, with its whitewashed cottages and the pine-covered hills surrounding it like a crown. The grass seemed to shine from the inside, and the sky took my breath away with its galloping grey-purple clouds. The air was so thin, so pure and clean it made me feel like I was breathing for the first time in aeons.

Leo, all wrapped up in a hoodie and with Pingu in tow, was holding Lara's hand. He was a bit unsure of the new place and clung to us. Lara, on the other hand, had a spring in her step after a rare night of unbroken sleep. My heart gladdened when, at breakfast, I'd seen her helping herself to a second jam croissant, light and buttery like only my mum could make. Her cheeks were pink in the chilly air, and she looked cute in leggings and the bright-red wellies Nonna had lent her. We just weren't equipped for the Scottish summer, but later that day we planned to visit the outdoors shop (aptly called the

Welly) to stock up on the right clothes and footwear for rainy days.

"Let's go to La Piazza and say hi to Michael," Lara suggested.

"Good plan," my mum said, taking Lara by the arm. I watched them walk on, Mum and Lara and Leo, and I thought they fit so well together, like three pieces of a jigsaw. Funny, how Leo and Lara were both quite unconcerned to be so far from their dad, for now at least. They were so used to it being the three of us, used to their father being away both in body and spirit, that they didn't feel there was anything out of place in that picture.

A surge of sorrow hit me. What kind of family were we? A family of three? Maybe Ash had been right in insinuating I left him out. And still, it was his decision to work all hours and play golf the rest of the time, I reminded myself. It was his decision not to spend time with us. But recognising his faults didn't make me feel better, didn't make me feel like I was in the right. The blame game had no winners. I tried to shake myself out of those gloomy thoughts, but there was so much going on in my head.

"Here we are," said my mum, pushing the door of her coffee shop proudly, making the wind chimes tinkle. I'd been so lost in thought I hadn't even noticed we'd passed the tiny hairdresser's, Enchant, then Peggy's shop – the local emporium – and arrived at the door of La Piazza. A delicious scent hit my nostrils as we walked in. It was only the second time I had seen my mum's and Michael's coffee shop, but when we first visited it was still a work in progress. They'd sent me pictures of the building when they bought it – it was solid and well kept but completely anonymous. Apparently it had been used as a tailor's shop for many years, but its previous owners now lived down in England and never visited, so they'd decided to sell. Mum and Michael had refurbished it completely, turning an empty shell into a warm, welcoming haven. They painted it bright white both inside and outside, and mounted a wooden sign over the door with La Piazza written in blue lettering. They ripped up the old flooring and covered everything in light wood; and brightly coloured photographs of wildlife and landscapes around the village, taken by a local photographer, decorated the walls. The bread and cakes they sold were beautifully displayed, and on the counter stood glass-covered plates of homemade goodies. The two fireplaces gave a lovely warmth and glow, and there was a corner with a soft, colourful rug and a box full of toys and books, where children could play while their parents drank their coffees. As a final touch, there were fairy lights – my mum's trademark – everywhere, hanging over the fireplace and the walls, and they made the place look enchanted. They had chosen artfully mismatched vintage china and flowery tablecloths – no two tables were the same. I could see that everything had been picked carefully and with love. My mum had a natural gift at turning everything she touched into something beautiful, and a great eye for colours and patterns. My dad always said I was like her in that way, that it was an Italian thing to have an instinct for beauty, but I felt that if I did have a gift I hadn't really used it in the last few years. As I looked around at what my mum and Michael had done, as I took in the fruits of their labour and commitment, I felt a deep, deep desire to see things blooming from my fingers again, to create and make and shape. To have something I felt truly *mine*.

"Hello, welcome!" boomed Michael from behind the counter. "So, what do you think?" He echoed my mum's words when she'd showed us our rooms. I was moved by how eager they were to impress us, to show us the outcome of all their hard work.

"I think it's wonderful." And I meant it.

"Can I have a chocolate muffin?" asked Leo. There was a big tray of muffins covered by a glass dome that was impossible to miss.

"Sorry, my son is right down to business!" I laughed.

"Absolutely. Aisling, a muffin for the gentleman. In the VIP area, please," Michael said solemnly, gesturing towards the corner with the toy boxes and squishy sofas.

Aisling played his game. "Master Ward," she said in a rolling Irish accent that surprised me, placing a chocolate muffin on a plate in the children's area. She was a stunning woman, with long black hair and moss-coloured eyes. She wouldn't have looked out of place in a fashion magazine.

We sat at a table near the window as Leo played and ate his muffin. Lara and Aisling were chatting behind the counter. Michael brought us each a cappuccino and two generous slices of cherry and almond tart. I could almost *see* the calories settling around my hips, but I could never say no to cake, not when it looked so lush anyway.

"I'm so glad to have you here." My mum smiled. She hadn't stopped smiling since the night before, it seemed.

"Me too. I just wish it were under different circumstances," I said wearily. "I'm so confused right now, I can't untangle my thoughts."

"Try and put Ash out of your mind for a few days. I know it's easier said than done, but it's way too early to be making decisions about your marriage anyway. You've only been apart for six months."

"I'll try." I looked into my lap. A frightening thought flashed through my mind: that a decision had already been made, that I was just failing to see it.

Failing being the operative word.

Right at that moment the door opened, the clear sound of the wind chimes above it filled the air, and a red-haired young woman with a laptop under her arm came in. There was something about her, something in her demeanour – maybe her vivacity, her spirit – that I imagined would make people do a double-take: it certainly made *me*. She was wrapped in a long cardigan and wore a woollen miniskirt, and she was small and slight.

"Hi, everyone! Do you mind if I stop here to do some work? My house is full of various in-laws up from Edinburgh, including Alex's five nephews. *Five*. I can't hear myself thinking! Can I have the first of half a dozen cappuccinos?" she said, piling her stuff on the table beside ours. She had a soft Scottish accent, the kind that sounds like a rippling stream.

"Coming up," said Aisling.

"That is Inary Monteith," my mum whispered. "Remember the book I left with you when I came down to London, the one that mentions La Piazza in the acknowledgments? *She* wrote it."

"Oh, yes, *The Choice*! I loved that book, I really did. Wow, a real-life author! I bet Lara would love to meet her . . . but she seems busy now."

"Don't worry, there'll be plenty of chances. She comes here a lot to work," my mum said conspiratorially. "She says she likes the peace and quiet."

"Okay. Mum, look what I brought." I slipped Nonna Ghita's

notebook out of my handbag. "I thought we could work from it a bit while I'm here."

"Oh! I haven't seen this in years!" she said, taking the little notebook reverently from my hands and opening it. The pages were yellowed, and there were little stains on them from many baking sessions. "Oooh . . . *baci di dama, torta di Nonna Rosa*, oh, you loved that one for your breakfast! *Amaretti . . . torcetti* . . . I haven't made these in ages!" The names of those delicacies evoked memories of beautiful smells and tastes, and happy times in the kitchen with my own nonna as I was growing up.

"Maybe we can offer some Piedmontese specialities here in the coffee shop. I'm sure we can try to stretch the local taste buds a little."

"Oh, yes. You'd be surprised how bold the local old ladies can be. I'm weaning them off scones and onto almond croissants!" she laughed.

"There's something else," I said as I slipped the notebook back into my handbag. "I was thinking. I'd like to find a job for the summer. Part-time only, of course, having the children . . ."

"You can work for us, Margherita."

"Oh, I see, having us come and stay was all a plot to get me up to bake for you!" I laughed.

"Absolutely. I'm glad you twigged!"

"You are very kind, and I will help out, but you don't need another person, you know that. You'd just be doing me a favour."

"Well, what's wrong with doing your own daughter a favour?" She shrugged.

"Thank you, but after the summer . . ." I began, and then I hesitated. *After the summer* was uncharted territory. I had no idea what was going to happen. "Whatever happens with Ash and me, I want to go back to work. My real job, what I trained for. Work as a chef." Every time I said that word aloud I got a rush of desire for a busy kitchen, the scents of yummy things cooking, the buzz and challenge of it all.

"That's a good plan. I never told you, but I could guess you missed your work. You used to enjoy it so much."

"I did. I'm glad I didn't work these last few years, I think it was the right decision and I don't regret it for a moment, but things have changed now. When I see what you did here . . ." – I looked around at all my mum's and Michael's hard work – ". . . it makes me feel like I have so much more to give."

"You do. And you should. I can look after Leo." My mum has always been so supportive of me and, once again, she wasn't letting me down. I felt very lucky.

"Are you sure?"

"Absolutely. Look at him, he's no trouble," my mum said, her gaze moving to little Leo over in the play area. He was building a Duplo castle with Lara's help, too busy to take any notice of us. "It would also give me a chance to spend more time with him. I've seen him so rarely for a year . . . This was my only qualm about moving so far away, you know. Anyway, you are here now. At least for a bit."

"Thanks Mum. If you're sure . . . You see, this could be a good chance to dip my toes in the water and get a few hours somewhere, just to start with. Tourists flock up in the summer, don't they? I'm sure there are a few businesses needing a hand. Like guest houses, or something. I mean, I would still help here, of course, and it would just be for a few hours a week—"

"I'm sorry, I couldn't help hearing your conversation . . ." said a voice beside us. It was Inary.

90

"That's what you come here for, don't you, Inary? Looking for stories," my mum laughed, and the red-haired girl joined in the laughter.

"You know me too well. Anyway, I heard what you were saying about a summer job . . . I think I might be able to help. You know my cousin Torcuil, up at Ramsay Hall?"

"Oh, yes, of course."

"He needs someone to help look after the house. Well, not the whole house, just the living quarters."

"Like a housekeeper?" I said. I was looking for something more focused on cooking, but I was open to suggestions.

"Yes, sort of. Mrs Gordon gave her resignation, you know, Agnes Gordon?" Inary said towards my mum. "She's now engaged to Malchie McNally, the former postman."

"Oh, yes. I know who you mean."

"Well, they're moving down south to dedicate themselves to ballroom dancing." Inary's lips turned up mischievously, and my mum laughed.

"Mrs Gordon, a closet dancer? And Malchie? Who would have guessed!"

"Oh, yes. Apparently, they're doing what they call Silver Tournaments, for dancing OAPs."

"Well, good on them. I hope I'm dancing when I'm their age!" my mum laughed.

"So yes, Torcuil has nobody to help, and you know how he's away in Edinburgh all week and he only comes home at weekends. It's been hard going for him. If you're interested, maybe I could pass on your phone number to him, Margherita? I'd give you his, but he never answers his mobile. He loses it a lot. Once he left his BlackBerry in the freezer."

91

"Frozen blackberries make great milkshakes. Sorry, I had to say it." I giggled at my own silly joke. "But yes, why not? It wouldn't be exactly what I was looking for, but it would be a start . . ." I hunted in my handbag for a pen and scribbled my number on a napkin.

"Perfect, she said, slipping the napkin into her canvas bag. "Well, I'm done eavesdropping; I'll get back to work."

"Work? Making up stories is not a real job," Michael chipped in.

"Ha ha." Inary smiled.

"Ignore him, Inary," my mum said. "Well, the universe is clearly giving you a sign, Margherita."

I wanted to believe it.

"Anyway, we must be off. We're going to the Welly to get some warm stuff for these two!"

"Say hi to my brother for me," Inary said.

"Oh, does your brother work there?"

"Yes, he owns the shop. Everybody is related here." She shrugged. "He's the one who took those pictures," she said, gesturing at the lovely framed photographs on the wall. "And Aisling, there, is his partner."

"For my sins," said Aisling, but there was a softness in her eyes that told me she was happy.

We rose to go; my mum leaned over the counter and placed a kiss on Michael's cheek. With a flurry of goodbyes we spilled out onto the street, and I was left wondering what it must feel like to be in the kind of relationship where you kiss them goodbye even if you are only walking down the road.

"Lara," I said as soon as we were out of earshot. "See that girl who came in, Inary? She's an author."

Lara's face lit up. "A real author?"

92

"Yes! You can show her your stuff," I said.

She blushed. "I don't know . . ."

"Why not? Your stories are great, Lara."

"You would say that, though, you're my mum."

"Well, no, I mean it. She's putting me in touch with her cousin for a summer job. Maybe you and Inary can meet up for a chat?"

"That would be *amazing!*" Lara loved the word *amazing*. Everything was either *amazing* or *awesome*.

Leo pulled at my hand. "Mummy!" He had his nose stuck to the shop window next door to La Piazza. In my mind, I called it The Shop That Sells Everything. I'd met Peggy, its owner, on my first visit to Glen Avich.

"Look! A fire engine," Leo said reverently, like he'd seen Spiderman himself materialise in front of him. Leo had a thing for toy fire engines, especially if they had lights and made noise.

"That's quite splendid," my mum said. "Can I . . ." She glanced at me.

I smiled. "Okay then. But just because he doesn't have many toys here with him. Let's not make this a habit."

"We won't. Promise. Sure we won't, Leo?"

"We won't!" he said, having no idea what he was talking about but clearly ready to say anything that would get him the fire engine.

"Sure Nonna can spoil you every once in a while," she said, leading us into the shop. "Hi, Peggy!"

"Oh, hello, Debora. And who do we have here? These are *not* your grandchildren, are they? How they've grown! Look at this boy!" Peggy was a kind lady, immaculately dressed and with a sweet manner.

"It's them indeed. Leo is now three and Lara is fourteen."

"Nearly fifteen," Lara specified.

"Here's a lollipop for you, wee man. And Lara, would you like one?"

Lara shrugged and smiled. "Yes, thanks," she said. Clearly being *nearly fifteen* wasn't too old for a lollipop.

"You know, my niece Eilidh has a wee one about his age."

"Oh, yes," I said. I'd met Eilidh and her son in passing when we first visited. "How old is Sorley now? Two?"

"Two and a half. Maybe they could get together for a play date, if you stay for a while?"

"Absolutely," I said. "I'd love that. Leo, would you like to play with Sorley?"

"With the fire engine?" he replied, placing both hands on the box in the window but without daring to lift it. I laughed. It was a clever way of reminding us why we were there in the first place.

"With the fire engine." My mum laughed too. "Thank you, Peggy," she said, paying for the toy. "I see Eilidh quite a lot at the coffee shop anyway, so we'll arrange something."

"Righty-o, see you soon."

Leo insisted on carrying his toy, even if the box was nearly as tall as he was. We walked on slowly, Leo waddling in front of us blindly, unable to see where he was going. Before long, he relented and let me take the box.

"Look after it, Mummy."

"I will, don't worry."

Our shopping trip to the Welly was successful. Logan – Inary's brother – kitted us out with some warm stuff for the Scottish summer. I bought an aqua-coloured zip-up fleece with flowery wellies, Lara bought a blue hoodie and a pair of bright-pink wellies, and Leo was now the proud owner of a pair of dinosaur-shaped boots and a little waterproof jacket with a hood. On the way home we stopped time and time again to greet people in the street. My mum seemed to be very well liked within the community, and people were keen to meet the children and me. I wasn't surprised. My mum has always been so open; she makes friends wherever she goes.

"Everybody knows everybody here!" Lara said.

"It's a small place. Many families have lived here for generations. Just like in Castelmonte," my mum said, recalling her parents' village.

"You never thought of moving back there, Mum?" I asked as the children walked ahead of us and out of earshot.

She shrugged. "I would have loved to. By the way, you know who moved back to Castelmonte? Your cousin Allegra. With her husband and children. I wonder how she's getting on . . ."

"Why did you not move back?"

"Well, that was the plan, when we retired. And then your father died. It just made no sense without him, with you and Anna over here, and Laura in Australia . . ."

"And then you met Michael."

"Yes. Michael will never leave Scotland. When his wife died, his daughter tried to convince him to move to Canada to be closer to them. She said it was absurd for him to be here alone. But he refused. He said this country was his home and that he would not go. And then we met, and here we are. We found Glen Avich and we took a leap of faith together."

"Well, it worked out." I smiled.

"Yes. I never thought I could be happy again, not without

your father. And not a day goes by that I don't miss him, Margherita."

"I know. Me too."

"And Michael misses Edith very, very much. But we have a life left to live, and we're living it. We followed our hearts."

"Yes. You built something special here. And look at me. My life is falling apart," I said bitterly.

"No it isn't. Your life is not falling apart. It's changing."

Changing without Ash, I thought. The man I married. The man I used to love. The man I still loved, in a weird way. Deep, convoluted roots of what we used to have together still burrowed into my heart. Still, I wished that none of this had happened, that our family was still together, but there was no way things could revert to the way they had been. Never. It seemed impossible now, but we used to love each other very much. We used to be happy.

Nothing would ever be the same, not even if, at the end of the summer, we were back in London, and back to reality.

"Is it okay if I go for a walk around the loch later?" Lara asked, interrupting my dark thoughts. I loved the way she said *loch*, making such an earnest effort to pronounce it correctly.

"Is it safe?" I asked Mum.

"Perfectly safe, as long as you don't go too near the water. The shores can be slippery."

"Nonna, I'm not a child!" Lara rolled her eyes.

"No, that's true. You are *nearly fifteen, tesoro.*"

"Exactly!" she said. And then, after a pause. "You're teasing me!"

"Just a little. Anyway, time to take Leo home for lunch."

"Yes, we haven't eaten anything for the last . . . half an hour. We'll die of starvation any time," Lara said.

"Are *you* teasing *me*, now?"

"Just a little," Lara said, and they both laughed, easy understanding and affection flowing between them.

At that moment, my phone chirped. "Oh. A text from that Torcuil person. *Hello Margherita. Torcuil here,*" I read aloud. "*It would be great if you could come up to Ramsay Hall tomorrow any time and we can have a chat. I'll show you where to kick the boiler.*" I paused. What?

Mum nodded. "That's good. But what does he mean by kicking the boiler?"

"No idea. But maybe he'll also show me where to punch the washing machine," I smiled, typing a reply.

"You're not going to say that, are you? He's a lord!" My mum was flustered.

"A what?"

"A lord. Lord Ramsay."

"Don't worry, I'll curtsey when I see him, Mum," I laughed.

Sure. See you tomorrow. Margherita.

"You can see it from here. Ramsay Hall, I mean," my mum said. "There, beyond the loch."

My gaze went towards Loch Avich, and there they were, nestled on the side of one of the hills, the grey stones of Ramsay Hall. Even from so far away, the place looked quite imposing. A little lump of anxiety settled in my chest, but I ignored it. I imagined Lord Ramsay to be a bumbling, pompous middle-aged man wearing a tweed jacket and sounding like he had marbles in his mouth. He was bit of a snob, probably. Not that it would be a problem. I'd quickly put him in his place.

10

Wandering

Lara

Dear Kitty,

So, this is what happened. We are in Glen Avich. I didn't write yesterday because we spent the whole day in the car and by the time we arrived my eyes were closing. My room here at Nonna's house is gorgeous, a real grown-up room with a writing cabinet (which is like a desk but cooler – that's where I'm writing now) and a lot of bookshelves. I even have a fireplace! Can you roast marshmallows on a peat fire? I must Google it. Here the signal is terrible, but hey, you can't have everything. And I found we have okay reception in the bathroom, so that's where I go when I need the Internet. I sit in the bathtub. Anyway, I met a real writer!!! Her name is Inary Monteith. She's a friend of Nonna's. I hope we can meet up for a chat.

Today I went to the loch (NB. it's loCHHH, not lock. They'll tell you off if you get it wrong and also I don't like pronouncing things wrong). I love wandering alone, thinking about things. Just walking around with nowhere to go, nothing to do. Exploring. There was only so much wandering I could do in London, and anyway there are people and shops and cars everywhere. Here in Glen Avich there are places where there's so much silence I can actually *hear* it.

My mum has a job interview tomorrow. Trust my mum to

have everything organised for herself in the space of forty-eight hours. She has this thing: she sorts people out, she sorts places out, she sorts herself out. It's like a magic wand she uses to go from chaos to order. I wish I had the same gift, but I seem to do the opposite. I go *from* order *to* chaos, usually.

The air here is so damp my hair has gone all frizzy. I can't believe I'm wearing a fleece in July, it's just *not right*. But everything is beautiful here and the air smells so lovely. Nonna has been great. She is the *best*. First of all, she feeds me loads, because she says I'm too skinny. I hadn't realised how *hungry* I was until I started eating. Risotto is my favourite. And her cakes!!! I could just eat and eat. This morning Leo had a special homemade cake called *torta di Nonna Rosa* for breakfast, and warm milk. Apparently, this is what Italian children eat sometimes for their *colazione*: cake! (That's Italian for breakfast.) Lucky things. Oh, I'm also learning Italian. And a bit of Scots from Michael: like, today is *dreich* (CH, same as in loch). It means that it's grey and drizzly.

Overall, things are good, though I heard my mum crying last night. Things with my dad are messed up. They always fought back home, every time he came round, but she misses him all the same. Weird.

Enough for now. Nonna is calling us for lunch (*tortellini – si grazie*) and then I'm going for a walk to the loch. Write later.

*

I'm back!

This place is like something from a postcard, a picture-perfect corner you'd expect to pop up in a fairy tale . . . but let me start from the beginning.

I went to walk across the bridge, but there was someone sitting on it. I was a bit nervous all of a sudden. There didn't seem to be anyone around, this being the residential area and not the high street with its hustle and bustle (I'm being sarcastic). Why would anyone be sitting on the bridge anyway? Are they watching all the people pass by? (i.e. nobody.)

For a second I wondered if I should stop and change direction. I'm a bit paranoid about these things because when I stayed with my dad I had to go to the corner shop on my own to buy food because my dad never bothered, and it scared me. But anyway, enough with the memories.

I decided to walk on. This is Glen Avich, not London. And I'm nearly fifteen, not a child any more. I pretended not to look, but I kept an eye on the stranger. It was definitely a man. A young man, I realised as I got closer. He was wearing a tweed cap. A young man in a tweed cap? Where does he buy his clothes? Unless it's ironic retro, as Polly would say.

"Hello," he said.

Against my better judgement, I stopped and said hello back.

"There's nobody around," he said, and he seemed a little bit lost.

Oh. I asked myself, does he mean, *There's nobody around so I can conveniently rob you and kill you and throw your body in the river*, and then my friends will set up a Facebook page for me and Ian will leave a heartbreaking tribute asking why, oh why he never realised how he truly felt for me. Or does it mean, *Morning, nobody around and such lovely weather blah blah* small talk?

The boy didn't look scary. Actually, he looked a little bit lost. His eyes were flint-grey (nice expression, eh? I found it in *Bride of Shadows*, the first in the Shadows series. *Awesome* book. The hero, Damien, has flint-grey eyes) and his arms were very white, Scottish white. You've never seen white skin until you've been to Scotland, honestly. He was wearing a white shirt and dark woollen trousers.

"No, that's true. It's very early," I said.

"I like it like this. It's peaceful. But I wish I saw more people. There's *always* nobody around."

I took a second to digest this strange statement. It sounded weird, but then a lot of girls in school say I'm weird, so I can hardly be judgemental. "Do you live in Glen Avich?"

"Yes. Up that way." His hand waved towards the loch in the distance. "Do you? I haven't seen you before."

"I'm just here for the summer. My nonna . . . *grandma* owns La Piazza, you know, the coffee shop?"

He looked at me blankly. "I've never tried coffee."

"Right."

Who hasn't tried coffee? Maybe his mum and dad are some kind of health freaks or something and they only drink herbal teas?

"What's your name? Who are your people?" he asked.

My people? As in, *My people will speak to your people*? Or as in *What's your tribe?* and I should say I am Lara of the Clan Ward?

I decided I *could* actually be judgemental: this boy was strange. Or maybe it was a Scottish thing, maybe they ask "who are your people?" as a matter of course.

"My name is Lara. My people . . ." I giggled a bit. "My mum's name is Margherita Ward and my dad's name is Ashley Ward, and I have a little brother called Leo. I also have three aunts, two uncles, several cousins and two sets of grandparents. They are my people."

101

"I've never heard of any Wards in Glen Avich." He looked about eighteen, but he sounded like Nonna's eighty-year-old neighbour. Apparently, when Nonna moved up to Glen Avich she said, "We've never had any Italians in this village" (pron. Ayetalians.) "Well, you missed out," Nonna had answered diplomatically.

"We are brand new here," I replied. "So, I'll just go, I guess . . . I'll see you around."

"Yes," he said, and his face lit up all of a sudden and he didn't look that bad. "I'm looking forward to seeing you again." He took his cap off and his hair was very dark, almost blue, and curly. A bit messy, in a nice way. "Maybe up at the loch. I'll show you my favourite places, if you like."

I shrugged in an attempt to look unconcerned, but I was kind of happy. "Sure."

I walked on across the bridge, and as I stepped off it I turned around for a second. He was still sitting there, looking at me. He raised a hand and waved it in the air with a sweet smile, the sort of smile I've never seen on Ian or any of the boys I know. It was then I realised two things: that I'd forgotten to ask his name, and that he wasn't wearing any shoes.

11

Dust

Margherita

Lara, Inary and I walked along the loch shore towards Ramsay Hall, its grey stones appearing and disappearing from view as we advanced, like an enchanted castle from a fairy tale. It was my first time near Loch Avich since I'd arrived and I was bewitched by its calm beauty. The afternoon was chilly and clear, and the water was shining green, rippling softly in the breeze. It was worlds away from my suburban home in London: another world, another life.

"Look! There's a little island there," I pointed out to Lara. In the middle of the loch sat a little mound of land covered in larches and pine trees, like something out of a mystical vision. "That's Innis Ailsa," Inary said, with her delicate Scottish accent. "But we call it Ailsa." I was still to get used to the local lilt – everything people said sounded like a song. The name of the island sounded something like "Eylsa", in that beautiful, mysterious language that is Gaelic. Gaelic was completely foreign to me and it wasn't in my blood; and still, there was a sense of weird familiarity to it, like I'd heard it somewhere before, in a distant past.

Lara smiled. "It sounds like a spell," she said. "Like something out of Harry Potter." She branded an imaginary wand, "Innis Ailsa!"

We walked on, the grass still wet and shiny with morning dew, mist slowly rising from the hills. The perfect silence was only broken by the noise of the water lapping the shore and the rustling of birds in the trees. It was so peaceful. Flashbacks of my life in the run-up to the summer hit me all of a sudden – busy days, packed schedules full of chores that somehow seemed all-important. When had my life become so frantic? For months, years even, it had felt like everything had to be done now, everything needed seen to at once.

I took a deep, deep breath, letting this new calm fill me up. It's only when you put your burdens down, I considered, that you realise how heavy they were, how hard it was to carry them for all that time.

"Here we are," Inary announced. We were in front of a stone arch with an iron gate at its centre; ivy-covered stone walls continued at both sides of the arch as far as the eye could see, semi-hidden by trees. There was a heavy chain threaded between the gate's halves, holding them together, but Inary opened it without a key. Lord Ramsay was expecting us.

We stepped onto a gravelled space with Ramsay Hall at its centre. Lara gave a little *oh*, and I looked around me in awe. Inary was smiling silently, aware of our admiration.

Ramsay Hall was built of beautiful grey stone, with a square central building and two wings at its sides, and ivy climbing up its walls. Its structure was symmetrical and harmonious, a jewel of perfect proportions. A copse of oak trees surrounded the house like a garland, and endless fields of grass rolled gently beyond them before turning into pine-clad hills. My stomach churned a bit, but I resolved not to be daunted by the mansion's size and by the title of its owner. After all, a bumbling old man in a tweed jacket could never intimidate me.

I imagined him calling me *dear*. Maybe he had a moustache. And a cravat, and knickerbockers. Okay, now I was getting a bit carried away.

We heard the low, gentle neighing of a horse coming from the outbuildings on the right-hand side. "Are those stables?" I asked.

"Yes. They have a riding school, if you want to take lessons," Inary replied.

"Not me . . . horses are *high*." I shook my head in horror. Horse riding is one of the many things I'll never even consider doing. "But maybe Lara . . ."

"Well, I don't know . . ." Lara said.

"Torcuil will show you the stables and then you can decide. I love horse riding," Inary said, which I suspected might swing Lara towards trying. Lara was starstruck by Inary, hanging on every word she said. It was very sweet and funny, and *so* Lara. "Come to the back," she continued. "Torcuil never uses the main entrance. Nobody does, really. Only Lady Ramsay."

"Oh, there's a Lady Ramsay?" I imagined the kind of groomed, genteel old lady who would appear on the cover of *Country Living*.

"Well, not as such . . . I mean, Torcuil is not married," Inary explained as we made our way towards the back of the house. "Lady Ramsay is his mother. My aunt, on my father's side. She's scary."

"Oh."

"Don't worry, she's not here. She lives in Perth. Thankfully," she added.

As we got closer to the house I noticed signs of neglect – unchecked ivy eating away at the walls, hedges that needed

105

trimmed, windows in dire need of a wash. It was a big house for someone to live in alone.

We walked along the back wall until we reached a small wooden door painted in black. It was garlanded by a stunning fuchsia plant, laden with flowers.

Inary tapped against the wood. "Hello! It's us!"

The door opened and on the other side was a man wearing jeans, an untucked chequered shirt and silver-rimmed glasses. He was probably a stablehand or a gardener. "Come in! Hi, Inary. And you must be Margherita . . ." he said, offering me his hand. His smile was warm and shy at the same time.

"And this is Lara, Margherita's daughter," said Inary.

The man shook my daughter's hand. "Hello. I'm Torcuil."

Torcuil? I blinked a couple of times, trying to adjust to the discovery. This man was Torcuil? But he was young. And he wasn't wearing tweed. And he had all his hair.

The old, bumbling, Colonel Mustard-type figure dissolved from my mind.

"You are Lord Ramsay?" I asked, just to make sure.

He ran a hand through his thick auburn hair and left it sticking up, like a little boy who'd just woken. "Yes, but don't call me that or I won't know who you're talking to."

At that moment, I realised I'd seen him somewhere before. He was the man who'd picked up Pingu on the night we arrived.

"You were there," I said. "I mean, you were there when we arrived. You picked up my son's toy."

"Yes. Yes, it was me. Funny that. Anyway. Tea? Coffee? My coffee is a bit past its best . . ." he said, lifting a jar of something that had solidified in a weird way, like a desert rose.

"A cup of tea would be lovely," I said, looking around me.

Everything was clean and smelled of bleach – I suspected a last-minute cleaning frenzy before I arrived, and the thought made me smile. There was a vast oak table in the centre of the room, half covered in piles of books and folders, and stone slabs covered the floor; from the window I could see what must have been a gorgeous garden but was now overgrown with unkempt bushes and covered in swathes of dead leaves.

He began filling the kettle, and I took the chance to observe him a little as his back was turned. There was a certain family air in his and Inary's colouring, with their auburn hair and fair skin, though Torcuil's hair was darker than Inary's. But the similarities ended at that – Inary was even smaller than me and very slight, while Torcuil was tall and well built.

"I hope you don't mind if we have our chat here in the kitchen?" he said. "It's the only place where my allergies don't act up. Here and my bedroom, but I couldn't interview you in the bedroom, it would just be dodgy." He seemed completely unaware of what was coming out of his mouth.

Inary burst into laughter. I looked at him with raised eyebrows, and a deep red colour started rising up his face.

"Okay, I should shut up. Sorry." He was nervous too, and for some reason I found this very endearing.

"Er, yes. So . . . you need a hand with the house?" I said, helping him along.

"Will you show my mum how to kick the boiler?" Lara asked, deadpan. I gasped inwardly, but Torcuil was unfazed.

"Oh, that. Yes, of course. You can just slam it if you don't want to kick it. It's up to you. It's just that it gets very cold in here all year round, and my housekeeper was the only one who got it right every single time. She was like a horse whisperer, only with boilers . . ."

"Why exactly would I have to hit your boiler?"

"Because the heating won't start otherwise," Inary intervened, handing me and Lara a cup of hot tea. "Milk and sugar?"

"Milk, one sugar," I said.

"Milk, four sugars," said Lara.

"Caramelised tea, my favourite," quipped Torcuil, and Lara giggled. "I have some biscuits as well." He brandished a packet of digestives as if he were showing us the Holy Grail.

Inary took hold of a plate. "Oh, yes please. You know, Margherita is a pastry chef . . ."

"Well, I was . . ."

"Oh, cool! I love food! I can't really cook it, but I love it. So anyway, have a seat, have a biscuit, let's *talk*." He moved several piles of books and what looked like essays.

I was smiling inside. He was funny. We all sat at the table, except Lara, who lifted herself up on the windowsill. Torcuil pushed his glasses up on his nose.

"Well, what I'm looking for, I guess, is just someone who could try to keep the living area sort of acceptable . . . I only use a few rooms; this place is enormous and heating the whole lot for just one person would be just silly. Every weekend I come back from Edinburgh, you know I teach at the university there . . ."

"Inary told me."

"Yes, so it makes no sense to come back every single weekend, let's face it, but I sort of have to. I can't stand to be away from here for too long . . ."

I was surprised at this sudden, unexpected candour. Inary had her hands around her mug, her head tilted slightly and a smile hovering on her lips. I had the feeling that Inary's affection for her cousin ran deep.

"You would have the place ready for me, you know, warm, groceries in, stuff like that. A cooked meal would be great, if it's not too much trouble . . ." I loved the way he pronounced the word *great*, rolling the *r* in the middle.

"Torcuil has an ongoing tab with the Golden Palace. You know, the Chinese takeaway," Inary explained.

"See, I can't cook to save my life," he said, running his hand through his hair once more. He was fidgety, forever touching his hair, pushing his glasses up – there was a sense of awkwardness around him, of shyness. "It runs in the family. I mean Inary here is just legendary when it comes to dodgy meals . . ."

"Excuse me!"

"No offence, honestly . . ."

"None taken." Inary grinned and dunked another biscuit in her tea.

"Also, I'm so busy all weekend trying to oversee the riding school and prepare for my teaching week . . ."

"So I would come in on a Friday morning, and maybe a Thursday too, depending on what needs done? A general clean, kick the boiler . . ." – Lara giggled and I shot her a glance – ". . . bring some food in, cook a couple of meals for you?"

"Yes. Does that sound reasonable?"

I thought it did, but I wanted to think about it for a bit, so I bought myself some time. "Would you show us the rest of the house?"

"Of course." He rose and beckoned us. "Follow me."

"Wait till you see this place. It's incredible," Inary murmured to Lara, taking her by the arm. I felt a tingle of anticipation.

We followed Torcuil up a few uneven stony steps and passed some rooms to our left, which he dismissed as his bedroom and bathroom, and then a small reception room. Every possible surface there was covered by stacks of books, and I could see by the amount of papers around and the jumper thrown on the sofa that Torcuil used this as his study. It was a mess, but a *lovely* mess, I thought, a sign of someone who was passionate about what he did. The same mess that's in a kitchen in the middle of a cooking session.

"And here comes the real thing," he announced as we stepped into a stone-floored hall. "That's the main entrance, and down here are the formal reception rooms."

From the high-ceilinged hall a marble staircase wound up to the first floor, dividing itself in two landings, both lined with portraits in tarnished gold frames. A row of coats of arms hung at the top of the staircase, and in the centre, bigger than the others, was what I guessed was the Ramsay coat of arms: a two-headed black eagle holding a shield.

"Is that the Ramsay coat of arms?" Lara asked.

"Yes. Our motto is *Dei Donum*, which means—"

"Gift of God," said Lara.

"Do you study Latin?" asked Torcuil with a smile.

"I've been taking some classes in school. Just for fun."

"That's my kind of fun too," Torcuil replied, and I saw Lara blooming under his praise. It warmed my heart. "So this is the posh side of the house . . ." he continued. It *all* seemed pretty posh to me.

We walked through room after room, each of them covered in dust, with the most beautiful pieces of furniture shrouded in huge white sheets, cobwebs hanging from the ceilings. Torcuil had started sneezing already.

"And this is what used to be ... *atchoo!* ... my father's study."

This was the only room that was clean and well kept, with framed maps on the walls and an antique globe on the desk.

"My dad passed away five years ago. He loved Ramsay Hall. He tried to spend most of his time here, though his work kept him away. It's history repeating itself with me, I suppose! Come. I'll show you the library."

"It's like the Cluedo mansion," Lara whispered. "Margherita, in the library, with a pastry cutter . . ." I had to laugh.

The library was lined with dark wooden shelves from wall to wall. There were hundreds of volumes in their glassed cases, like a book aquarium. I could *feel* Lara's excitement.

"Some titles are impossible," Torcuil said. "Like an eighteenth-century encyclopaedia of all Scottish plants in five volumes . . . but some are more modern and very readable. I know, because I spent half of my childhood here . . . I mean literally *here*." He patted a dark-brown leather sofa in a corner.

"And the other half in the stables," Inary intervened.

"Exactly. So, Lara, if you want to come and explore the library, you are very welcome."

"That would be amazing," she said. "Thank you so much."

"I can't wait to show you the ballroom!" said Inary, taking Lara by the arm.

"Ballroom?" I said, swooning already. I was dying to see it – images of mirrors and gilded ceilings and frescoes on the walls and a mosaicked floor rushed through my mind. I wasn't disappointed.

Torcuil opened a double wooden door and led us into a grand hall. It was even more beautiful than I'd imagined, its ceiling painted blue and dotted with silver stars, and baby angels sitting on clouds and playing musical instruments. At each corner, a group of them was singing. I couldn't take my eyes off the ceiling, and I wandered around for a while, looking up.

"The fresco is incredible, isn't it? My grandfather had it restored, so it's in good condition. You can't say that about much else at Ramsay Hall."

"I'm trying to imagine how it must have looked like long ago . . . The music, the dancing, candles shimmering all over . . ." said Lara dreamily.

"The last time wasn't that long ago, actually. My grandparents still had receptions here. I remember attending one when I was about seven . . . They sent me back upstairs very quickly, though!"

"I remember. I was here with Logan. Our sister Emily was too young. He was eleven or so . . . he was made to wear a kilt and he danced with Lady Diana, remember? She was nice to him," said Inary.

"Oh, yes," Torcuil laughed.

"I used to go to my parish discos in the chapel hall. Sister Maria gave us Smarties out of a jar and we danced to eighties power ballads," I said.

"Mine were mostly like that too! Not like the landed gentry here . . ." Inary teased.

Torcuil put his hands up. "The landed gentry here used to sleep with a woollen jumper on because it was so cold in this house, so really—"

Inary made a sympathetic face. "Aw, Oliver Twist!"

"I wish . . ." Lara began, and we all looked at her. She stopped abruptly.

"What do you wish, Lara?" said Torcuil gently.

"I could go to a ball here," she said softly, and gazed out of the window at the surrounding trees. And then, "Oh!"

I stepped beside her. "What is it?"

"Look!" she said, and her face was all lit up. I followed her gaze out of one of the windows to the little copse. At first I couldn't see what she was pointing at, and then, entwined with one of the oaks, I saw a tiny wooden house nestled on a cradle made of branches, and connected by a small rope bridge to another, smaller house on the oak tree just beside it. "That," she breathed, "is *amazing*."

"Oh, that's our tree house. It's still in one piece, and safe to use. My nephews played in it just a few weeks ago."

"We used to play there all the time," said Inary.

"Yes. I remember falling off it and on you, once."

"I remember that too. It's burnt into my memory, Torcuil," Inary laughed.

"It's the perfect place to read in, Lara. You're very welcome to use it."

Lara beamed. I think words were failing her. She looked at me and I read her eyes – *please take this job.*

Inary intercepted the look that Lara was giving me. "So, Margherita, what do you say?"

"Feel free to say no . . ." Torcuil hastened to add. "I mean, I know it's not really your line of work—"

"Yes," I said.

"—and I know it all looks a bit . . . *dusty* . . . and it's quite isolated . . . but it's not like you'd have to do anything heavy . . . Did you just say *yes*?"

"I'd love to do it." I smiled.

"Oh. Oh. That's great. That's really, really great. Oh,

wow . . ." He looked at Inary and opened his arms as if to say, *So that worked out.*

Lara and I exchanged a glance. She looked so happy. I knew then that I'd made the right decision.

"I'd love to show you the grounds and the stables, but I need to go back to Edinburgh tonight," Torcuil said, shooting a glance at his watch. "If it's okay with you, you can start this week."

"Sure. No problem."

"So, it's all sorted. What shall I call you? Do your friends call you Maggie?"

"Nobody who holds their life dear calls me Maggie."

"Oh. Oh. Sorry. Margherita, then?"

"Yes." I liked the way he said my name. He rolled the *r* a bit, ever so subtly, and made it sound like something not quite Italian but at the same time not English. It made it sound like a Scottish name. Like he skimmed all the consonants and melted them into something softer.

"Aha!" Lara exclaimed, picking up something tiny from the floor.

"What?"

"A red sequin. Somebody has been dancing in here very recently," she said.

Torcuil and Inary looked at each other. "Mrs Gordon!" they said at the same time.

We left Inary at Ramsay Hall and walked home by ourselves in the late morning. The day had brightened up and a soft, golden sunshine made the loch shimmer. Lara was so excited she was nearly skipping.

"Do you think he has a wife in the attic? A Mrs Rochester?" she asked.

114

"What?"

"Well, it would make sense."

"How would it make any sense? It only makes sense in your crazy imagination," I said, tapping my head in jest. "I don't think he has a wife in the attic, no."

"How do you know?" she said dramatically.

"Lara."

"Yes?"

"You read too much."

12

And there she was

Torcuil

Memo to self: under no circumstances shorten her name. Do not, I repeat *do not*, call her Maggie. Once you remember that, you'll be fine.

She really has the biggest eyes I've ever seen. I'd caught a glimpse of them that night, but the light of the lamp post was so dim I couldn't see her face properly. They are so dark they're nearly black. She looks Italian, but then when she opens her mouth a London accent comes out. She has small hands, and a wedding band on her middle finger. Inary said she and her husband are separated. Not that I have any ideas about her, obviously, no interest in her at all. This kind of thing doesn't tend to work out with me anyway, not since Izzy, so there's no point even thinking about it, really.

God, those eyes.

She is yet another reason why I can't wait to get back to Glen Avich next week – but I shouldn't be thinking that, of course. In fact, I didn't just think that at all; it was just a ripple of the mind and I've already forgotten it.

"So that's you sorted. For the summer, at least," Inary says as I pack my bag to go back to Edinburgh.

"Yeah. Funny how papers that fitted my bag on the way here don't fit any more on the way back . . ."

"You like her," Inary says abruptly.

"Shut up. She's married."

"Separated. And you are quite a catch, Torcuil."

"I'm every woman's dream," I say. It's meant as a joke, but there's an edge of bitterness to it. These last few years have been . . . how can I put it? I don't want to say *lonely* and sound whiny. They have been *cold*. Yes, cold is the word.

Bone-chilling, to be honest. But I just don't seem to be able to feel anything for anyone else. A vague goodwill, or physical attraction, or fondness. But love, no. Not love, never again.

There was someone, long ago. Eleven years ago, to be precise. It's a short story: I loved her and she loved me, but clearly not as much, because she left me for someone else.

In those eleven years there have been other women of course, but they never really worked out. To be precise, it was *me* who didn't work out. I suppose you would say I'm wary of letting my guard down, after having been so badly betrayed – but I have another theory: that I just didn't care enough for any of them. I mean, I *cared* for them, but I didn't love them. Not the love I'd felt for my fiancée, which had been so much more than friendship, so much more than a crush, so much more than attraction or being compatible or having a laugh together, and all other parameters of what love should be. My love for her was about my soul reaching for hers and wanting to be with her and never be apart again.

Maybe it had something to do with her having been hurt in the past, I don't know – this desperate need I had to house her within me, to be her home and place of peace.

Nobody else could compare.

"Want a lift back?" I ask my cousin as we make our way to the car.

117

"No thanks. It's a lovely afternoon, I'll walk. See you soon."

Since she moved back to Glen Avich when Emily died, Inary and I have become very close. Considering the non-existent relationship I have with my sister and the fact that I hardly ever see my brother, though he only lives down the road, this is good news to me. To be fair, my brother Angus and I *are* close; it's that with Isabel's health getting worse and his job taking him all over the world, it's hard for him to get away. Sometimes it feels like I am quite alone.

I am now thirty-six years old and on my own. I am drifting.

I am drifting and I think that the only thing that's keeping me from getting lost at sea is this house, Ramsay Hall. My sister often says that this place is an albatross around our necks, but she's so wrong. To me, Ramsay Hall is a buoy. It's what saves me from drowning. I have this overwhelming feeling that if I save Ramsay Hall I will, somehow, save myself.

13

He stood there in the mist

Lara

Dear Kitty,

The tree house sold it to me. The library was awesome, and the ballroom was a dream! But the tree house was just the best. Forget the wandering and reading at home, I want to spend a good chunk of my summer up there with a book.

Thankfully my mum accepted the job. She'll take things in hand, of course, sort the guy AND the house. Lord Ramsay (I know he said not to call him Lord Ramsay, but I like the way it sounds, like he's out of a novel) is nice. Really nice, and not bad-looking at all, for his age. He won't know what's hit him when my mum gets stuck in. She's going to revolutionise the place, bring it all back to order.

I wonder if I should tell Dad about all that we're doing here. Since we arrived I've phoned him twice from our bathroom but sometimes it felt awkward to be talking to him. He asked me questions about Mum. I think he should ask *her* stuff, not me. But they haven't spoken since we arrived. He never mentioned wanting us back, or missing us. To be fair, I never told him I miss him. As I write this I realise how sad it sounds.

Anyway, on to Inary. She is awesome. When I'm her age I want to be like her: have books published, a boyfriend and a home and her *hair*. I want red hair. It's not really red, though, it's somewhere between red and brown, like autumn leaves. She invited me for lunch at her house next week. I can't wait. In fact, I made a little calendar and I score every day that passes. Five days to go now.

I've been looking out for the boy in the tweed cap every time I pass the bridge, but he's never been there. Then, on the way back from Ramsay Hall, I thought I caught a glimpse of him across the loch. He was far away, but I'm nearly sure it was him: he had the same clothes, and I recognised the way he stood. I wanted to wave at him, but then I thought what if I'm wrong? So I didn't. Now I feel bad about it, because I think he saw me and we sort of looked at each other across the water, but I didn't call to him or make a gesture or anything. Neither did he, though. He just stood there, looking exhausted. And sad. Maybe he was fishing or something, because he looked covered in mud; I could see that even from far away. Also, my mum was with me, and I didn't want her to get all friendly with him and "oh hello, so you are a new friend of Lara, and what school do you go to, what do your parents do, where do you live etc etc", you know the way she gets. I wanted to keep this to myself.

Looking back, though, it was funny the way he just stood there in the mist, not moving. Like he wasn't sure where he was. He looked lonely.

I hope to see him again soon.

14

Butterfly summer

Margherita

The fire was glowing, the fairy lights around the fireplace were on, and from the window I could see twilight slowly turning into night. Everything was so serene, so beautiful. Lara was across at my mum's helping to bake for La Piazza, so I had the cottage to myself and I was free to reflect on all that had happened. I lay on my bed beside Leo, stroking his hair until he fell asleep suddenly and deeply, tired as he was after a long day of exploring Glen Avich with Nonna and me. He was adorable in his blue PJs with the little helicopters on, clutching Pingu.

The job at Ramsay Hall was a new beginning for me, and I couldn't wait to get started. But I was hurting from Ash's silence. My absence – *our* absence – was not devastating him. Where his longing for us should have been, there was only silence. I knew Lara had phoned him a few times. She'd simply told me that he was fine and he was happy that we were fine too. Just like that, like an exchange you'd have with a stranger – *How are you? Fine, you? I'm fine too*. He'd never asked to speak to Leo.

But after that text in the middle of the night to tell him we'd arrived, I hadn't contacted him either. I could have picked up the phone, after all, instead of waiting for him to do it.

But every time I thought about calling him, every time I tried to force myself to press the green button on my mobile, my stomach churned. The simple thought of hearing his voice was enough to make my head throb with stress, and still there was a void in my mind from the absence of him. Because in all these years we've been together, all these years we've been married, we've never gone without talking in some form or another for more than a few days, even if sometimes it was just harsh words, just arguments. It was like having been chopped in half, and although the half I'd lost had hurt me so much, I still missed it.

It was all new, and frightening, and immensely sad, especially because Ash didn't seem to want to speak to Leo. The chasm between them was deeper than I had realised, I thought as I tucked the duvet around him protectively and rested my arm across his sleeping form. Our noses were touching. He smelled sweet and warm; he smelled like love itself. My baby boy. I would do anything to keep him from pain.

Leo didn't seem that fazed by his father's absence. He had only mentioned him once, when Michael made a roast for us and he said that was his daddy's favourite dish. That was it. But how could I know what the long-term consequences of this would be? And since we'd arrived in Glen Avich, Leo had just looked so happy. His nonna and Michael spoiled him rotten. They took him around the village like a trophy, holding one of his hands each, and he basked in the attention.

Night had now fallen over the hills. Venus was shining bright in the black, black sky, and it occurred to me that for some reason, down in London there had been never time to look at the sky. Here in Glen Avich time seemed to have stretched and slowed, expanding until it seemed there was heaps of it.

Maybe because I wasn't in a hurry any more, I did a lot less and observed a lot more. Days seemed so slow and peaceful, in comparison with the breakneck speed at which I'd been living my life – and what was I doing anyway? Rushing around on a million little errands that I'd set up to fill the emptiness I felt. My whole being began loosening up, bit by bit. It seemed impossible that after such upheaval, after the silences and arguments back in London, such an easy rhythm could come naturally to us; it seemed impossible that when everything in my life was up in the air, and things had changed so deeply, my mind was calmer than before.

From the cottage I could see right inside my mum's kitchen. Lara was stirring a bowl and my mum was taking a tray out of the oven, laden with something I couldn't quite make out. I moved Leo to his own bed, careful not to wake him up, and wrapped myself in the creamy mohair cardigan my mum had loaned me. I grabbed Nonna Ghita's notebook from my bedside table and made my way through the fresh, breezy Scottish summer evening and inside the kitchen. The baby monitor was on, so I could leave Leo on his own. The scent of baking was mouth-watering, and now I could see what my mum had been taking out of the oven – croissants.

"Is he asleep?" my mum asked me, slipping another tray of croissants into the oven.

"Yes. I've come to give you a hand," I said. "What do you say we try something from here?" I waved the notebook.

"Yes, why not? You choose . . ."

"You're on." I took off the cardigan, rolled up my sleeves and slipped an apron over my clothes in a ritual I'd known since I was little. "What about *brutti ma buoni*?" *Brutti ma buoni* literally means "ugly but tasty", and they live up to the promise. They're gnarly little biscuits that lack beauty but have a heavenly nutty, sweet flavour.

"If we have all the ingredients, yes, sure," my mum agreed.

It was such easy, earthy happiness to be in the kitchen with my mum and Lara and to bake together; a bit like when I was a little girl and my mum, Anna, Laura and I spent so much time in the kitchen. And now Lara was there too. It wasn't just about food; it was about companionship. For Italian women the kitchen is so much more than a place to rustle up quick meals – it's the most important room of the house, where we chat and bond and laugh and rest our souls. I seemed to have forgotten that, but it was all coming back to me, like the scent of my Nonna Ghita's cakes.

After an hour of work and fun and laughter, my mum had finished and the *brutti ma buoni* were ready too.

"Oh, Mum, why did you not make these before?" Lara said as she tasted a still-warm, knobbly little biscuit.

"Honestly? I don't know," I said, and I allowed myself one short moment of dismay as I had a quick look at my mobile – still no missed calls, no texts.

It looked like Ash was letting me go.

15

Little love (1)

Margherita

I made my way along the loch shore early on a misty, chilly morning, towards Ramsay Hall. The silence was so complete that I could hear every little noise: the wind in the trees, little creatures scurrying in the bushes, the crackling of gravel under my feet. It felt like there was just me for miles around, approaching this enormous house.

Then, all of a sudden, I heard someone call my name and I jumped. I brought a hand to my chest to try to quieten my heart, as I turned around and saw a woman approaching. She was in her fifties, with short blonde hair, a weather-beaten complexion and mud-covered boots.

"Margherita?"

"Yes, hello," I called, walking towards her.

"Nice to meet you, I'm Fiona." She crushed my hand, and I had to hide a wince. "I work at the stables, as you probably guessed. Sorry, just making sure you were really *you*! I mean, Torcuil told me you were coming up today so I was keeping an eye out."

"Yes, it's me. Not a burglar or anything."

She laughed a warm, roaring laugh. "Have you seen the stables?"

"Not yet."

"Well, if you have a minute, I'll show you."

"I'd love to, thank you," I said and followed her down a small path towards the stone outbuildings. Unlike the house itself, the stables were immaculate and perfectly kept. The smell of horse hit me at once – strangely pleasant in an earthy way. There were five horses peeking from their stalls, their huge brown eyes looking at me. I've never been into horses much – they've always looked a bit scary to me – but the last one of them made me do a double take. Fiona saw me staring.

"That's Stoirin, Torcuil's horse."

"Story?"

"Sto-reen. It means *little love* in Gaelic."

"Not so little!" I smiled. It seemed huge to me, with a warm, chestnutty coat and a blonde mane.

"You should have seen her when she was a foal. She was tiny, and so cute. That's why Torcuil named her Stoirin."

"So she's a mare?"

"Oh yes. And very girly too. Look at her eyes."

Stoirin and I looked at each other in the eye for a moment. Fiona was right, I could see it now – she was, somehow, girly. Womanly, more like, although I can't quite explain why. She wasn't moving or making a sound; then, suddenly, she snorted delicately and came forward in her stand. Without thinking, I laid a hand on her silky head, then on her muzzle – she was so warm, and soft. She rubbed herself against me ever so lightly, as if she were saying hello.

"You seem smitten." Fiona smiled.

I couldn't look away from Stoirin's eyes. Finally, I forced myself to take a step back. "I'd better get on with it," I said, turning away . . . and then turning to look at Stoirin again.

"You must have made an impression on her too. She doesn't

let just anyone touch her. She's sweet, but not *that* sweet. Why don't you come back and ride her? I mean, ask Torcuil first. Stoirin is his; we don't use her for the school."

"Oh, no, that wouldn't be for me. Honestly. I don't ride horses. They are . . . *high*."

Fiona burst into her deep laughter again.

"I'd better go and get some work done," I told her. "Thanks for the tour. See you later."

As I walked on, I crossed paths with a group of mums and little girls in horse-riding gear. Fiona was going to be busy. Something made me turn around once more before the stalls were completely out of sight. I can't swear by it, because it was quite a distance away, but I thought I saw Stoirin's sweet, dark honey eyes following me.

I made my way into the kitchen. The place looked tidy and clean enough. Again, I suspected he had cleaned for me, because there was once more there was a faint hint of bleach underneath the damp, mouldy smell that was omnipresent at Ramsay Hall. On the kitchen table, there was a note.

So sorry about the mess in a rush as ever
looking forward to seeing you at the weekend
please put the heating on or you'll freeze
T

Clearly, he was too much in a rush for punctuation too. I grinned, picturing Torcuil running out of the door, clutching stacks of paper.

He was right about the cold; there was a shiver building up in my body already. Somehow, the temperature inside was lower than outside. I switched on the thermostat in the kitchen and then I made my way down to the one of the cellars as he'd showed me. I went down the stony steps and opened the door to the basement. It was dark and silent in there, and quite spooky, with the bare light bulb hanging from the ceiling and cobwebs everywhere. *I* am not easily spooked, though, so I walked down the steps resolutely.

"Sorry, mate," I said to the huge, old-fashioned boiler as I banged it a few times. No joy. Hopefully Torcuil would change the heating system one day ... but in a house like this, that would cost a fortune. I went on kicking, and it felt quite satisfactory to let out some steam. I was about to kick it again when a low humming began emanating from the thing. Clearly, the dancing Mrs Gordon wasn't the only one with the magic touch. I was about to turn around to go back upstairs when the door of the basement slammed closed, making me jump in fright. I silently cursed the draughts in that chilly old house, and ran up the steps to the door. For a moment, I had a vision of it having locked itself and me being stuck there until Torcuil came back in two days' time – and then, as I turned the handle and the door opened, I laughed at my own silliness. Clearly, I was taking a leaf out of Lara's book, turning every situation into a mini gothic novel. To be fair, at Ramsay Hall it wasn't hard to do so.

I made my way back upstairs and ransacked the cleaning cupboard in the kitchen. I hesitated at Torcuil's bedroom's threshold; I had never cleaned anyone's house before except mine, so it felt strange to intrude in somebody else's space like that. His scent – wood smoke and pines and a hint of something else, something fresh and pure that reminded me of sea air – was everywhere. For a moment I stopped, and something in me responded to the scent. Like a long-lost memory, somewhere I'd been once and wanted to go back to . . . And then I shook myself.

My eyes fell on a photograph on Torcuil's bedside table: two little boys wearing jeans and woollen jumpers, both on horses. One of them had bright-red hair and freckles and looked thin and small. There was a bright smile on his face and an aura of mischievousness and fun around him. It had to be Angus – he looked like the typical younger brother, I thought. My younger sister, Laura, the baby of the family, had the same look about her. The other boy was, without doubt, Torcuil. The picture must have been taken when he was about eleven, in between childhood and the beginning of young adulthood. He was tall already, with wavy, thick auburn hair and a wistful look in his eyes, like an old soul inhabiting a young body. He had a serious demeanour, like someone who already felt responsibility on his young shoulders.

There wasn't much to do for the day. In fact, after cleaning all I could clean and opening all the windows I sat on the little bench against the back wall. Tomorrow I would bring groceries in and cook a feast for when Torcuil came back at night. In fact, I might even use him as a guinea pig for the baking experiments I had in mind. It was a warm day – by Scottish standards – and I closed my eyes for a moment, enjoying the breeze. A lovely scent of roses came to me. I opened my eyes and contemplated the garden. For the first time I noticed a few rose bushes lining the flower beds in the back of the garden, towards the trees. I made my way towards them, stepping onto the little gravel paths between the flower beds.

Dotted here and there were small ornamental statues,

their shapes softened and blurred because of the exposure to the elements and the moss and lichen covering them. The boundaries between flower beds were blurred and the gravel paths in between them overrun with weeds. I wondered why Torcuil had let the garden fall into such disrepair – there seemed to be a stronger reason than not being able to afford a gardener. It was more of a sense of . . . defeat. He said he cared so much for Ramsay Hall, but I felt that part of him had given up, in a way. Like part of him didn't believe this place could ever be restored to order, to its old beauty. To life.

It was a sad thought, and I wandered around in the fresh summer breeze, trying to dispel it. The roses in the flower beds, though left to their own devices, were beautiful – some of them were a colour I had never seen before, a mixture of pink and yellow and orange on the same rose. The yellow ones with pink tips looked like they were blushing, and the pink one with the touches of yellow seemed bathed in sunshine. I bent forward to look at them better and inhale their scent, when something moving at the edges of my vision made me straighten up quickly. It must have been a bird taking flight from a windowsill in the upper floor . . . but no, there it was again. There was something moving behind the furthest window on the right. A shadow. The curtain flickering. And then nothing. The fuchsia wrapped around the back door swayed gently in the breeze and a shower of pink flowers fell on the stony ground. But nothing else moved.

I dismissed the shadow as a trick of the eye. But as I unearthed a pair of gardening gloves and began tugging at the weeds, I kept my eyes on the windows and never turned my back to the house again.

16

Kindred spirits

Lara

Dear Kitty,

I've had the best afternoon ever. I went to Inary's house for lunch, and it was great. She burnt our toasties and we ended up having cornflakes because she'd run out of everything else. Nonna would have had a fit, but I loved it. This is what I always imagined writers would be like, I think: they just focus on their work and forget about everything else. I mean, I'm sure Charlotte Brontë didn't stop writing to make herself a nice risotto, don't you think? They go on and on into the night as well and are completely possessed by their art. It's all very romantic, and Inary has just the right looks for it: her hair looks like a painting, so bright and wavy. Not like mine. Frizzy. She said my hair is gorgeous. Obviously she was just being nice, but then she showed me in the mirror in her room, and it was weird but as she untied my ponytail and let my hair fall, it didn't look so bad.

Inary's house is exactly the way I'd like my house to be, one day. Full of books and with a study all for myself. I don't know what I want to do when I grow up, be a writer or a teacher or a librarian, but whatever I'm going to do, it must have something to do with books. Also, Inary has a gorgeous boyfriend who looks like an actor. He's had to go to London so I didn't meet him, but I saw a picture and he has raven hair, like Damien in Bride of Shadows.

Inary is going to read my Bride of Shadows fan fiction. I'm so excited.

I *so* wish she lived in London, then I could speak to someone who *understands*. She used to live there, but she came to see her sister, who died young, and then she decided to stay. Her boyfriend followed her. She said she loves living here, though it's so small. She told me that there are a thousand and five hundred souls living in Glen Avich, and a few more floating around. I think she means commuters.

After having been to Inary's house, I decided to go down to the tree house at Ramsay Hall – Torcuil said I can go any time I like. I wandered around for a bit first because I was sort of hoping I'd meet that boy again.

As I walked, I felt strange, like he was just at my shoulder all the time. And then, there he was.

"Lara," he said, and I was startled.

"Yes. Hello. You are silent as a cat!"

"Sorry. I didn't mean to scare you. Where are you going?"

His eyes are really grey. As in, properly grey. A shade I've never seen before. I don't even think that Damien has eyes as grey as that. And his hair is so black. I didn't think someone with skin so white could have hair so dark.

"Up to the Ramsay Estate. Do some reading in the tree house." I showed him my *Wuthering Heights* and the blanket I'd sneaked out from Nonna's cupboard.

"I like reading too. There aren't many books around, but the schoolmaster always lends me some."

"You mean your teacher?"

"Yes. I go on Ailsa with my boat. I bring some food and a book and spend hours there, reading. Just me, alone with the loch. My father gets cross at me because I read instead of helping him. He says I'll become a priest or a schoolteacher." He smiled. When he smiles he looks different. He looks like he's shining from the inside. It doesn't happen often; usually he seems sad, or troubled. "Sometimes I write poems."

"A priest?" Seriously?

"Yes. But I don't enjoy the Bible much, so I don't think that's ever going to happen!"

Okay. Sometimes he says strange things. I mean, the Bible? What teenager reads the Bible? Unless you come from a super-religious family. I suppose that's possible.

"Want to come up with me?" I asked, and then I was scared. In case he said no.

But he said, "Very well," and we walked together in silence, and it wasn't awkward, it was just peaceful. Every once in a while he looked at me and smiled.

And that was all, a walk with no words, until we climbed up the tree house and sat there cross-legged.

"Are you sure Lord Ramsay doesn't mind we're here?" he said.

"I'm sure. He told me—"

Suddenly he grew very pale, and once again he seemed scared. But why? Why was he so frightened again, like last time? It's hard to explain; it was like the weather had turned all at once, like it does here in Scotland, going from clear to rainy in the space of a heartbeat.

"I have to go now," he said in a voice so soft I could barely hear it, rising to his feet.

"Will I see you tomorrow?" I asked, and I regretted it at

once. Maybe he didn't want to see me, maybe I was making a fool of myself.

"I hope so," he said, and crawled to the little door.

Suddenly, I remembered. "Hey . . . you never told me your name."

"My name is Mal."

And who are your people? I was about to ask, just like he'd done to me the first time we met. But I didn't get the chance, because he disappeared down the rope ladder. I crawled to the little door and looked out, but a thick white mist was rising from the fields. I could only make out a blurry shape for a few seconds – and then he was gone.

So now I know his name.

17

Ramsay Hall

Margherita
The next day I arrived at Ramsay Hall bright and early, with two bags full of groceries for Torcuil's weekend. I made my way into the kitchen and began putting them away, when I heard a noise coming from inside the house. I froze.

It was probably a mouse. Or one of those weird noises you hear in old houses, like the building settling or things creaking all by themselves. Or the wind around a window. It was nothing. So I started working again.

And again the same noise made me jump. And then another – a thump, like something falling or someone putting something down forcibly ... And steps. Steps that moved towards the kitchen. Steps that moved towards me.

There was someone in the house, and whoever it was, was coming to get me.

And then he began to sing. Very loudly. It was a Miley Cyrus song – I recognised it from Lara's playlists.

"We can't stop, we can't stop! OH OH OH ... We can't STOHOP ..."

I knew that voice.

"Aaaah!" Torcuil jumped as he walked into the kitchen, only a second before oblivious to my presence and singing away.

I was standing with a packet of pasta in each hand, trembling from head to toe. So much for not being easily spooked.

"Oh God. You gave me a huge fright there," he said. He was wearing an Edinburgh University T-shirt and a pair of woven cotton pyjama bottoms.

"So did you! I thought I'd *die!*"

"It must have been my singing," he replied with a smile.

"Yes, that alarmed me for sure. What are you doing here?"

"I came back last night. It's a bank holiday today. Did I forget to tell you?"

"Yes! Anyway, no harm done. Apart from having lost five years of my life."

"Did I scare you as much as that?" He looked genuinely concerned. For a moment, I considered telling him about the shadow I'd seen yesterday; then I changed my mind. It had been a trick of the eye, not worth mentioning.

"No, of course not. I was joking."

"That's a relief. What are you doing here?"

"Working. It's Friday. Remember?" I grinned and put away a few tins of peas.

"It's a quarter to eight in the morning! It's a miracle I'm dressed."

"And I'm thankful for that," I laughed. "I'm a morning person, what can I say?"

"Well. It's good to have you here. Is that food?"

"Yes. And all for you. I was going to make a lasagne for you to find tonight."

"Homemade lasagne, oh yes. I loved Mrs Gordon's homemade lasagne. Well, homemade by the Co-op in Kinnear. Cup of tea?"

"Yes, I'd love a cup of tea. And maybe I'll make pancakes

with maple syrup, what do you say?" I showed him the bottle of maple syrup I'd bought. "I was going to leave it for you to find, for Saturday morning breakfast."

"Oh, that is good. Very, very good. I'm always starving at the weekend; I was thinking I should start going down to La Piazza—"

"I lost my mum a customer!" I laughed, mixing eggs, flour and milk in a bowl.

"But that's a lot of food," he said, peeking into the cupboard. "Let me know if you need more money for that . . ." He looked all worried.

"Not at all. Staples cost a lot less than takeaways."

"I haven't bought anything but bread, ham and biscuits in a long time."

I rolled my eyes, whisking the mixture. "You're the stereotype of the hapless man!"

"It's not really about being a man. My sister is the worst of us three. Her children are being brought up on cheese sandwiches. Nobody in my family seems to cook much."

"Just the opposite to my family, then! We cook and eat a lot. Maybe too much, I suppose," I said, putting a hand on my curvy hips, and then regretting it immediately. It probably wasn't appropriate to bring attention to my hips. Only the conversation had been so friendly that I'd forgotten myself.

"Not at all, you look . . . great," he scrambled, and it was my turn to blush. "Oh, no," he said, all of a sudden.

"What's wrong?"

"I just remembered I don't have a pan."

"I know you don't. I bought one. Well, two," I said, taking them out of my bag for life. "Ta-da!"

He smiled. "You're stocking up my kitchen!"

"Listen, any normal human being owns a pan. I had to get it."

"You need to tell me how much—"

"Shush!"

"Okay. Okay. But honestly—"

"I won't buy any more stuff. Promise."

"Deal. Goodness, you are quick . . ." he said as I buttered the pan, placed it on the fire and began producing picture-perfect pancakes.

"I used to do this for a living."

"I can see that," he said admiringly, and I was pleased. Very pleased. In fact, I was surprised at how much I relished that little bit of praise.

"Oh, I forgot about the tea," he said, switching the kettle on and fishing two mugs from the cupboards.

Five minutes later, I had a stack of syrupy pancakes ready. He sat at the table, folding his long legs underneath it. I noticed once again how tall and broad-shouldered he was, and suddenly the kitchen table seemed a lot smaller.

"These are gorgeous," he gushed, taking a big bite.

"Why thank you." I had to agree. "So, anyway, of the three of you . . . I mean you and your siblings . . . you were lumbered with this lot." I opened my arms, to signify Ramsay Hall and the land around it. "Where do they live? Can they not help with Ramsay Hall a bit?"

"Sheila lives in Perth near my mother. She's not remotely interested. To her, Ramsay Hall is just a money drain. That's what my mother thinks, anyway, and Sheila lives under my mother's command. If it weren't for the riding school, my mother would have sold the place already."

"Command?" I laughed. I had a vision of Lady Ramsay in a military uniform, shouting orders.

138

"Yes. You don't know her."

"She sounds scary."

"Mmmm." He nodded. "She *is*. My mum and my sister aren't my favourite people in the world. I know it sounds terrible . . ." – he ran a hand through his hair: he did it a lot, it was an unconscious gesture, like pushing his glasses up his nose – ". . . but hey, that's the way it is."

A sudden ray of sun shone through the clouds and through the glass and made its way onto our table. It made the syrup bottle glimmer like liquid gold, and Torcuil's hair shone russet.

"No, not at all. I understand. Families can be a difficult thing. My husband . . ." I hesitated. Just thinking of Ash gave me a knot in my stomach, of both resentment and longing. "My husband has a really complicated relationship with his own mother. I think that my mother-in-law and your mum are probably cut from the same cloth. She's quite horrible to him, actually."

"That must be hard. I mean, that *is* hard. I know it from experience."

"It's very painful for him, yes. I think . . . I think it *scarred* him." And more deeply than I'd realised.

"So, you are separated."

I swallowed. "Yes. For a bit. Maybe forever, who knows? Everything is up in the air at the moment, I don't know what's going to happen . . ." I realised I had begun ripping the napkin into a million pieces, so I stopped myself.

"I'm sorry, I shouldn't have asked," he said.

"No, that's okay, don't worry. Tell me about your brother."

"Well, Angus is five years younger than me. He's a fiddler. He's so talented; I must take you to hear him playing."

"He lives here in Glen Avich, doesn't he?"

139

"It's AviCH. Not Avick," he laughed.

"Sorry, I do my best! I'm English-Italian, remember? Scotland for me was just somewhere I saw on TV before my mum moved here. I haven't had time for Scottish elocution lessons!"

"You sound like a Londoner, you really do."

"That's what I am. In a way."

"Do you speak Italian?"

"I don't, but I understand it. Actually, my grandparents didn't even speak Italian as such; they spoke Piedmontese. It's a French-Italian dialect. Anyway, you were telling me about Angus . . ."

"Oh, yes. Angus does stay in Glen Avich, but he never really lived here at Ramsay Hall. He went to boarding school and then to Glasgow to study music."

"Did you go to boarding school?"

"They didn't send me, thankfully. I really wanted to stay anyway. I went to the local schools and then to university in London. I had terrible asthma, so I was kept at home."

"Oh . . . that's why you said the kitchen and the bedroom are the only places where you can breathe! *Everywhere* is full of dust!" I was alarmed. What if he had an attack when he was here all alone? Yes, I barely knew him, but I cared already.

"I know, I know, but it would take weeks to clean the whole house and all the knick-knacks and books and paintings . . ."

"Lara and I will start on it. Okay, probably just me. Bit by bit. Mind you, I'm terrible at housework."

"Oh, that bodes well, considering you're supposed to be my new housekeeper."

"Sorry!" I laughed, taking another bite of pancake. "But beggars can't be choosers. I'm joking, of course."

"You are joking as in you are actually very good at housework?"

"No, I'm terrible at it. I was joking about the beggars can't be choosers thing. I bet there were quite a few people who would have loved this job. I mean, it's such a lovely place—"

"I don't think so."

"Why?"

"Well, a lot of people think that Ramsay Hall is spooky."

"It is. But in a nice way. If it was done up . . ."

"We can't afford that. People think the Ramsays have heaps of money, but it's not true. Angus is a musician; I'm a lecturer. Enough said." He shrugged. "We simply can't afford to restore this house."

"Have you thought of opening it up to the public?"

"I can't."

"Why?"

"There are ghosts."

I laughed. "That could be a tourist attraction! A real haunted castle."

"Yes, well, try living with them."

I laughed some more.

Then I remembered the shadow through the window and the basement door closing, and the laughter died on my lips. If I told him, would he think I was mad?

"Torcuil?"

"Yes?"

No. It was too weird. "Nothing."

"Tell me."

"No, it's fine. Honestly."

"There's something on your mind," he said, pushing his

chair back and standing up. His concern touched me, and all of a sudden, as I looked at him leaning against the windowsill with his cup of coffee, his feet bare, his hair still damp from the shower, my heart gave a little jump.

Which really wasn't good.

"You don't mean it, do you? You haven't really seen a ghost?" I blurted out.

Torcuil opened his mouth as if he was about to say something, but then clamped his lips shut. "Of course not. Don't be silly."

I felt completely stupid for having asked that question. I decided to change topic quickly.

"I met Stoirin, yesterday. Fiona showed me around."

His face lit up. "Stoirin is beautiful, isn't she? My brother's wife, Isabel, was the only one who was allowed to ride Stoirin, apart from me."

I noticed he was using the past tense. I wasn't sure whether to ask what happened to Isabel. He must have read my expression, because he explained.

"My sister-in-law . . . she's not very well. She can't really leave the house."

"Oh . . . I'm so sorry to hear that."

"Yes. She's been like this for a couple of years now and hasn't been outside in six months. She's fine physically, but . . . there's something in her mind that . . . cripples her. The doctors say it's some form of anxiety thing, but who knows."

"Oh. Oh, I see." Poor Isabel. My heart went out to her. "If there's anything I can do . . ."

"You are very kind. But I don't think so. There's nothing anyone can do," he said, and there was such sorrow in his

142

words and on his face, it was like a cold, black cloud had entered the room. He seemed to care about her a lot.

"Did you see what I did in the garden?" I said hastily, to try to lighten the mood.

"No ... I came home last night when it was dark, and I haven't been out today," he replied, and stood to look out of the window. "Why, what happened?"

"Have a look." I smiled. He opened the door and walked outside – it was a drizzly morning and the sky was grey, but he didn't seem to notice and he walked out in his bare feet. That's Scottish people for you. They seem immune to cold and damp. He looked around, and a smile danced on his face.

"You cleaned it up. Thank you," he said. And then, "Thank you," he repeated in a small voice, and looked away, to the grey skies.

That night, as we baked for La Piazza, I couldn't stop thinking about Isabel. I made a batch of *amaretti*, the bittersweet almond cookies. To me, *amaretti* signify the bittersweetness of life. I slipped some into a little paper bag and tied it with a ribbon. *For Isabel,* I wrote on it with a silver Sharpie.

I tried to phone Torcuil to ask if I could drive up and leave the parcel with him, but there was no reply. I had no idea where Isabel lived, so I walked to Inary's house in the windswept evening sky, grey clouds galloping above me.

She welcomed me with a smile. "Oh, Margherita, come on in."

"It's okay, I just came to—" I began, and then Torcuil's face peeked from behind her.

"Hello," he said, running his hand through his hair as usual.

"Torcuil is here, we were just having a wee whisky," Inary said. "Join us?" She stepped aside to let me in.

"Honestly, I can't. I have to help my mum clean up; you know the way she does the baking in the evenings. I made these for Isabel, I wanted to drive up to Ramsay Hall but you didn't answer the phone . . ." Oh, God, I sounded like a nag.

"Torcuil is not the most reliable when it comes to phones, Margherita!" Inary said.

"Sorry." He seemed flustered and I felt terrible about it.

"No, that's okay, really, it was no bother to walk up here, and anyway, there you are. Night!" I left the sweet-smelling parcel in Torcuil's hands and practically ran away.

As soon as I arrived home, my phone chirped.

I'll keep an eye on my phone from now on. Thank you for Isabel's biscuits. Night. T.

A little bubble of happiness rose in my chest, and I wondered why.

18

The gift

Torcuil

I'm still reeling after Margherita's appearance at Inary's door.
I would have loved her to stay. I *should* have asked her to stay. I
stand in the hall with the parcel of biscuits she made for Isabel
and I don't quite know what to do.

"Torcuil?" Inary is grinning. "Come, I'll pour you another
one."

I guess I am *that* transparent.

And now she's going to ask me questions. Questions I can't
answer because I don't even know myself what I'm feeling or
what I'm thinking.

I mean, it's *not* normal to be thirty-six and to have a crush,
is it? It's okay if you're fifteen.

So please, Inary, don't ask me questions, not now, I say to
myself.

"That was lovely of Margherita, wasn't it? To bake
something for Isabel. Did you tell her the situation?"

"Yes. Sketchily, I suppose."

Please, please, please *enough*. Miraculously, Inary has pity
on me and changes the subject entirely.

"I wonder if things have been happening in the house with
Margherita there. You know what I mean."

I know what she means, yes. Because when I told Margherita that Ramsay Hall was full of ghosts, I wasn't lying.

"Probably."

"And will you explain?"

"Well, I told her about the ghosts, and she thinks I'm joking, of course. I'll let her believe that. Mrs Gordon thought the weird things happening . . . like you know, things moving place, stuff like that . . . were all down to her being scatty, and I left her to believe that."

"That's so mean!" she laughs. "You convinced Mrs Gordon she was losing her marbles!"

"I didn't convince her of anything of the sort! She thought so herself, and I didn't contradict her, that's all."

"Mrs Gordon is in her sixties. Margherita is young. If the same things start happening, she won't believe it's her being scatty and forgetting things, she will wonder what's going on. What will you do then?"

"I'll play it by ear, I suppose. If I tell her the truth she won't believe me anyway."

"She might . . ."

"It's unlikely."

"Yeah, I suppose so. Do you remember Lewis, my former fiancé?"

"Oh yes. The idiot who left you."

She smiles. "Thanks for your loyalty. Anyway, I told him. That's why he left me. I mean, of course there must have been other reasons, but that was the main one. He said I needed help. Basically, he said I was crazy. He just put it in a slightly more delicate way."

"That's terrible. What a complete—"

"So yes, I know what you mean when you say Margherita

wouldn't believe you, because Lewis didn't believe *me*. He could have never believed me, had we stayed together. He would have kept thinking I was hallucinating or hearing voices."

"And does Alex know?"

"Of course he does. He thinks it's amazing," she smiles. "That's my point. Lewis didn't believe me, but Alex does. You just have to choose the right person to tell. Did Izzy . . . Oh." She stops abruptly. "Sorry, I don't mean to pry . . ."

"I would have told Izzy, but there was never a right time, and then she was gone. Only my parents and siblings know. And you. That is it."

"And what about when you find someone again?"

"It's not likely I'll find anyone."

"Why not? Why shouldn't it happen to you?"

"Oh, Inary, I don't know. So much of it is down to luck, isn't it?"

"Yes, but you also have to *want* it, Torcuil. If you never put yourself forward . . ."

I really, *really* want to change subject. "So anyway, you asked me if I'd tell her, this phantom woman I'll probably never meet? I don't know, is the honest answer. I kept it from you for years, remember?"

"And I never suspected, of course. Men are not supposed to have the Sight; it only goes down the female line."

"I must be some sort of genetic abnormality."

"Is that what you feel it is? A genetic abnormality?"

I shrug. "I don't know. Maybe."

There's a moment of silence and we both take a sip of whisky. Oh, it feels good. Warm and comforting, like everything in the world shines gold.

147

"Inary?"

"Yes?"

"What if I tell Margherita and she reacts just like Lewis?"

"Then she's not worth being told."

On my way home, I type a text to Margherita.

I wish you'd stayed. Sweet dreams, T.

But then I edit it to *I'll keep an eye on my phone from now on. Thank you for Isabel's biscuits. Night. T.*

I send it with a sigh.

19

Little love (2)

Margherita

The following Friday, after finishing all my work at Ramsay Hall, I waited for Torcuil to return from Edinburgh. All week we'd exchanged text messages, simple and short conversations that mainly revolved around saying good morning and goodnight and discussing the weather. But I cherished those texts. They had filled my week with companionship, somehow. Anna and I made long, long calls to each other and spoke for ages, dissecting what had happened to us, how the children were, down to the littlest details, but Torcuil's messages, somehow, were becoming nearly as precious.

But that afternoon he never turned up, and there were no texts. I was disappointed, and quite cross with myself for feeling that way. At five I had to get home to look after Leo and let my mum take a break before we started the baking for the next day. So I walked home, crushed and also frightened at the intensity of my disappointment.

I'm sorry I missed you earlier, things crazy at work, just arrived. How about coming to the stables on Sunday with Lara and Leo?

The text flashed on my mobile as Leo, Lara and I were sharing buttered toast in my mum's kitchen, before putting Leo to bed and getting on with the baking for the coffee shop. Butterflies fluttered in my stomach as I read it.

"Who is it, Mum?" Lara asked.

"Just Torcuil," I said nonchalantly, and then gazed at her quickly. She was busy cutting Leo's toast into smaller bits; she didn't seem up nor down about Torcuil's text, thankfully. "He's asking if we want to go riding on Sunday. Would you like to go and see the horses, Leo?" I said.

He beamed. "Yes! Can I go on a horse?"

"Well, maybe, if Fiona holds on to you very very tight and the horse goes very very very slow. We'll see. You up for it, Lara?"

"Sure!" she said brightly, and bit into her toast. Her hair was in a braid resting on one side of her head, and she was wearing a bright-yellow miniskirt with black ballerinas and black tights. Inary had given her some clothes she didn't wear any more, and it was a treasure trove for Lara. Once again I noticed how much cheerier she looked these days, how rested, with the unbroken nights' sleeps she'd been getting since we arrived. There had been no sign of her anger, though to be fair she'd never unleashed her rage on me, her dad or Leo before. It only usually happened in school. Or with my beloved mother-in-law.

"What?" she said with a smile.

"Oh, sorry. Have I been staring?"

"Yes! *Again!*"

"Sorry!" I put my hands up. "Just, you're very pretty."

"You are very pwetty," Leo echoed.

"Mum! Stop it! Stop it, you too!" she said, and leaned over to give us both a kiss before she disappeared through the French doors.

★

150

On Sunday, Leo was the first up. I was still asleep when he jumped on my bed.

"Mum! Wake up! We are going on a horse! Can you help me put my wellies on?"

"It's a bit early, darling . . ." I forced myself to sit up. Lara wandered into the room, bleary-eyed.

"What's the time?" she slurred.

"It's very late. It's time to go," Leo said cheerily. "I need to bring my Transformers."

"You won't be needing those, I don't think."

"Please, Mummy!"

"Okay, okay," I relented, and looked at my watch. "It's barely seven o' clock!"

"I'm going back to bed," said Lara grumpily.

Leo took her by the hand. "But you can't! The horses are waiting!" I had to laugh. That was what I always said when we were running late for nursery – *Your teacher is waiting*.

"The horses are all asleep. Torcuil told us to go around nine. That's three hours away," I said reasonably. "Why don't we relax here for a bit, have a little play and—"

"I need my wellies on."

He was unmovable. I had to relent and get up. I decided to take Leo to La Piazza for breakfast to try to kill time. Michael was always there early on a Sunday to prepare the lunch specials. I tried to be as slow as I could in getting ready and managed to stretch the time to just past eight o'clock.

Leo ran down the little alley and into the coffee shop's kitchen.

"We are going horse riding!"

"You're here early, young man!" Michael said. The kitchen smelled beautifully of coriander and nutmeg.

151

"Yes, because the horses are waiting," he explained.

"Sorry about this. We have to be up at Ramsay Hall around nine and this boy has been awake since seven."

"Well, somebody is keen! Help yourself to breakfast, Margherita. You can use the coffee machines, can't you?"

"Oh yes. Can I make you an espresso or something?"

"No drinking when I'm on duty." He smiled. "Also, if you make coffee like your mum, I can't drink that. I wouldn't sleep for a week."

I helped myself to coffee and some *torta* I'd made the evening before with Mum, and fixed Leo and Lara some hot milk and a generous portion of *torta* each. Leo was so excited he couldn't sit still. Finally, it was time to go.

"We're off then, see you later!"

"Have fun!" Michael winked at me.

He *winked*.

Why was he winking?

Because he was nice! That was all. I was being paranoid. That was all.

"Say hello to Lord Ramsay from me," he called as we walked out of the door.

I take that back. I wasn't being paranoid. Michael was *teasing* me. And I would most certainly ignore him.

Poor Leo was made to wait even longer, as all the horses were taken up by pupils of the riding school for the next half an hour. Torcuil was in full riding gear and wasn't wearing his glasses; he was holding onto Stoirin's reins loosely, as if they were holding hands. The bond between them was clear to see. Every once in a while, Stoirin nuzzled the top of his head. She was even more beautiful as I saw her out of her stand for the first time: her coat glimmered in the sunshine with a warm shade of brown, shiny and immaculately clean, like she'd been washed with some exotic oil. Strands of her mane flew gently in the wind – there seemed to always be a breeze at Ramsay Hall.

"So, what do you say? Do you want to ride her?" Torcuil offered, lifting the extra helmet he had in his hand.

"Come on, Mum!" Lara encouraged.

"Come on, Mummy!" echoed Leo, whose little hand kept patting Stoirin's side.

"I don't know . . . I've never been on a horse before . . ."

"She won't throw you. I guarantee that," said Torcuil.

"I know, I know she wouldn't. You wouldn't, would you?" I said sweetly, caressing Stoirin's mane. But she was so big. "Look, maybe another time."

"I'd like a go," Lara said, and looked at me.

"Go for it!" I smiled.

Torcuil handed her the helmet. "There," he said.

I was so proud of her and just a little bit apprehensive as she stepped on the stirrup and lifted herself up, with Torcuil's help. Stoirin snorted and swayed a little but was otherwise unfazed.

"How does it feel?" I asked unnecessarily. Lara was *beaming*.

"Brilliant! Wow! Can I . . . go somewhere?"

"Well, you could, but Stoirin isn't used to sticking to a circuit, she'll be off. Are you okay with that?"

"I don't think you should, not the first time . . ." I protested. "Mum!"

"She'll be fine. Honestly, Margherita. I promise. She's a mellow girl, aren't you, Stoirin?" Torcuil looked like he knew what he was doing, so I relaxed a bit. He wouldn't put my daughter in danger.

"Lara, if you feel like she's going too fast, pull the reins back . . ."

"Will it hurt her?"

"Of course not," said Torcuil. "It's like speaking to her. You're simply telling her you want to slow down a little."

"Okay."

"Ready?"

Lara nodded. Maybe she was ready: me, not so much.

"Off you go, Stoirin, good girl," Torcuil said, and patted her side.

"Oh!" Lara's face broke into a big smile as Stoirin began trotting over the gravel and into a field. My heart was in my throat and my knees were wobbly, but I pretended not to be afraid.

"Don't worry. She'll be fine," Torcuil said with authority. The knot in my stomach loosened ever so slightly, but not completely.

Lara sat on Stoirin like she'd been riding horses forever. I saw her increasing the pace a little, then pulling on the reins as Stoirin went too fast. She looked in control. I was so full of admiration for her.

"She's a natural," Torcuil said, echoing my thoughts. "And soon it'll be your turn, won't it?" he said to Leo.

"Yes! I want to go on the very big horse!"

"No way, you are going on the very small pony!" I retorted, my eyes not leaving Lara as she trotted across the fields.

"He can ride Sheherazade," he said, pointing to a small mare Fiona was leading by the reins. "The lessons always finish on the hour, so it's almost time." He glanced at his watch.

"Mum! Look! It's Peppa Pig!" Leo pointed at Torcuil's arm. And indeed, he was wearing a Peppa Pig watch.

154

"Torcuil? Are you a fan of Peppa Pig?"

"Oh, that? It's just temporary. My watch broke, and this was left behind at the stables and nobody claimed it, and I hate shopping . . ."

"Oh, I love shopping. I hope to make it to Aberdeen with Lara and my mum soon. Before the summer is over and we go back to London."

He hesitated for a moment, like what I'd said had upset him, or surprised him. "Sure, there will be time for that," he said. "There's plenty of time. Before you go back, I mean."

"Yes. Of course," I hurried to say. But he didn't reply, just looked away, and there was a moment of silence between us.

The lesson was over and the little girls were dismounting the ponies. We waited until they were on their way with their mums, and walked over.

"Fiona, do you think we can have Leo riding Sheherazade for a little bit?" Torcuil asked.

"Absolutely! Come on, young man," she said, and took him by the hand, leading him towards a pile of little helmets resting on the wooden bench. She chose the smallest one and fitted it on Leo's head. He was so thrilled he couldn't stand still.

My heart was in my throat as Torcuil lifted him and placed him on top of Sheherazade, who didn't stir and didn't move. The pony was the picture of placidity as Fiona began leading him slowly around the circle, while Torcuil held on to Leo, a hand on his back.

"Mummy! Look! I'm on a horse!"

"Yes you are! Clever boy!" I called, half proud, half terrified. I threw a glance to Lara, who was still trotting with Stoirin and looked perfectly in control.

We walked slowly round and round, and a thought that had

been whirling in my mind for a while finally bubbled up to the surface. "Torcuil, I was thinking . . ."

"Yes?"

I hesitated.

"What if I came up to Ramsay Hall an extra day a week? You wouldn't need to pay me, of course. I'd like to . . ." I shrugged, trying to explain my desire to see Ramsay Hall rescued from its decay. My hands were itching to sort out all the beautiful, neglected corners of Ramsay Hall. ". . . help sort things out."

His eyes widened, and for a moment he stopped walking. "It's a huge job. You could never do it in six weeks . . ."

"Not all of it, no . . . but some of it, at least. It would be a beginning."

"I couldn't ask you—"

"Mum!" Lara's voice interrupted us. I jerked my neck, my heart pounding, fearing she'd be in distress – but she was trotting back calmly like she'd been riding Stoirin forever.

"How was it?"

"Amazing! Please can I do it again soon?"

"Of course. Come any time," Torcuil replied, helping her to dismount. "What about next Sunday?"

"We can't ask—" I began.

"You just offered to help me with Ramsay Hall. Let me offer you this in return. I'll teach Lara to ride Stoirin and Fiona will give Leo lessons. Why don't we do it this way?"

Lara's head was turning from me to Torcuil and back again, and I could see she was desperate for me to accept.

"It sounds good to me," I said.

"Thank you, Mum!" Lara was overjoyed. "You are so lovely, aren't you," she said, throwing her arms around Stoirin. "I'll

156

be back to see you soon." The mare nuzzled Lara's neck just as she'd done Torcuil's, and Lara closed her eyes in bliss.

"And here we are." Fiona's voice came from behind me. She was helping Leo to dismount. "Sheherazade has another lesson now, but you did so well, Leo!" she said kindly.

Leo slipped his hand in mine. "Did you see me? Did you see me on the horse?"

"Of course I saw you! I was just here! You were *splendid*," I said and ruffled his hair.

"Can I come back?"

"You'd be very welcome, Leo," Torcuil said solemnly, and Leo nodded just as formally. It was funny, and heart-warming, how this childless man could instinctively relate to a three-year-old he'd never met before. How relaxed he was in Leo's presence, the way he looked at him and laughed at the funny things he said, made me wonder why he was alone, without a family of his own.

We walked home in the midday sunshine, and I couldn't stop thinking about Torcuil's reaction when I mentioned the time we had left in Glen Avich. That summer, a season that seemed endless when it started, would draw to a close at some point – short like a butterfly's lifetime. My time in Glen Avich was a moment of respite, a little *pause* symbol in between notes on a music sheet. Our *real* life was still awaiting us in London, and, sooner or later, we'd have to go back to reality.

We dropped by at La Piazza on the way back, to share the details of our horse-riding day. Leo and Lara were beaming.

"So you had a good time then?" My mum smiled.

"Yes! And we're going back next weekend!" Lara said, taking off her sweatshirt in front of the warm fire.

"Well, I think I might have to take you, then, because your mum might be busy."

What? How did she know about my offer to do some extra work at Ramsay Hall?

"Well, I'll only work an extra day a week, I'll still be free at the weekends—"

"Work an extra day a week? What do you mean?" My mum was dumbfounded.

"I offered to help Torcuil with Ramsay Hall. That's what you were talking about?"

"No!" My mum smiled smugly, the *I know something you don't know* kind of smile.

"What is it then?" I was beginning to feel a spark of excitement.

"Well, remember those *torcetti* you made yesterday? This woman was here with her friend, and she loved them. She's doing a book launch in Aberdeen on Sunday afternoon and she asked me if you'd like to cater for it!"

I was speechless for a moment. "Seriously?"

"Oh Mum, that's fantastic! You have to do it!" Lara said.

"Of course she will!" My mum bent down and disappeared behind the counter for a moment, only to emerge with a card in her hand. "This is her business card. She said to call her for details and that she's sorry about the short notice, but it'll be a small event, so not to worry."

I looked at the card. It was black with a bright yellow and pink bird in the corner.

"*Carlotta Nissen,*" I read. "*Author – reiki practictioner – life coach – yogini*. Oh, cool!"

"I *know*! It's for the launch of her latest book. Something about liquid sunshine, I can't remember exactly. She's

Danish, by the way. Do you want to give her a phone now?"

"Oh yes, please!" I said and stepped into the back. The kitchen faced a little courtyard, and I sat on the stone wall around it to make my call. It was so strange, how things were happening for me.

"Carlotta?"

"Yes?"

"Hello, it's Margherita here, from La Piazza."

"Oh, hello! I'm so glad you called!" She had the hint of an exotic accent, mixed with a Scottish lilt. "I loved your biscuits. What were they called . . . *Torseti*?"

"Nearly! *Torcetti*. Did you try any others I made?"

"I think I had some of those little cakes filled with coffee ganache . . . they were incredible!"

"Oh yes, the *bignole* . . ."

"*Bi* . . ."

"Bi-ni-ole," I said.

"If you say so! I was hoping, if you're not too busy, maybe you could make a variety of cookies and little cakes for me? I'm launching my first book on Friday at the Waterstones in Aberdeen. I know it's short notice . . ."

"No at all, when I worked at the restaurant I had to rustle up desserts for eighty people in the space of a few hours! Really, there's plenty of time."

"That's great! I was hoping you could do some savoury bites as well to be had with wine . . ."

"Sure! I can continue the Italian theme if you like? *Salatini, pizzette*?"

"I'm not sure what they are, but they sound good! Especially the way you say it . . ."

"And what about little mini favours in transparent bags?

159

You know, with a nice ribbon and a thank-you-for-coming label . . ."

"That would be fantastic. If you could make, say, sixty of them? It'll be a small launch, but quite a few well-connected people . . ."

"Certainly. Thank you so much for this. It's such a great opportunity . . ."

"No, thanks to you. I can't believe I've been so lucky. I mean, when I tried those biscuits they were so good I thought the person who made these can't possibly have time to do my launch!" Carlotta's accent was lovely, like a cheerful sing-song, her voice going up at the end of every sentence.

"Well, I'm just here for a little while. I'm not working as such at the moment . . ."

"Yes, your mum said. But I think you should make some business cards to bring to my launch. I suspect you're going to need them."

20

Something was lost

Margherita

I could barely sleep that night for excitement. I had enrolled Lara to design the thank-you-for-coming labels on Michael's computer, and I'd trailed the Internet for the equipment I needed – little transparent bags, ribbons, ink and printing paper. The next day I drove to the La Piazza suppliers and bought extra ingredients so that I wouldn't raid my mum's kitchen and leave her cupboards bare.

"There was no need to buy all this yourself, Margherita. You should have asked me to help . . ." Michael said, lifting a five-kilo bag of flour from the boot of my car.

"You're busy enough!"

"Never too busy for my stepdaughter," he said.

"Thanks for letting me use your kitchen, Michael. I really appreciate it."

"It's just so good to see you happy. And this is just the beginning!"

Was it? I thought about what Carlotta had said about preparing business cards, and butterflies fluttered in my stomach. It was all exciting, but a bit daunting too.

Just for a start, what address would I put on my business cards, if I decided to have them made?

Glen Avich was just temporary, of course, I said to myself.

And then I recalled the short exchange I'd had with Torcuil at the stables, and once again I felt a hand squeezing my heart.

"If you need a guinea pig for your creations, I'm available!" Michael said as he rubbed his hands together after handling the floury bags.

"Noted. Well, I'm off . . ." My hands were itching to start experimenting, but I'd promised Torcuil an extra day at Ramsay Hall and I thought it would be better to just get that over and done with and concentrate on getting organised on the four days I had left.

"You are? I thought you were keen to start straight away."

"I am, but . . ." I was about to say I needed to go to Ramsay Hall, when I remembered Michael's weird winking the day before. I didn't want to give him any more ammunition to make fun of me.

"I . . . have stuff to do. For a few hours."

"Are you sure? Your mum is more than happy to look after Leo, I'm sorted at La Piazza, so you can get going . . ."

But I had already placed a quick kiss on his cheek and was out of the door with a heartfelt *thank you*.

Catering for a sixty-person event was nothing compared to what needed to be done at Ramsay Hall. The short guided tour that Torcuil had given us had revealed only a fraction of the mansion's wonders. I was determined to convince Torcuil to open it to the public, whatever reasons he had not to, whatever real concerns his jokes about ghosts wanted to hide.

I was sitting in the kitchen in front of a pile of botanical prints I was cleaning one by one, making a mental list of the cookies I wanted to include in Carlotta's favours. I had already done so much work that morning and I was very

162

satisfied with myself. It mainly involved getting rid of tons of dust to help with Torcuil's asthma and opening dozens of windows to let the fresh air in. In the next few days I planned to tackle the windows. I had taken the chance to sit-down with a cup of tea when from the pile of wood-framed prints came a cheery tune that bounced against the walls and resounded all over the house. I jumped out of my skin and it took me a few seconds to realise it was my phone, sitting on the table beside me as I wiped the prints' filthy frames. It was Torcuil.

"Lord Ramsay?" I said, a hint of teasing in my tone.

"Margherita. Thank goodness you replied."

I was alarmed. "What's happened?"

"I need to ask you the biggest favour ever. A *huge* favour."

"You can try," I said, resting a picture of a petunia on the never-ending pile. How many prints of plants, flowers and roots can a family own?

"I'm doing a guest lecture today at the Scottish Medieval Society. It's a mega-important gig and it took me weeks to prepare. The notes for the lecture are saved on a memory stick, which I left at Ramsay Hall. And I am in Edinburgh. You can see the problem. The lecture is in . . ." – a little pause – ". . . two hours and twenty minutes, so I couldn't drive there and back again."

"Did you not save the notes on your laptop?"

"No."

"Why?" I decided to leave him on a knife's edge for a minute.

"Because I'm an idiot. And I also need my handwritten notes too, which are in the same folder. Please save my life. I'd ask Inary, but she's on deadline with her manuscript and—"

"And you thought, hey, what would Margherita have to do this morning apart from cleaning seventy-two botanical prints from my family collection?" I laughed, screwing the cap back on the wood polish.

"Seventy-two? Do we have that many?"

"Yes. I counted them. Anyway, sure, no problem. I'll just give my mum a phone to let her know and I'll drive down. Where is the memory stick and your notes?"

"On my desk, in a bright blue folder."

"Oh," I sighed, as I began to make my way towards Torcuil's study.

"Yes, I see where you're coming from, but I tidied up a few weeks ago, or was it before Christmas? Anyway it should be—"

"Torcuil? Torcuil?" I called. The line had gone down. The signal was funny at Ramsay Hall: it came and went in waves and you could never predict where it would pop up or go down next. As I walked into the almighty mess that was Torcuil's study, my phone rang again.

"Yes, hello again. I'm looking for the folder on your desk. It's like an archaeological dig here . . ." I said, moving around the piles of paper and books.

"It's bright blue. You can't miss it."

"Torcuil, you could miss a fluorescent-orange *tractor* in this mess. Oh, wait . . ." All of a sudden, the piles of documents and printouts seemed to shuffle and rearrange themselves, and a glimpse of bright blue appeared among the papers. I blinked. Was my mind playing tricks on me, or had the papers just moved?

"Did you find it?"

"Not yet. I need two hands to dig into . . . this. I'll call you back."

"Okay."

I eyed the piles of paper suspiciously, then moved them around some more until I could see again the flash of cobalt blue peeking from in between printed sheets. I grabbed hold of it quickly as if to stop it from moving – as weird as it might sound – and looked around me.

It wasn't the first time that something like that had happened. My cleaning materials never seemed to be in the same place. And something had happened with my handbag a few times now: it was never where I'd left it when I first arrived at the hall. If I left it on the kitchen table, I would find it on the window seat. If I left it on the window seat, I would find it by the door. It played musical chairs by itself. I hadn't mentioned anything to Torcuil or to Lara. I was worried in case they said I'd gone mad. I didn't want Lara's imagination to run away with her, especially after her jokes about a Mrs Rochester locked in the attic.

I refused to believe there was anything untoward going on, apart from me forgetting where I'd put things. But I'm not the forgetful type. Or maybe it was Torcuil's cats. Though cats don't really get hold of handbags and move them around.

There was a little alarm bell going off in a corner of my mind, but I couldn't allow myself to listen to it. The whole thing was too weird.

With the folder safely in my hands I walked back to my mum's house to get the car. There was nobody home – they were probably all at La Piazza. I texted her quickly to let her know where I was going and to check that everything was fine with the children.

We are all well. Have fun with Torcuil, she replied. It was exactly what Michael had said when I'd taken the children horse riding – *have fun with Torcuil.*

I decided to ignore her too.

The drive to Edinburgh was beautiful. The colours of August, especially its lush, heavy, vital green, painted a landscape right on the cusp and about to fall, its ripeness a sign of an impending end. There was a hint of autumn in the air even if it was just early August – or maybe the Scottish summer was so chilly this year it was fooling me into thinking it was already over.

I negotiated my way around the city and managed to locate somewhere to park, which felt like a bit of a miracle because the place was packed with tourists. Torcuil had arranged to meet me in front of the Scottish Medieval Society, a beautiful Georgian building in what they called the New Town.

"I can never thank you enough," he said. "Listen . . . If you have to go back to Leo and Lara it's fine, it's okay, really it's okay, but . . . No, you probably have to get back. You do, don't you?"

"Well, not really. My mum has the children, and I was due to be out working at yours anyway." I shrugged, and looked around. "I think I'll take some time to have a walk." I'd never been to Edinburgh before. The little I'd seen was so beautiful and atmospheric, I wanted to see more.

"Oh. Oh, that's good. So maybe you could wait for me somewhere . . . and maybe we could meet up . . . and maybe we could have a spot of lunch? Maybe?"

I hoped for him that his oratory skills would be better during the lecture than those he'd just demonstrated.

"That's a lot of maybes! Sure, why not?"

"Good! Great." He ran a hand through his hair, his nervous gesture again. "Do you have a good sense of orientation?" he said in a serious way that made me laugh.

"I'm a homing pigeon. See the woman in the satnav? That's me."

"Really? I could get lost in my own house."

"Most people could, given where you live."

"I suppose that's right. So, anyway, I'll be finished around one, maybe we can meet somewhere away from the madding crowd. I think I know just the place."

"Perfect."

"Good! So I can unleash you on the city and see you back here at half past one?"

"You certainly can. See you later. Good luck with the lecture!"

"Thank you," he replied, lifting the little memory stick for a moment, as a thank you. I recalled the way the papers on his desk had seemed to move, revealing the memory stick underneath, and I wondered once again if I should tell him.

A couple of hours later we were sitting in the Dovecot Studios, an art gallery with a coffee shop tucked away from the main tourist haunts. Edinburgh was full to the brim with tourists and performers – the Fringe festival was about to start. The atmosphere was exhilarating, chaotic and full of life and excitement, with its startling contrast between the buskers and entertainers and the grey, heavy buildings.

"It's like a carnival has exploded in a cathedral, if you know what I mean," I said to Torcuil.

"That's exactly how it feels like and looks like! Lots of people complain that the festivals are a hassle, the city just fills up and you can't move for people shoving leaflets in your face, but I love it. It's so . . ."

"Vibrant."

"Exactly!" Torcuil's face was animated as he spoke. It was the first time we had sat down face to face for a long time, so I had the chance to notice how his eyes changed colour with the light. Sometimes they were light blue, sometimes green . . .

Oh.

I wasn't really supposed to notice the changing colour of his eyes, was I? Or how the dark-blue woollen jacket really suited him. And I wasn't really supposed to be so happy we had some time together.

A sense of unease filled me for a moment, but Torcuil kept chatting and somehow I forgot. I forgot to feel awkward. I forgot to feel inappropriate.

To be with him, to speak to him, was just so easy.

". . . so I sort of stopped there for a moment, but thankfully I recovered myself. I've been doing this for years and I still get nervous. I don't know how Angus does it, getting up on stage with all those people looking at you . . . Oh, here we are. Thank you," he said to the waitress, who rested two steaming bowls of Cullen skink, a smoked-fish soup, in front of us. "You are going to love this, Margherita. I can't believe you've never tried Cullen skink before."

"It smells beautiful. I want to try haggis soon too. My stepfather is going to cook it for me."

"Hmm. I tend not to eat stomachs, really."

I laughed. "You don't eat the stomach! It's just offal and oatmeal cooked inside the sheep's stomach. I shouldn't be explaining this to you, you're the native, not me!"

"I don't eat guts either. What do you think of the soup?"

168

"It's beautiful. We have something like this where I come from. It's called *minestra bianca* . . . soup made with milk, rice and vegetables."

"Sounds good. So, you were a chef?"

"In a previous incarnation, yes. A pastry chef. And by the way, I've got news in that department."

"Tell me."

"I was asked to cater for a book launch in Aberdeen this Friday coming."

"That's fantastic! You haven't been here a month and you're already in demand." He wasn't flattering me – he sounded honest, truthful.

"This girl tried my biscuits at La Piazza and, well, she loved them. I'll still do what needs done at yours this weekend, of course . . ."

"Don't worry about that. As long as I get to see you . . ." A heartbeat as we both realised what he'd just said – and then he hung his head, confused, as soon as the words came out of his mouth.

As long as I get to see you.

"Well, I'm sure . . ." I began, equally flustered.

"Why did you leave in the first place?" he interrupted, and I was grateful for a change of topic.

"You mean why I did I leave my job? To be at home with the children."

"That's what my sister did. She lasted a year before she was tearing her hair out with boredom. I'll rephrase that . . . before she was tearing *our* hair out with *her* boredom."

"It's not for everyone, but I loved being at home with them. Now . . . well, now things have changed for me. I'm ready to open up to the world again. You see, I thought I could juggle a part-time job around my children, but Lara has always been . . ." I hesitated. Usually I was reluctant to share the details of Lara's story with people. I didn't want her to be labelled *the one who was adopted*, as if her past defined the whole of her – it didn't. I always let people assume she was my biological daughter, and if she felt like talking about it then she would make that decision for herself. But with Torcuil, it felt different. He seemed so . . . kind. And steadfast. Like someone you could speak to, who wouldn't betray your confidence. Someone who wouldn't spread harsh, thoughtless words around later, behind your back, like seeds of unrest.

"Lara was adopted when she was six. She always needed me. A lot. So that's why I left my job."

Torcuil nodded, while I waited with some apprehension to see what he'd say next. "It seems to me that there's something special about Lara. She is very bright and imaginative. And very clever."

I smiled. He'd said the right thing.

"She is. She is very talented. She's taking extra classes in school . . . English and creative writing. I'm so proud of her."

"I can see that. Your eyes light up when you talk about her."

"We waited for a long time for Lara. She was . . . a gift. My family means everything to me," I said, looking into my soup. Those were intimate words, and difficult to say out loud. "Things aren't working out exactly like I'd planned . . ."

Torcuil nodded. "I know exactly what you mean."

I debated for a moment whether or not to ask. "Have you ever been married?"

He smiled and shook his head. "No, no, never."

"Oh, sorry. Just when you said you knew what I meant . . ."

170

"As in, I know what it's like when things don't work out the way you planned."

Sadness shadowed his face for a moment; it was time to change subject. "Well, I have my eye on one of those . . ." I said, gesturing to the array of cakes on display.

"Do you think they'll be as good as yours, or your mum's?"

"Never. But they'll do this time," I laughed.

I chose a slice of apple and cinnamon cake, while Torcuil ordered another coffee. An older couple sat at the table beside us, all wrapped up in heavy jackets, though it wasn't that cold. I identified them immediately as tourists. The woman looked towards me.

"*Guarda che bella signora scozzese . . .*" she said to her husband.

I giggled.

Torcuil smiled. "What's funny?"

"The couple beside us," I whispered, leaning over towards him so they wouldn't hear me. "They are Italian. They just said I'm a beautiful Scottish woman!" I giggled again. "They got it all wrong."

Torcuil looked straight into his coffee, like there was something very, very interesting inside his cup. "Well, not all of it. The Scottish bit is wrong."

I had no answer to that.

As I was driving back, I found myself wishing that Friday would come soon, so that I could see him again – and immediately an overwhelming sense of guilt and shame drowned me for a million different reasons.

But it had been so lovely. It had been so good to just sit there and chat and laugh and be listened to. Like what I said mattered. Like my company brought joy and pleasure. I couldn't remember the last time I'd felt that way, and now that bit of my heart had been opened again, I knew it would be hard to close.

Thank you for today. Night. T.

His goodnight text, simple as ever, came that evening.

Thank you. I hope I'll see you sometime before next Friday. I mean, there isn't much time left before the end of the summer and we go back, and I had such a good time today . . . I began typing. And then I deleted it.

Thank you for your company. Goodnight. M.

It was all I allowed myself to say.

21

Still waters

Lara

Dear Kitty,

I spent hours printing and cutting out little labels for my mum, and I loved it. I think the favours are going to look amazing and I'm so excited to go to a real book launch. Inary is coming too, so that's going to be perfect.

When I finished, I went wandering. Not that I went looking for Mal, obviously, I was just strolling and it was a lucky coincidence I happened to bump into him. He was beside the loch again. He was standing still and looking at the waters. His face lit up when he saw me, and so did mine. Obviously I didn't see myself, but I felt it. Like a lamp going off in my head and making everything bright.

"Hello," I said, and just then a gust of wind glued my hair to my lipgloss.

Awkward, awkward, awkward.

But he didn't seem to notice as I unstuck the strands from my lips.

"Hello again. How are you, Lara?" He lifted his head on one side, in that way he has. Like he's really listening, like he's really interested in your reply, not just asking for the sake of it. You know, like the kind of people who actually mean, *Hello, how am I?*

"I'm good. I was doing some work for my mum, and then I came out. Just for a walk, you know. No reason in particular. You?"

"I don't know."

"You don't know what?"

"I don't know how I am."

"You're here. With me," I said. I rubbed off a smudge of mud from his cheek and I took his hand; the look of confusion seemed to disappear from his face.

"Never mind," he said, and squeezed my hand. "Come. I want to show you something."

"What?" I asked.

"You're going to have to wait and see," he said with a smile.

He led me along the shore all the way past Ramsay Hall, and nearly to the other side of the loch. We walked in silence, the sound of my breathing echoing. I noticed how quiet his step was, how he moved on the grass and on the pebbled shore barely making a sound.

Suddenly, he stopped and put a finger to my lips. It felt strange, for him to touch my lips, and I think I must have blushed, because my heart leapt a little and my cheeks felt warm. I nodded.

He took my hand again, and we stepped so close to the shore we were nearly in the water. It looked like he was leading me inside the loch, and I suppose I should have been a bit nervous at that point, but I wasn't.

For some reason, I trusted him.

He squeezed my hand and pointed along the reeds.

And there, in a soft nest made of weeds and grass, lay an otter curled up and asleep. Nestled against her body there was a little pup, its fur wet and glistening and its tiny nose baby pink. I sucked in my breath in wonder and smiled silently. I could feel Mal's joy in seeing my reaction, and for a moment we were inside one another – if that makes sense. I can't think of a better way to describe it – but it was like we were one.

And I was happy, but very cold. Very, very cold all of a sudden. I'm not sure why. A shiver ran through me.

Suddenly the spell was broken – the otter mum woke up and began to stir. I glanced at Mal in alarm, but he shook his head and squeezed my hand again, as if to say, *It's okay*.

The otter slid into the water so smoothly she barely made ripples, and her pup was left alone in the nest. It made a high-pitched sound, calling for her – and my heart was ready to break when its mummy emerged from the loch and gave it a little nuzzle. I think she was saying, *It's okay, I'll be back soon*, and the pup must have got the message because it curled itself up again into a little ball and didn't call again.

Mal pulled my hand softly, and we stepped away.

"They make their nest there year after year," he whispered. "I go say hello once in a while."

I opened my mouth to say something – anything – about how cute the baby otter was, but something else came out. "You know what?" I looked down. I was probably scarlet at this point, but I didn't care.

"What?"

"I was hoping you'd be there. I sort of came looking for you."

"You know what?" he said.

I kept looking down, but I heard a smile in his voice.

"What?"

"I was there because I was hoping to see you."

He took a strand of my hair and tucked it behind my ear. And then he stroked my cheek.

Nobody has ever done that to me before.

I mean, no boy has ever done that to me.

I thought I'd melt.

He took my hands in his – they were freezing, and I held them tight, trying to warm them a little – and he folded me into him. It was perfect.

Until I felt him shivering, a shiver so violent it jolted him.

"Lara. I think I need to go, now. I'm sorry," he said, just like that, without warning. Another one of his sudden exits.

"Oh. That's okay," I said. But I was *crushed*.

"It's just that I'm very tired now."

Tired? Was he ill or something?

"It's okay, really. I'll just . . ." I threw a hand behind me, to say I would just get back by myself.

"So will I see you again soon?" He was nearly pleading, and I felt sorry for him, though I didn't even know why.

"Yes, of course."

"Promise? Because *everybody else is gone*."

"Of course. It's a promise . . ." I said, but before I could take the next breath he was gone already, away and into the trees in that silent way of moving he has. His dark hair and jacket melted into the darkness of the woods, until they were one.

And that was it, Kitty.

I made my way back alone, and I'm already counting the hours till I see him again.

I'm just happy he exists, you know?

I'm just happy he's in this world.

22

Time for us

Margherita

Lara and I were baking from Nonna Ghita's notebook, trying different recipes to decide what would make the cut for Carlotta's launch. The results of our labour were lined on the kitchen table, cooling, wafting off a wonderful scent – little cakes and biscuits, mini-pizzas of different flavours and *salatini* made with puff pastry. Lara was standing across from me and sieving icing sugar on our new creation – we'd tried our hand at *tortine di mele*, apple tarts, and they had come out lush and light. We'd also made *paste di meliga*, a traditional Piedmontese biscuit I hadn't made in a long time.

"The *tortine* can't be used for the favours, they're too moist, but we can serve them at the launch anyway. Don't you think?"

No reply. She'd been at Inary's earlier, and her mind was somewhere else; she was lost in thought. I glanced at her, and once again I considered how beautiful she was, though she was so completely unaware of it, so convinced she wasn't. Her wavy hair, to her, was frizzy; her light-blue eyes, as blue as the summer sky, to her were common; her long limbs were too skinny; the near-invisible freckles that dotted her nose in a way that I found irresistible, to her, were just plain ugly. She couldn't see what everyone else, not just me, saw: beauty blooming slowly, until the day she'd grow into herself. In fact, I had a theory: that Lara's looks were one of the reasons for Polly's and Tanya's – and their cronies' – cruelty. They reminded her constantly of how much more attractive they believed they were in case she got ideas above her station. I was so glad that Lara was away from them, at least for a while.

When I told her this, she didn't believe it. After all, what teenager believes her own mother when she tells her she's beautiful?

"Lara?"

"Yes? Sorry, what did you say?"

"Just that the *tortine de mele* are too moist for the favour bags."

"Oh, yes. That's true," she replied, like that was the last thing on her mind. What was troubling her?

"So, will you see her again soon?"

"*Her?*"

"Inary, I mean." Who else could I be referring to?

"Yes." She smiled, a genuine smile, and gently wiped off some icing sugar from the side of one of the plates. "We're going shopping in Aberdeen together."

"That's great," I said, but a little sting of jealousy nipped me. *I* wanted to go shopping with Lara. And then I silenced the little jealous voice in my head; it was unfair to think like that, and Lara needed new friends. Inary was so much older than her, but to me they seemed like kindred spirits.

"That sounds good. So when do you think you'll do that?"

"Well, I was hoping to go to Aberdeen with you first, Mum. After the launch, I mean."

I smiled inwardly. As petty as it was, I was happy that my daughter wanted to go shopping with me first.

"I'd like to give contact lenses another try." Lara had been dreaming of contact lenses for a couple of years now and we'd visited the optician twice, but both times it hadn't worked out. She said that putting something in her eyes *creeped her out.*

"Sure. Why not? I'll find a Boots in Aberdeen and sort an appointment."

"Thanks . . . I hope they don't touch my eyeballs this time."

"Well, you sort of have to touch your eyeballs in a way if you want to put lenses in."

"Urgh . . ."

"Hey, you'll be fine. You know your *zia* Anna wears lenses and she loves them. This time it'll work out, I'm sure."

"I hope so. And also . . ."

"What?"

"I'd like to have my hair cut," she said, ruffling her soft, wavy locks and leaving a trace of icing sugar in them. I'd always thought her hair was the colour of ancient gold, like the frame of an old painting.

I was crushed.

"Oh."

"Mum, I'm not a child any more and my hair is like a ball of straw!"

"It's not! Your hair is lovely!"

"Mum. I've made my decision."

I sighed. "Right. It's your hair . . ." I said, feeling my own heavy, dark mane that I wouldn't have cut for the world.

"It is," she said mutinously.

"But it's so gorgeous . . ." I tried again.

"Mum!"

"Okay, okay." I put my hands up.

179

I had to admit to myself it was hard to see Lara growing, turning into a young woman, but there was no point in resisting the change. Also, I suspected that this makeover thing she'd asked for had something to do with the mysterious Mal. She'd mentioned him in passing one day when we were baking goodies for La Piazza.

"So, is this Mal a new friend of yours?" I'd said, trying to sound nonchalant.

"Yes," Lara had said briefly. Just like that, without elaborating.

"Right. Is he a nice boy?"

"Yes, of course he is! I wouldn't be friends with someone nasty, would I?" she'd snapped.

"Okay, okay. Sorry."

"Yeah, well."

"Just maybe it'd be nice to meet him . . ."

"Mum!"

And that had been the end of the conversation. I'd looked at her pleadingly one last time, but she glared at me, so I left it.

With the intention of keeping an eye on this new friend of hers, it goes without saying.

"I'm sure Lara will introduce him to us when she gets the chance," my mum had said diplomatically when I'd brought it up with her. I thought back at the grief my sisters and I had invariably got from my dad every time we mentioned a boy, and I didn't want to be as possessive as my dad had been, although he'd always been loving with it. It was sort of endearing, looking back. But I had to try to let Lara have her own experiences.

Within reason.

"Listen, Lara, why don't we make a day of it? We can go

and have contact lenses fitted and your hair cut, and do some shopping to round off your new look?"

"I'd love that! This weekend maybe?"

"I'll ask Nonna if she's okay to look after Leo. If she says yes . . ."

"She always says yes," Lara said without a hint of jealousy. She was more confident than I'd seen her for a long time, and revelled in her relationship with my mum and Michael.

"That's true, yes. And now let's see how these *tortine* turned out," I said, taking a bite.

23

New beginnings

Margherita

Carlotta was standing with a microphone in her hand, confident and commanding the attention of the whole room in spite of being a small, slight woman. She had a pixie cut and smiling brown eyes, and she was wearing a bright-yellow minidress that made her look like she, herself, was liquid sunshine. Copies of her book, *Drinking Sunshine*, were piled on the table behind her and displayed all around a poster with her photograph and the cover of the book.

"Your labels are perfect," I whispered to Lara, who was standing beside me. They were a bright-blue sky with fluffy clouds as a base, with a tiny yellow sun in the corner.

She beamed. Our favour bags full of tiny biscuits, kept closed by blue ribbons and decorated with Lara's labels, made a pretty sight on their tray beside the books, while my mum's vintage plates displayed our creations beautifully. I couldn't wait for the guests to tuck in, although I was also a bit nervous.

"I wanted to encompass my experience as a life coach with my research on Eastern philosophy . . ." Carlotta was saying, but I couldn't concentrate on her words; all I could think about was the moment when the guests would approach the little tables arranged at the back of the room and sample the food I'd made with so much love and care. Part of me knew that I had nothing to worry about, that we had sampled everything and it was all delicious, but another part of me wondered what if they didn't like it? I couldn't help it. ". . . to help my clients identify what I call Core Needs and to reach their Point of Achievement . . ."

Finally, the presentation was over – with a deep-breathing exercise that left me gasping for air, ironically, and Lara giggling – and the guests gathered around the food and drink. I tried to be inconspicuous as I mingled with the crowd and kept my ears open for any comments.

"It looks like they're polishing off the lot . . ." I whispered to my mum, looking for reassurance.

"Absolutely! Why wouldn't they? It's delicious and you know it."

"They'll only leave the crumbs. And then lick the plates," said Lara.

"Now that would be a bit much . . ."

"And there you are!" Carlotta approached us, flushed and happy after her thank-you speech and all the congratulations that came her way. "Abby, this is Margherita. Margherita, Abby needs . . . I'll let her tell you herself."

A young woman with smiling eyes shook my hand. "So you are the famous Margherita!"

"I don't know about famous . . ."

"Well, Carlotta raved about your creations and now I know why!"

"Thank you. They aren't really my creations as such; they're old recipes, just not very well known outside of Italy."

"We'll spread the word! I was thinking, I'm having my hen do soon . . . We're having a spa party at my parents' house. It'll be in a couple of months' time. Maybe, if you're not too busy . . . I mean, there will be quite a few girls there, it could be quite good networking for you as well as a gig."

"Oh, that's a pity, Abby. I won't be here in two months' time . . . I'm only in Glen Avich for the summer."

"Oh, no! I had my heart set on it . . ."

"Why don't we give you this for now and see how it goes?" said Lara, taking a small white card from her bag. "My mum's business card."

My business card? Had Lara made business cards for me? I thought we hadn't decided on that one.

"Oh, thank you. Can I have two? My cousin is having her son christened soon and you never know, I suppose," Abby said. "It was nice to meet you, I hope we speak again soon!"

"And you," I said. And then, to Lara: "Business cards?"

"Courtesy of Prontaprint! They're a bit amateurish but it was the best I could do in less than a week."

"Amateurish?" I laughed. We hardly had a professional business established! We'd just baked a few biscuits and put them into bags, really.

"They are lovely," my mum said. And they were: pure white with blue lettering, recalling the colour scheme of La Piazza.

Margherita Ward
Catering and Cakes
Italian Recipes and More
c/o La Piazza
Glen Avich

"I thought I'd keep them simple. Less is more," said Lara solemnly.

"This was such a thoughtful thing to do, Lara! I had no idea!"

"I wanted it to be a surprise," she said with a smile.

"How many did you have made?"

"Two hundred and fifty."

"*Two hundred and fifty?* But it says Glen Avich on here! And we're leaving in a few weeks . . ."

"Well, I—"

"I think I'm late. There's no food left." It was Torcuil, standing at my side all of a sudden. Lara turned around and walked away, reaching Inary on the other side of the room. We'd discuss this later, but I could guess what she was trying to tell me . . .

"What are you doing here?" I asked Torcuil.

"I'm looking for a life coach, did I not tell you?"

"You are?" I laughed.

"Sure! I need to find my Core Needs and Points of Achievement . . ."

"Shhh!" I laughed. "I didn't see you in the crowd."

"I was hiding in the gardening section doing my breathing exercises."

"Shut up!"

"Honestly! And I think I have identified my Core Need for a cup of tea—"

"Lord Ramsay! It's an honour!" Carlotta had zoomed in on Torcuil.

"Oh, hello. Congratulations on your book, Carlotta," he said warmly.

"Thank you. I didn't know you'd be here! Wait till I call the photographer, we must have a picture taken together . . ."

I watched while Torcuil stood for pictures like you would stand on a bed of hot coals.

185

"Oh, don't tell me you already bought a copy! I would have given you a complimentary one. Why don't I give it to you anyway, you can pass it on to your girlfriend?" Carlotta said, eyebrows rising at the end of the sentence. She was fishing, I could see it. And it was oh-so annoying.

"I'll be sure to do that," Torcuil said, and Carlotta's face fell almost imperceptibly. She recovered herself in the blink of an eye.

"Oh, good. So she's not around tonight?"

"Oh, my, look at the time! I'd better go. It was lovely meeting you, Carlotta," Torcuil said quickly, and, as soon as she left, he turned to me. "Nosy . . ." he whispered.

"Well, you are quite a catch!"

He rolled his eyes. "Don't. I hate it when Inary says that."

"But it's true! Did you see the way she was looking at you? And you must admit she's pretty."

"I didn't notice." I considered how unlikely it would be for any man not to notice Carlotta's fair, pink-cheeked Scandinavian beauty. "Also, she's too . . . too upbeat for me. Like she swallowed a disco ball."

"She's a life coach, she has to be this way! All cheerful and enthusiastic."

"You could plug her in."

"Stop it! Anyway . . . were you working today? Did you come all the way from Edinburgh?"

"Yes. I'm off home now. Need a lift?"

That sounded very casual. Like, *Need a lift? If you don't it's all the same*.

"I—"

"She does, yes," my mum said. She had walked over to us with two elderly ladies from Glen Avich, Maggie and Liz.

They were part of the blue-rinse brigade that patronised La Piazza – looking for chats as much as for tea and scones, and almond croissants it seemed. They were nearly as well informed as Peggy, and a lot chattier. Whenever there was something happening in Glen Avich, they had to be there to oversee the proceedings – and sometimes they branched out, like today. They were both wearing their Sunday coats and carrying their best handbags, and I could guess Maggie had had her hair blow-dried at Enchant that afternoon. It sat immobile and, surely, was highly inflammable.

"Maggie, Liz and I are going for errands after this and I think Lara is planning to go with Inary." My mum gestured at Lara and Inary chatting animatedly in the corner.

"Hello, Torcuil, how are you? We haven't seen you in a long time in the village," Liz said.

"Well, Mrs Ritchie, you know, I'm busy with my work. But I should come down more often."

"And tell me, do you have a special someone at last?" Maggie intervened.

"No. No special someones for me, Mrs Bell."

Liz raised her eyebrows. "And why is that, I ask myself, when there are so many pretty girls in Glen Avich?"

"No one as pretty as you ladies," said Torcuil, completely sidestepping her question. I kept trying to smother laughter, but I wasn't sure how long I would last before my mirth spilled out.

"Oh, you've always been so charming. Since you were a little boy! So, where are you off to after this, *Margarayta*?"

"Well, I do have some stuff left to do at Ramsay Hall," I said. "I just didn't have much time this week . . ."

"But that's okay, don't worry, honestly!" Torcuil reassured me.

"Well, it's her job, isn't it? She needs to go and sort the things she hasn't sorted yet," said Maggie. "Not come *gallivanting* with us, don't you think, Maggarita?"

What?

"That's true. You go with your young man, Margaret-ah," Liz said. My name isn't that hard to pronounce, is it? But both Maggie and Liz seemed unable to . . . wait – did she say my *young man*?

"I'm not that young, Mrs Bell," said Torcuil.

"Oh, when you're my age you'll know what old is really like!" She laughed a wistful laugh. "Enjoy it while you can. Off you go, you two . . ." she said, and she literally pushed me and Torcuil towards the door.

We were left with no choice but leave together, with a brief goodbye to Lara.

They'd set me up.

"So, what are we going to do?" Torcuil said as we stepped out of Waterstones.

"What do you mean? Aren't we going back to Ramsay Hall so I can do the work I didn't do today?"

"I didn't come and get you so that you'd do more work for me! I'm not a slave driver!"

"No, I know, but—"

"I'll tell you what. It's a beautiful evening, let's go for a . . . oh."

"What?"

"I felt a drop on my hand."

"Oh . . . me too. It's starting to rain . . . so much for the beautiful evening . . ."

"Okay, let's go for food then."

"That's always a good idea! Where? Oh, wait! I know. I'll take you to this place I know . . ."

"Do you know restaurants in Aberdeen?"

"Well, my mum and Michael told me about it. It's not far from the Trinity Centre. Wait . . ." I took out my phone and checked out the route on Google Maps.

"What's the name?" Torcuil asked.

"I'm not telling you, because you'll know it for sure and I want it to be a surprise."

"Okay, I'm up for it."

We only had to walk for a few minutes, thankfully, because it had begun to rain in earnest.

"Oh, La Lucciola!"

"See? I knew you knew it!"

"Well, I've never been. And you can educate me on Italian food."

"I'll be happy to!"

Sitting across Torcuil, I considered how he made every table and chair look smaller when he sat. Tonight he was wearing a light-blue shirt with his sleeves rolled up – he always did that, I'd noticed. His eyes, so changeable, tonight were grey.

"So . . . you were interested in Carlotta's work?"

"Not in the slightest."

"I suspected!"

"I came to see you," he said, looking over my shoulder. I hung my head immediately, and we were like two awkward teenagers.

"I'm sorry you didn't get to try any of the stuff I made. I have a few bags left at the house," I said, trying to dispel the awkwardness.

"You've been in Glen Avich a matter of weeks and you already have two jobs." He smiled.

"I know. Crazy. Look what Lara made for me . . ." I took out the business cards from my bag.

"She's a thoughtful girl . . ."

"Are you ready to order or do you need five minutes?"

"The lady is ordering for both of us," Torcuil said, and smiled at me.

"Oh, that's a big responsibility! Well, we'll go for . . . *risotto ai funghi* for me and . . . *tagliolini al tartufo*?"

"No idea what that is."

"Trust me."

"I certainly do."

"And *antipasti misti* to start, please," I said, fully satisfied with my choices.

"You look like the cat who got the cream," he laughed.

"Oh, I know! I'm more than a bit obsessed with food. It's in my genes."

"So, we were saying . . ." – Torcuil lifted the little card I had handed him – ". . . but wait, she put your Glen Avich address? But you're leaving in a few weeks' time . . . though I really don't like thinking about it."

"I know. It's like . . . it's like she's trying to tell me something. That she doesn't want to go."

"And what do *you* want?" The candlelight was flickering and dancing between us, giving his skin a golden hue and making his eyes sparkle blue again.

I didn't know how to answer that. He looked at me like he was trying to look all the way into my soul, and something stirred inside me that had been dormant for a long time.

24

Life itself

Torcuil

I sit across her while we eat. She is life itself, her cheeks pink in the candlelight, her eyes liquid, rejoicing in the sensual pleasure of the food. She's chatting, animated, talking about anything and everything with that lovely London accent of hers.

And then the moment comes when I'm speaking, but I don't know what I'm saying; I'm listening, but I can't hear the words.

A fire has started inside me, warm and bright, like the light you would see in a window on a cold winter's night. And the warmth and light are calling me home.

I leave her at her mum's house in Glen Avich after a silent drive – she leaned her head against the car seat, tired after the excitement of the day. Her eyelashes cast a little shadow on her cheeks and one of her hands was uncurled on her lap – she had small, slender fingers, tiny as a starfish.

Ramsay Hall seems even colder and darker – my bed is cold too. Dreams of Margherita take my hand and lead me through the night, and the last thing I see behind my closed eyes, just before sleep conquers me, is her face.

25

Union

Margherita

I was driving back from Aberdeen after the day out I'd promised Lara, and my head was full of thoughts and doubts and questions. I was still reeling from the success of my catering and from the woman I met, Abby, possibly offering me another gig. And, of course, from dinner with Torcuil.

It was just a dinner. It didn't mean anything.

But I had loved every minute.

And the way he looked at me . . . like I was something precious. Something delicate he held in the palm of his hand and that he would never let break or fall. Thoughts of him followed me through the day with Lara, though I did my best to put them out of my head.

Our day out shopping, just the two of us, had been a success. In the space of a morning she had managed to finally get contact lenses in ("No, I won't get you purple-coloured ones; yes you told me that Ophelia in *Bride of Shadows* has purple eyes, but you're still not getting them), her hair cut (my heart broke with every strand of gold that touched the floor) and a few new items of clothing ("Yes, I know you're not a character from *Little Women*, but that skirt suits you so well . . . No? Okay, let's go for skinny jeans instead . . ."). I was exhausted, like any sane human being would be after shopping with a teenager for three hours, and I needed a cappuccino break, but Lara was set on me buying something for myself.

"Let's go to Next. It's a shop for older people," she said.

"Right, thanks. I'm thirty-eight, I'd like to remind you."

"Yes, that's what I mean."

No point in arguing. Lara was adamant I should buy something to dress up with, but I wasn't sure. I didn't have anything planned, and it seemed wiser to buy some everyday clothes I could get more use out of. But Lara would not be swayed. She was determined to get me some *glad rags* (she got the expression from Nonna). I tried on a few dresses, but I always felt that, being so short, dresses swamped me a bit. Finally, I found a bright-red tunic that reminded me a bit of an Indian sari, and thin, soft black trousers. The red called to me.

Suddenly, I remembered what a surreal experience packing for Scotland had been. I'd slid open the doors of my wardrobe and wondered at the rows of blues and greys and blacks, the same dark-coloured or muted tops reproduced dozens of time, in slight variations – short sleeves, long sleeves, cotton or wool – but fundamentally the same. And a sea of jeans. It was like I'd been wearing a blue and grey uniform for years, like an oversized schoolgirl. In the end, I'd only filled a third of my suitcase – I would have loved to leave all those depressing colours behind.

"Mum. You are stunning," Lara said when I tried on my tunic.

"Well, I don't know about that . . ."

"You are! You're so . . . *beautiful*."

Suddenly I remembered when she first told me that. It had been in the first few weeks she'd been with us, when we were curled up together on her bed, reading a story. She'd touched my face with her little hand and said, "You are so beautiful," and me, still new to motherhood and the emotion it brought, had to stop myself from bursting into happy tears.

Laden with bags, I finally sank into a Costa sofa while Lara ordered us coffee. I gazed at her as she stood in the queue. Thankfully she'd decided to just trim her hair and not do anything too drastic: it sat in an artfully messy bob that framed her delicate face. She had decided to wear her new clothes straight away: an oversized jumper with a wide neckline that showed one of her white shoulders, teal-coloured skinny jeans and silver ballerinas. The outfit fitted her long, slender figure like a glove. But she looked so much older all of a sudden. Like a young woman.

For a moment I longed to see her in her Hello Kitty pyjamas and her blue-rimmed glasses, my little girl once more. But I couldn't stop her from flying, and I didn't want to. I had to embrace this gorgeous young woman, as much as I missed my baby.

"You look so lovely, Lara. You really do," I said as she sat beside me.

"Do you really think so?" she replied in a quiet voice.

"Of course! Are you okay?"

"Yes, it's just . . . I don't know," she shrugged. "Today has been perfect. Things are going so well. It's different, here. I get to be myself. Not worry about what people think so much. I'm just . . . happy."

"But that's a good thing, right?"

"It's just that when things go really well I'm always scared that something will happen."

I knew exactly what she meant. Someone like Lara, who'd

spent her early years treading on thin ice and seen it break many times, found it hard to accept happiness. I could understand her, but I struggled to fully grasp this way of looking at things, because I always had an optimistic outlook and never really dwelled much on possible catastrophes around the corner. Everyone in my family was like that. But then, we hadn't gone through what Lara had endured as a child, when she was still so vulnerable.

"I think that in life something always happens," I began, trying to choose the words carefully. "Good or bad. Things change, all the time. They never stay the same. It can be unsettling, but it also means that when a situation is disastrous there's always a good chance it will improve."

She nodded. "Like in *Bride of Shadows* when it looks like Ophelia is the only person who can stop the curse on herself, but she can only stop it by sacrificing herself, and what use is it to have your curse lifted if you're dead? And then it turns out Damien takes the curse on himself and offers to be sacrificed and he is, but he can't die because he's immortal, and so he saves the day?" she said eagerly, and suddenly she was my bookish little girl again.

"Yes, something like that," I said, my heart overflowing with tenderness. "Lara?"

"Yes?" She looked at me, eyes wide – at her age, so much of her happiness depended on me and my choices, and sometimes the responsibility felt overwhelming.

Would you like to stay in Glen Avich? The words nearly came out. And then I stopped them.

Yes, my mum and I had spoken about a leap of faith – but this was too much, too soon. I was too scared to take a leap and never reach solid ground again.

I took Lara shopping in Aberdeen today.

Was it good?

It was great. She looks different. Grown up.

A bit shocking but inevitable? Thankfully little Leo is a long way from being a teenager!

Yes. He's now sleeping with Pingu on one side and a Transformer on the other.

Bless him. Night, Margherita, sweet dreams. PS. It's a long way to Friday.

Night Torcuil. Yes, five days seem very long.

Five days ARE very long. Leave it with me. I'll see what I can do.

Our goodnight texts had evolved.

26

Blooms

Lara

Dear Kitty!

I HAVE CONTACT LENSES IN!

I can't believe I made it.

And I took them out and put them back in TWICE! The optician made sure I could do it myself. I can't stop smiling!

Afterwards Mum took me to Topshop to buy clothes and then to Debenhams to buy some make-up. I got shimmery eye shadows, purple, green and blue, and bright-blue nail polish. I was shocked because everything I asked for, Mum said yes. She looked so happy. I think it was because *I* was happy. And then I made her buy a red top and she looked awesome.

I sort of hope Torcuil sees her in it, but I didn't tell her, of course. She would have bitten my head off.

Anyway, we had the *best* time. I love shops, I love the lights and all the pretty things lined up on the shelves. I was looking at dressy clothes when I saw a blonde girl, her hair all nice and done up and make-up on and huge blue eyes. I thought wow, she's pretty.

And then I realised it was my reflection.

I couldn't believe it.

I wish I could show Polly and Tanya. No, actually, I don't. I don't need to show them and I don't care.

The person I really would like to see me like this is Mal.

Then we went for a cappuccino and I felt a bit strange. I was happy. I *am* happy. It's a weird feeling and I'm not used to it. It's just like I feel I never know where the next blow will come from, but there certainly will be one. Mum spoke to me and she knew exactly what to say to calm me down.

Maybe there are no blows coming. Maybe happiness is here to stay.

By the way! Which is not a by the way at all! It's actually very important, but I was sidetracked by the excitement of today. I spent a couple of hours with Inary yesterday – she needs to hand in her new book in two weeks' time and I GOT TO LOOK AT IT! I actually saw a book BEFORE it's published!

I printed some of my Bride of Shadows fan fiction with a nice font, tied it with one of the blue ribbons I had left from the favour bags and gave it to Inary. I can't wait to hear what she thinks, but at the same time I'm a bit nervous! What if she hates it?

I want to write more. I'm thinking of stories that are only mine, not just fan fiction. Maybe they'll have a grey-eyed hero in them.

No, I'm not thinking of Damien.

I'm thinking of Mal.

27

Bread and roses

Margherita

I was making *baci di dama* – ladies' kisses, melt-in-the-mouth little biscuits with chocolate cream in the middle – for the coffee shop when someone knocked at the door. It was Torcuil, and seeing him made my heart sing – I tried to hide it, but my smile gave me away.

"What are you doing here?" I said, pretending I wasn't hoping he was there for me. "Why aren't you at work? Are you skiving?"

"I had stuff to do here," he laughed. "For the Glen Avich History Association. Are you busy?" he said, looking down at my flour-covered hands.

"No, of course not! I mean, I am now, but I'll be finished in twenty minutes. Come on in."

"What are you making?"

"Ladies' kisses."

Awkward silence.

Okay. Say something, anything.

"What are you doing with the History Association?" I said quickly, stepping back into my mum's kitchen.

"Well, there's this soldier from Glen Avich. He died in Ypres in 1916. He was lost for years . . . His nephew asked for our help and we tracked him down. He's buried in Belgium and we're trying to get him back. I'm helping the family with the paperwork."

"That's so sad. I'm glad you found him. Glad he's coming home."

"Yes, it's very sad. He was only eighteen. He died of pneumonia."

"Poor boy," I said, thinking of his mother, and we were silent for a moment.

"Can I try one?" Torcuil said eventually. "A kiss, I mean?"

Oh God.

"I'll give you a bag of them when they're ready," I said gruffly, to hide my confusion, and strode to the sink to wash my hands. "Let's go for a walk!" I called, slipping my jacket on.

"But were you not . . ." He gestured to the half-finished biscuits on the table.

"Just need some fresh air. Oh, wait. Do you need to go? To the History Society?"

"No. Actually I don't need to be there until this evening. I came home earlier. To see you."

"Oh, really?" I said, as if nothing could have been further from my mind.

We kept brushing against one another as we walked down to the loch. We were sitting on the pebbles at the loch shore, in front of the quiet waters, when he finally took my hand.

I was frightened. I don't know why, I just felt something coming.

So frightened I started shaking.

"Are you okay?" he whispered, feeling me tremble.

I could only nod.

"There's something I want to tell you," he said as we sat watching the waters, my head on his shoulder.

I sat up. "Oh my God. You're secretly married with six children."

He laughed. It was a joke, but I felt really apprehensive. My heart was pounding. What was he about to say?

"Remember when I told you about my ex-fiancée? The woman I was about to marry?"

I nodded. For a moment, I thought he was about to tell me that she was back in his life. My face must have been a picture of worry and shock, because he took my hands in his. "Hey, no, there's nothing bad. Nothing to worry about. I just want to tell you who she was."

"Okay."

"Her name is Isabel, and yes, it's *that* Isabel, my brother's wife."

My mouth was a perfect circle. Isabel. The woman he'd told me about, but whom I never saw.

So Lara was right – there *was* a woman in the attic, so to speak. A Mrs Rochester.

"Your brother's wife?" I repeated.

"Yes – how's that for a plot?" He smiled a muted smile. "Life can be just like a film or a novel. Minus the happy ending, obviously."

"Well, sometimes there *is* a happy ending in life, I suppose."

"Well, there was one. Only it was for them, not for me."

"She doesn't seem very happy," I said, and immediately regretted it. I didn't want him to think I was being cruel.

"I suppose. Anyway, she's in the past now. I love her like a sister," he said, and I studied his face as he said that. I felt sure he was telling the truth; I saw it in his eyes. "But I wanted to tell you."

For a moment, I debated whether I should not press him for more, if this revelation had been hard enough for him. But he continued of his own accord.

"Back then, I never saw it coming. To be fair, I don't think Angus did either. He had always been my baby brother, you know? Isabel never really noticed him. Then, one Christmas, he came home from a tour – and you know him, he's the glamorous one in the family, he has enough charisma to turn compass needles . . ."

Sure, Angus had a fascinating job. But if you are in love, somebody else's charisma will not work on you. Privately I thought that for Isabel to turn away from Torcuil like that she probably hadn't loved him that intensely in the first place. But I didn't say anything. It wasn't the time to start passing judgement. And anyway, I couldn't be objective.

"It was like Izzy saw him for the first time . . ." – so that had been his nickname for her. *Izzy.* I felt a little bit sick. Sick with jealousy. How absurd, to feel jealousy about his past. To feel jealousy about him at all – ". . . though they'd known each other all their lives. I saw it happening before my eyes, them falling for each other." He opened his arms and once again I could see how much this hurt him.

"Angus left again at the end of the holidays. He told me that he would not be back, that he couldn't bear to do this to me. That he had told Izzy as much, that he was sorry, that they were sorry. That he wished us all happiness and he hoped we could rebuild what we had. That nothing happened between them. Not physically, anyway."

But betrayals of the heart were just as bad, I thought. If not worse.

"I knew that things between Izzy and me could never be the same again. I was sure of it. And when I spoke to her . . . Well, I could read it in her eyes. She was in love with him. And I couldn't bear to do this to them. I couldn't keep them apart, could I? They got married a few months later, and they're still together, as you know. Isabel's illness started a couple of years ago." I noticed how, as he spoke about his brother's wife, he called her Isabel again – she wasn't his Izzy any more. "It's destroying her, and my brother with her. She has now stopped going out of her house entirely, and she can't cope with having anyone over, apart from me and this woman who helps her when Angus is away. Nobody else. My heart breaks for her, and for Angus. I just can't believe it's got as bad as this . . ."

"I'm so sorry, Torcuil. I'm so sorry she hurt you and I'm sorry she's unwell."

"It's a mystery, isn't it? How the human brain works. I have no idea what's happening to her. She must have a . . . a sort of darkness inside her I never saw."

"But you were drawn to her."

"Yes . . ." He looked at me. "What do you mean?"

"Well, you seem to have your own darkness. From what you told me about your mother. Maybe you were drawn to her because she could understand that. Because you were similar. I don't know." I smiled. "Sorry."

"No, I think you might be right, actually."

We sat in silence for a few minutes.

"And you?" he said finally.

"Me, what?"

"Do you have darkness inside you?"

I smiled. "No. Not a speck."

"Lucky you," he said, and began studying the ground around us. Shadows were falling on the waters as the day

203

melted into dusk. I sat and contemplated the loveliness of the loch, taking in the silence and the sweet-scented air.

"For you," Torcuil said finally, and handed me a white pebble from among the many grey ones scattered all around us. "To remember the moment."

"Thank you," I said seriously, and slipped the white pebble in my pocket.

I was barely in the cottage when my phone chirped. It was a text from Torcuil.

I was scattered in a million little pieces. You picked them all up again and put them back together. Of all those little pieces, one I gave to you to keep. A white pebble from the loch shore. Of all the little pieces of me, this one belongs to you, and you only.

I read the text over and over again, quite shocked by the depth and intensity of it. Then another text appeared, and I braced myself – but it simply said:

I forgot to say, Angus is playing in the village hall tomorrow at 8, are you free?

Sure, I said simply.

I made my way inside and placed the white pebble on my mantelpiece, on top of the business cards Lara had made for me and among the fairy lights.

The words of Torcuil's text went round and round in my mind until I fell asleep, cradled by my son's soft breathing.

28

I saw the dangers, yet I walked

Torcuil

My brother's talent always manages to surprise me, even if I've listened to him a million times, even if I grew up hearing him play. His violin speaks and sings and cries, and the whole hall is silent and enraptured. Margherita is not here yet. I keep looking at the door, hoping she'll walk in at any moment . . . And finally she does, all dressed in red like an exotic flower. Her hair is down – I hadn't realised it was so long, it nearly reaches her waist, a cascade of black. Suddenly, my life seems as if it were a sea of muted colours, the grey of the loch and of the stones of Ramsay Hall, the grey in my mind – until she arrived like a little flame, to set everything on fire.

The music keeps going and nobody stirs at her entrance, while it seems to me that everything should stand still now, everything should be ablaze, because that's how it feels in my mind. The fire she kindled in me when we had dinner together in Aberdeen, and on the loch shore, is burning again, even stronger.

She catches my eye and smiles, and I look down. She comes to sit beside me, and her perfume – something flowery and deep, something that makes me think of night in a warm country – envelopes me. She closes her eyes as Angus's bow dances on the strings, and I see her melting to the music. I have to resist taking her hand – too many eyes watching – and all my muscles freeze in the effort not to touch her.

When the concert is finished an insane amount of people want to say hello to me. That is what happens in small villages, especially if you don't show your face that often. Finally, I manage to extricate myself and reach my brother, who's standing with the band, his violin still in hand. Though he lives twenty minutes from me, he's always travelling and we don't see each other as often as we'd like. What happened years ago with Izzy left no trace in our relationship – not on my part, anyway. I have no resentment, but I know he feels guilty towards me. But he shouldn't. He didn't look to destroy my happiness, he never meant it to happen.

"That was wonderful, Angus," I say, looking into his eyes. Angus looks straight out of a history book – he's a Viking, with reddish-blond hair, ice-blue eyes and a straight, proud nose.

"Ah, I don't know. Thanks anyway."

My brother never accepts a compliment.

"This is Margherita . . ."

"Hello, how are you?" They exchange hellos and nice-to-meet-you's, while my gaze goes from one to the other and I wonder if my brother *knows*.

I wonder if he knows that I'm falling in love.

Shit.

I'm falling in love.

". . . so I'm not here often . . ."

". . . it's my mum's coffee shop, yes . . ."

Angus and Margherita are having a conversation, but I have no idea what they're saying. I can't follow. I hear myself saying "See you tomorrow" to my brother, and find myself outside the village hall under a sky full of stars.

"So, thanks for coming," I scramble.

"It was lovely. Really, really lovely. I haven't heard live music for ages, and I've never heard Scottish music before, I don't think, unless you count the *Rob Roy* soundtrack and that was a tragic film, wasn't it, but then I love a good tear-jerker and . . ."

Wait a minute. She's rambling. She's *nervous*!

I'm not the only one who's nervous!

That's a relief.

"Are you walking?" I ask her.

"Yes. I mean, it was too close to take the car—"

"But too far to walk on your own at night."

She laughed. "It's not night. It's not even ten o' clock. Check your Peppa Pig watch."

"I bought a new one, see? This one is not pink and has no pigs on it." I show her my new grown-up watch, feeling like an idiot. "Anyway, let me walk you home . . ."

"Yes, that'd be safer. You never know what might happen in Glen Avich, with its criminal underbelly."

"Was that gritty drama not set in Glen Avich, what was it, *The Wire*?"

"*The Chicken Wire*, you mean."

"Oh, yes, that one. Like *24*, with Malchie McNally standing in for Jack Bauer."

"Terrorists threaten to kidnap Mrs Gordon . . ."

"Who's a secret agent in disguise . . ."

"But Malchie whisks her away with his post van and saves the day."

We chat as we walk. Music, food, how Scotland gets these

incredibly beautiful summer days and then it pours for three days after . . . All throughout I keep trying to catch a glimpse of her profile without looking like I'm staring. This is all extremely complicated and not at all straightforward. If only there was a rulebook . . .

"Well. Bye, then. Thanks for a lovely night."

Oh. We are in front of her house. Oh no. She's going to go now.

How do I stop it?

"Oh, no problem. Bye, then," I say, and then another little "bye".

And then she turns around, and without a word she takes me by the hand. She leads me away from the houses and the streets, across the bridge and into the woods.

29

Falling into him

Margherita

It happened. I fell into him.

It must have been the music. Music always does strange things to me. Life was flowing through my veins and I couldn't stop it. I was full of joy and fear all mixed together, and I didn't care about anything but that moment. We stood alone in the shelter of the woods, and the night was so still, like we were the last two people on earth. From a distant tree came the hoot of an owl.

I kissed him, my eyes closed and my heart wide open, and it was perfect – there was no way I could have stopped myself – and then, all of a sudden, he pushed me away.

Gently – but he pushed me away.

"I'm sorry, I can't do this," he whispered.

To feel him going away from me left me *mourning*.

It left me freezing, like my heart was going to ice over and then break into a hundred pieces. Why? Why was he pushing me away? I couldn't possibly have misunderstood what was happening between us.

"No. Of course. Of course, sorry," I forced myself to say.

"You don't understand . . ."

"Of course I do. I *completely* understand . . ." I was mortified as tears began to fall down my cheeks. Oh, the shame. How could joy turn into humiliation so quickly?

And most of all, what was I doing?

What was I doing here in the Scottish night, away from my children and kissing someone who wasn't my husband?

"No, you don't."

"I do! I do! I'm sorry. Honestly, it's okay. I'm just going to go home—"

"You need to let me explain. I don't want to do this because—" He shook his head.

"Because it's wrong, I know!"

"No. Because it's *right*. Margherita, when you and I are together, I feel . . . alive. Like I haven't felt in years. I've already fallen too far. If we do this now, and then you go, I couldn't bear it. I will only do this when you promise me you won't go. Can you promise me that?"

I stood in front of him, my mouth agape.

"If I kiss you now, if I take you home with me, if you stay the night, can you promise me that tomorrow morning you won't go away from me?"

Slowly, I shook my head.

I couldn't. My life was completely up in the air, and I couldn't make promises. To anyone. Not even to myself.

I couldn't take this kind, kind man's heart in my hands and then let it fall.

"That's what I thought."

"I'd better go," I whispered desolately.

"Let me walk you home—"

"No. No, it's okay. I'm fine on my own, honestly."

Tears were still flowing down my face as I stepped away from him, and then a hand closed around mine and pulled

210

me back. Without a word, Torcuil held me close to him, like he never wanted to let me go. I nestled against him.

"I can't promise what you asked," I said. I wanted to, but how could I?

"I know. But you can't stop me from hoping."

30

Only the wind knows

Lara

Dear Kitty.

I have been kissed.

My first kiss.

Apart from when that boy in summer camp tried to smooch me when we were seven, and caught my nose instead, and then he tried again and I whacked him with a Frisbee. Yes, I know I'm nearly fifteen, how come it never happened before, etc. I have no idea why. I've only liked Ian since we started High School, and he never really saw me, let alone fancied me.

But now Mal is in my life.

With Mal, everything is different.

Everything makes sense to my heart. Everything makes sense in my life.

We were beside the water, really really close to each other. He seemed so sad.

"I'm cold. Will you hold me?" he said. So I did: I wrapped my arms around his neck and I held him close, trying to warm him up. We stayed like that for a while, and I could feel him trembling.

"You won't let me go back there?"

What *back there*? Whatever it was, it didn't sound good.

'No. Never. You'll stay here with me."

And then his lips looked for mine, and he kissed me.

Mal's lips were very soft and cold, but his hands were rough. Not like *he* was rough, not at all – he was so gentle, and sweet, and perfect. I mean, his skin was rough, like someone who works with his hands.

I think I DIED there and then.

I am so thankful I had no glasses on. It was so much better with him being able to touch my face without knocking my glasses off or leaving fingerprints on my lenses and everything turning from beautiful to embarrassing.

The Ian thing seems so childish now: this is *serious*.

I'm not sure if we are together as such, though. I'm not really sure if he's my boyfriend, but I'd like him to be.

We kissed for a little while, and then he said he had to go, that he couldn't stay long. He was shivering and looking quite ill. Maybe he caught something. If he did, now I have it too, but I don't care. What's a cold when you've just been kissed by someone who is perfect?

Like he's come out of a dream.

Oh. I'm not sure I like that thought. Because dreams end when you wake up, and I never, never want to wake up from this one.

31

A leap of faith

Margherita

Torcuil left me on my doorstep with one last, heartbreaking embrace and a kiss that was too quick, too gentle.

I was reeling. I couldn't find peace as I stepped through my mum's house quietly, careful not to make too much noise. Leo was sleeping with Nonna tonight, because I'd been out for the evening, while Lara slept in the cottage. I wished I could just switch all the lights on in the kitchen and start cooking, to drain away some nervous energy, but I couldn't wake everybody up.

I felt my lips with my fingers – they were still tingly and soft, and it was torture.

I was too old for all this. I was supposed to be settled at my age, and there I was, having left my husband, pining for someone else, with two children whose well-being depended on me. I looked through the window up at the sky – it was full of stars, not a cloud in sight, which was uncommon for Glen Avich. The beauty of the sky brought tears to my eyes again, and I hated myself for it. I'd turned into a heroine from one of Lara's books, crying and swooning. This wasn't me. I had to pull myself together – and then my phone rang, impossibly loud in the silence of the night, making me jump out of my skin. I rummaged in my bag to find it and switch it off as quickly as I could, and my heart sank as I saw Ash's name flash on the screen.

I couldn't believe it. He hadn't phoned me in weeks. Why now? Did he have some strange radar that told him I had actually got close to another man?

As the thought formed in my mind, the full realisation hit me. *I kissed Torcuil.* I had kissed a man who wasn't Ash.

I'd never thought I could do something like this, never. Not with the way I'd been brought up, not with the way I'd planned to live my life.

And yet, it happened. And it had been magical, and perfect.

How long had Ash and I not kissed, anyway? Apart from a peck on the cheek at Christmas and birthdays? We were always too busy, or too tired, or just not thinking of it at all.

So now my phone was off; Ash couldn't reach me any more. But then I felt terribly guilty. Maybe something had happened. Maybe he needed me. He did have my mum's number, of course, but would he use it?

And anyway, I had to speak to him sooner or later. I couldn't just blank him. It might as well be now, when the guilt I felt was at its highest. I deserved to be struck back into reality. I walked to the back of the cottage and switched the phone back on. As it came to life, I was surprised at how intensely *I didn't want* to speak to my husband.

I didn't want to hear his voice.

I didn't want to be plunged back into self-doubt and loneliness and recriminations, which was the effect he always had on me.

And yet I couldn't just ignore his call.

I braced myself, my heart pounding as I pressed the little green icon.

Hello, Ash Ward here, I'm not available right now but leave a message and I'll call you back. Ta.

For a moment, I wanted to put the phone down. But I resisted the impulse.

"It's me. I'm sorry I missed your call. We are all well . . . I hope you are okay. Right. Speak soon."

I dragged myself inside and took off my bright-red tunic – a thought flashed through my mind, a memory of a film I'd seen about an adulterous woman forced to wear a scarlet letter. I went to the bathroom and looked at myself in the mirror.

I looked different. It wasn't just the red-rimmed eyes and that my lips were a bit swollen after his kisses; it was something in my eyes.

I'm not sure what.

I brought my fingers to my lips once again, remembering Torcuil's kiss . . . And then a loud chirp made me jump. I had forgotten to switch the phone off again, and the bathroom was the only place inside the cottage where it worked. It was a text from Ash.

Sorry, the phone was in my pocket. I called you by mistake.

32

The bridge

Margherita

The days after were a blur. I took Leo to the play park, I baked for La Piazza, I tried to keep myself busy. So much had happened, I had to digest it all.

I kept thinking of Torcuil.

And of the mistaken phone call.

For once the play park was empty, so I decided I could chance a whispered call with Anna. I looked at the watch – it was early morning in Colorado, so maybe she had a moment.

"Anna? It's me," I said, as I always did.

"Hello, sweetheart. How are things up there?"

"All good. Yes. All good," I lied.

"Something happened. Tell me."

"You're getting worse than Mum! Honestly!"

"Yeah, well. Shoot."

"I sort of . . . I don't know how to put it."

"You slept with Torcuil? Oh my God!"

"I *what*? No! *No way!* How . . . What . . . *Anna!*" I was outraged.

"Well, you are separated! And you have been for a long time!"

"Six months is not a long time! Not in my book anyway."

"Yeah, well. So tell me what happened."

"We didn't sleep together. You have a sick imagination, honestly."

"Okay, okay, bloody Jane Austen. Your glove dropped onto the ground and he picked it up and your fingers touched and now you're all in a flurry!"

"Stop teasing me. We kissed."

"That is so romantic!"

"Anna. I'm married. And a mother of two."

"You are separated. And you might be a mother of two, but you're also thirty-eight, which makes you too young to never have a relationship again."

"It's not a relationship! It's a kiss!"

"*It started with a kiiisss ... it started with a kiiisss ...*" she began singing. I could have strangled her.

"Anna!"

"Sorry, Margherita, I have to get the boys up; we're going on a hike. I swear my feet are falling off, Paul's family here are mental. They take us hunting in the mountains every day – it's like I'm training for the SAS. I'm going to call you back as soon as I can and you can tell me the rest."

"There's nothing more to say, I think."

"You are joking? I want to know about the kiss! Was it wonderful? Was it? Or was it meh? Or was it whatever, not that good but not that bad either?"

"It was ... it was wonderful."

"Oh my God! Oh my God! When do I meet him? Okay, I know it's too soon, but—"

"It definitely *is* too soon. He said he doesn't want anything more to happen anyway."

"Oh. Why? That is ... that is ... oh! How can he be not interested? Is he *blind*?"

218

I smiled at my sister's loyalty.

"No, it's not like that. It's that he wants to be sure my heart is really in it before he commits."

"But it was just a kiss ... I mean, is he talking about commitment? Is it not a bit intense?"

"He doesn't see it like that. He's been hurt in the past and he doesn't want to go back there. He wants to be able to trust me."

"So he put an end to it? Unless you can commit?"

"Well ... he kissed me, and then ... he kissed me again. So I don't know what's going on, really. He's very ... he's very kind. I can't explain." My heart softened as I thought of him. "It's like he doesn't open his heart easily and if he does ... Well, he doesn't want to be hurt again."

"So what are you going to do?"

"Well, I told him I can't make promises right now. And I can't. I'm confused and ... I don't know. I don't know."

At that moment, a local mum sat beside me on the bench, while her two toddlers spilled out into the play park. "I have to go too. Speak soon."

"Bye Margherita. And congratulations," she added absurdly. *Congratulations for what, you crazy woman?* I texted her at once. My phone chirped in reply and I was ready to see what Anna was saying ... but it was Torcuil. It was hard to hide my confusion as I felt the colour rising to my cheeks – I stood up and wandered off, away from the bench.

Are you okay?

Yes. A bit confused, but okay. You?

I want to get into the car and come see you and talk things through, but I can't, I'm in Edinburgh.

This comforted me a little. That he still wanted to see me.

But I wasn't supposed to see him.

Oh, I was getting all worked up again.

It's okay. I'll see you on Friday, I texted back, and my phone chirped once more.

I said congratulations because you started living again. Anna.

Had I? Really?

Because it felt like I was just messing everything up. I waited a bit for a text from Torcuil and I wasn't sure whether I was relieved or desolated that there were no more.

33

Ablaze

Torcuil

What I said to her makes no sense.

About needing a promise, and that without that promise, I couldn't let myself fall.

Because I've fallen already.

Because love doesn't come with conditions. To say *I'll only love you if you won't leave me* means it's not love in the first place.

The only way to love is *no matter what.*

It's forgetting every fear.

It's a leap of faith.

How could I have deluded myself to this extent? How could I have deluded myself that I needed a promise before I let myself burn, when I was ablaze already?

34

Lara's world

Margherita

I was relieved when finally night fell. I'd spent the whole evening making *nocciolini* and *paste di meliga* to serve at La Piazza, Leo was drifting off to sleep, and Lara was reading in her room. I'd said to Mum and Michael that I was tired and I'd have an early night. My mum had been studying my face, of course, and several times through the day I saw her looking at me when she thought I couldn't see her. She suspected that something was going on, but I wondered if she was aware that Torcuil was involved. I wasn't ready to talk about it. I dreaded what she would say if she knew I'd got so close to Torcuil.

I was lying on my bed with Leo beside me, trying to read but really lost in thought, when Lara tiptoed in, careful not to wake her brother up. There was something in her face that made me do a double take. She was worried about something, I realised at once. As always with anything regarding Lara, anxiety swept through me. I worried about her so much more than I did about Leo, though I loved them just the same.

"Fancy some chamomile tea?" she whispered.

"That would be lovely," I murmured back, stroking Leo's hair.

Lara went to make some tea in my mum's kitchen and came back with two steaming mugs and a little plate of the *paste* we'd made that afternoon. I followed her into her room. We sat cross-legged on her bed, clutching our warm cups. It felt good to have our little ritual again – like a lighthouse in the storm of my thoughts.

"This is lovely," I said in a low voice.

"I put honey in our tea," she said. We were dancing around what was to come; I could feel it. I knew she was getting ready to speak to me.

"Mum?"

Here we go. "Yes?"

"He wasn't there again today."

"Mal?"

She nodded. "Yes. I haven't seen him for days now. We've been meeting almost every day, and—"

"Every day, Lara?" I asked, slightly alarmed. I hadn't realised things were so serious. I silently berated myself for not probing her more about Mal.

"I said *almost* every day."

"Right." I stopped myself from saying more. She needed my support, not the third degree. "Look, he'll be there tomorrow, I'm sure . . ."

"I hope so."

". . . and I'd like to meet this boy."

"Mum!" The colour rose in her cheeks and she put her cup down on her bedside table.

"Well, when you're ready, okay? If you're seeing each other every day and he's so important to you . . . You're only fourteen, Lara. I need to at least see him once."

"Fine! I'll ask him if he can come and get me at the house one day so you can say hello, okay?"

"Okay."

Pause.

"Is he from Glen Avich? Or is he here just for the summer, like us?"

So much for not giving her the third degree. But I couldn't help myself.

She grabbed her mug again and she leaned back on her pillows.

"He lives here," she said.

I was holding my breath, hoping my request hadn't made her clam up. We sipped our tea in silence until, finally, she spoke.

"You see, last time we met, he said something."

"What did he say?"

"That he didn't know how long he'd be able to stay for. At the time I thought he just meant he had to get home soon, but now I'm not so sure."

"Did he elaborate on that?"

She shook her head.

"Maybe they're moving away?"

"Maybe."

"Can't you just ask him?" I said, gesturing at her mobile phone on the desk beside me.

"He doesn't have a phone. Can you believe it?" Lara replied, her eyes wide behind her glasses.

"Seriously? He must be the only person left on the planet."

"Yeah ... he's not into modern things much. He didn't know what an iPod was when I showed him mine."

"Well, Glen Avich is a little bit backwards compared to London, but not *that* backwards. It seems to me that your friend is a bit of a technophobe."

"He loves books," she said, and her face brightened up.

"Oh, that's good."

Lara nodded. "Yes. He's a lot like me. He doesn't have many friends."

Her throwaway comment squeezed my heart. "You just haven't found the right people, yet."

"I don't even know if the right people for me actually exist," she replied, biting a *pasta*. "Nonna wants to introduce me to a couple of kids from Kinnear High, but I don't know. Mmmm. This is heavenly ... Anyway. I just hope Mal will be there tomorrow."

"I'm sure you'll see him again soon. You meet at the bridge, don't you?" I said casually. I needed to know she wasn't going somewhere isolated with this guy. I knew she was streetwise and not likely to do anything silly or dangerous, but I wanted to make sure.

"Yes. And around the loch."

"Lara—"

"I know what you're thinking. And you *really* don't need to worry. Mum, I'm going to do a bit of writing before I go to sleep."

The time for confidences was over. But I had one last question.

"Lara, I was wondering ... do you know his second name?"

"So you can do your research?" A smile was dancing on her lips.

"Not at all. What makes you think that?" I laughed, gathering the cups and the plates back on the tray.

"I don't know his second name. I never asked him."

"Nothing like a man of mystery," I teased. I resolved to ask my mum and Michael if they knew something about this enigmatic boy.

"Mum, stop it!"

"Sorry. Anyway, I'll be off watching TV with Nonna and Michael." I'd given up on an early night; my mind was too agitated. "Just come through if you want some company," I said, and gently swept away a tiny crumb from her cheek, letting my fingers linger for a moment on her beloved face.

Her school would open again in three weeks' time. Soon our butterfly summer would be over. But I couldn't bring myself to mention that aloud, because it would upset Lara and it would upset me.

None of us was looking forward to going back.

We sat in my mum's house until late, but Lara didn't join us. From the window I saw the light in her room shine for a little while, and then it was all dark. She'd gone to sleep.

"Mum, you know the way I told you that Lara made a friend? Well, they're meeting nearly every day, apparently," I said.

"Yes, you mentioned it."

"Is he really just a friend, though?" Michael pondered. "Are you sure?"

Mum laughed. "Don't fret, Michael."

"I'm not fretting. I'm just saying, when my daughter was fifteen I had to fend them off with my rolling pin."

"I'm sure they were terrified." Mum laughed again and I couldn't help joining in. "Did you throw biscuits at them?"

"A biscuit can hurt, if aimed correctly," he quipped. Once again, I saw how much my mum and Michael were in harmony with each other, how deeply comfortable in each other's company. And once again, together with the joy I felt for Mum, a vague heartache filled me, to see what I had wanted to build with Ash and somehow failed to.

"She told me he's just a friend," I said. "But I'm sure they're sweet on each other."

"Well, that's good. I'm happy for Lara," my mum said.

"So am I, but I really want to meet him. I don't feel comfortable not knowing who he is. I mean, if we were in London I'd never let her meet someone I don't have a clue about . . ."

"Of course, but here is different. Everybody knows each other and there are ties with the villages around as well. Young people here don't have much chance to do anything secretly," said my mum. "Is Mal is short for Malcolm?"

"Probably. Lara says he definitely lives here in Glen Avich."

"I don't know any boys by that name personally . . . Do you, Michael?" He shook his head. "But I'm bound to know somebody who does. I'll ask Peggy. She knows every single soul around here."

"Including pets, guardian angels and everybody's ancestry," Michael chimed in. "She's like a human Google for the Aberdeenshire area."

"That's a good idea. I need to get a few things at her shop anyway, tomorrow. I'll ask her myself."

As I got myself ready for bed, I realised that I hadn't thought about what happened with Torcuil for a few hours, after having obsessed about it since the day before. It was a blessed relief, but I ended up replaying our kiss in my mind over and over again as I drifted off to sleep, in spite of the guilt. I found myself counting the hours to when I'd see him again – wishing the days away until he came back to Glen Avich. But nobody, nobody ever needed to know. It would be a secret for me to keep.

The next morning Leo and I went out with the excuse of running errands, but I was hunting for some more information

227

about Mal. It was a beautiful day and Leo skipped happily by my side. We dropped by Peggy's shop, which was, fortunately, empty – no curious ears to hear what I was asking. I didn't want to tell her the real reason for my curiosity in case any gossip about Lara started, so I kept it vague.

"I was wondering . . ." I began as I helped Peggy slip my groceries into a canvas bag. "I've met a few people since I arrived, but I can't quite place this boy . . . His name is Mal. Maybe short for Malcolm." I didn't specify how I'd met him, and Peggy didn't ask.

"Oh, yes. It could be Mal MacLennan," she said, and I smiled inwardly, remembering Michael calling her Google for the Aberdeenshire area. "A lovely lad. He's doesn't live here, though. He lives in Glasgow. They come back to the village every summer. They stay with the lad's grandmother, Morag MacLennan, two houses down from me. You know the wee lassie, Ruby, the one with the head of curls?"

"Oh, yes. Leo played with her a few times."

"Well, Ruby is Morag's youngest granddaughter, so Mal is actually her uncle."

"Right." My head spun a bit at the intricacies of Glen Avich family ties. "Do you know if he's still down for the summer or if he's gone back to Glasgow?"

"No, the McLennans didn't come at all this summer . . ."

Oh. Dead lead.

". . . Morag told me they'd gone to visit their eldest daughter in Arizona and stayed there all summer. It's a shame. She misses them this year. I suppose there's always the October week . . ." Peggy kept chatting as my mind wandered.

"You don't happen to know any other Mal? Or Malcolm?"

"A few, but they're all my age. Malcolm is an old-fashioned

name, isn't it? They don't tend to call little ones 'Malcolm' any more. My friend's granddaughter called her son Wingo. Seriously! That poor wee mite having to live with that for the rest of his life."

"Maybe he's a tourist?" I tried to steer the conversation away from Wingo and on to Mal.

"Maybe. I'll ask around, if you like? Tourists always end up at the Welly anyway – you know the outdoor shop? Inary's brother owns it. That'd be Logan. I'm his grand-aunt, you know . . ." She'd lost me. She could see it on my face, and she laughed. "Never mind, dear! Maybe Logan knows your Mal. I'll ask Eilidh, anyway."

"Thank you, Peggy," and I went to go before she tried to explain to me any more genealogical trees.

"No bother, dear." Her eyes wrinkled all around as she smiled warmly. For a second I thought she'd ask me where I'd met Mal, but she didn't. I was grateful for that. Maybe she'd guessed, who knows. One thing was sure: if she didn't find out for me, nobody could, and this Mal was a figment of Lara's rich imagination. Or he went by a false name, I joked to myself, and I was immediately freaked out by my own joke. I hoped with all my heart to meet him soon and dispel all my fears.

On my way back to La Piazza, I debated whether to speak to Inary about this. Maybe she knew something and she could ask her brother. But I wasn't sure it was right to do that. After all, in spite of the age difference she and Lara were friends, and it really felt disloyal, like going behind Lara's back.

"Would you like to go to the play park?" I asked Leo. How easy to please he was, a three-year-old puppy who just needed cuddles and fresh air. A universe away from the complications

229

and complexities of a nearly fifteen-year-old girl. And of a thirty-eight-year-old woman, for that matter.

"Yes!" Leo jumped up and down, and pulled on my hand.

As I sat on one of the play-park benches in the morning sun, feeling a gentle breeze on my skin, I decided to wait and see, and keep close tabs on Lara in the meantime. I didn't want my beautiful, sensitive daughter to ever get hurt. Though I knew that all women do, sooner or later, and her turn would come. I just hoped it wouldn't happen too soon, before she knew how to protect her heart at least a little.

As for me, I was lost. I couldn't make any decisions, because I didn't trust my confused heart to make the right one.

35

Chill

Lara

Dear Kitty,

I'm very worried. I haven't seen Mal in three days now. I've tried everywhere: the loch, the bridge, the tree house, but he's nowhere. I've spoken about him with Mum, even if I was determined to keep everything to myself (by the way – I didn't tell Mum we go to the tree house sometimes, in case she drops in on us while she's at Ramsay Hall . . . by *complete coincidence* of course). This worry is too heavy to bear on my own. She reassured me a little bit, but now she has wants to know more about Mal.

And I can't tell her more about him because I know very little too.

I know *nothing at all* about him, really. And still if feels like I've known him forever, if that makes sense.

I'm just back from another long, long walk, looking for him. I'm all kind of blue.

I miss him so much.

And there's something else. I don't want to go back to London.

The summer is drawing to an end. None of us is mentioning it aloud, but it hangs between us. Yesterday I heard Mum saying to Nonna that when we go back we'll have to go to John

Lewis because my school blazer will probably be too small for me. I felt sick. Just thinking of going back to that school . . . Maybe I should speak to Mum? Maybe she'd like to stay?

But what about Dad?

Last night he actually phoned me, for the first time since we arrived. I asked him why he'd never phoned me before – I couldn't help it, I just had to. He said it was because I always called him first, so he never really had the chance. I'm not sure I believe him, but anyway he did call me in the end. He told me he can't wait to see me and Leo. It took him a month to realise that, which is a bit strange, but hey, I'll take it. He said it's been a long time and he misses us. I asked him why he never calls Mum. He said it's because Mum doesn't want to speak to him. If she did, she would have never left in the first place.

I'm pretty sure he's rewriting history here. They both agreed to take a break from each other. He forgets that I'm fourteen, not ten, and I see and understand a lot more than he gives me credit for.

I'm all confused now. I want to see Dad and I don't want him to be upset. But I'm so much happier here. I hate the thought of going back to my old school and facing *them*. I haven't checked social media all summer; maybe they put up more stupid cartoons of me. I'm dreading it.

And Mum seems so happy. Her face *shines*, if you know what I mean.

The way she was in London, always rushing and frowning and like there was a big weight of worry on her shoulders, it seems so far away now. She was like . . . *dimmed*. Yes, like a light that had been dimmed.

Here she is *bright*.

Having said that, in the last few days she's seemed a bit troubled. I think I know why: it's the end of the summer, and she's worried. I told her what Dad had said about missing us, about wanting us back. She didn't say anything. She just went very pale. I don't think she wants to go back either.

It's all messed up.

Kitty, the bottom line is: I want to see Mal again.

For now, that's the only thing that's clear in my mind.

36

Nowhere

Lara

Dear Kitty,

I'm in my bed, and I don't want to see anyone.

He's gone.

We went to the tree house, and it was just the two of us in the whole world. The wind was very strong and it was howling outside the little window. The tree house was creaking a bit, but I was too perfectly happy to care about that, or anything else. We sat really close to each other and he held my hands. He always did this thing, Mal – he held my hands. Like he was holding on to me, in case I disappeared.

"When I was wee, me and my brothers slept in this room with a big window," he said. "When the wind was blowing strong it made a strange noise around the window, like something hissing. I was frightened, so my mother used to come and sing to me. She sang a song about a bird flying in the wind and then coming home safe."

"When I was little my mum wasn't there. She died," I blurted out. Just like that.

I don't even know how I came out with that. I never speak about my family. I mean, my birth family. It's too painful. But this time I did. I have no idea why. It's just that I trust him. I trust him with my secrets.

"But did you not say you came here with your mother?"

"She's my adoptive mother. She adopted me when I was six. My birth mother died when I was two. My dad looked after me for a while, but he didn't do a very good job."

People I've discussed these things with:

1) My mum
2) My dad
3) Sheridan.

Nobody else in the world, *nobody*. I couldn't believe I was talking about it with Mal.

"I'm sorry," he said, and I hate people pitying me, but with him it didn't feel that way. So it all came out.

"They put me in foster care. I wasn't adopted for ages because they hoped my dad would sort himself out, but he never did. He tried, but not hard enough. Living with him was horrible. I had to be very quiet because if I made any noise – even just walking around with my shoes was too noisy for him – he got mad at me and shouted at me and he hit me in a way that left no marks, so that nobody knew. He told me never to tell anyone otherwise they were going to send me to a really mean foster family because that's where you go if you're noisy and naughty. I had to fend for myself. I only ate biscuits because there wasn't anything else in the house or I had to walk to the shops alone and I was scared. Then one day my dad fell asleep smoking and set the house on fire, so they took me away again . . ."

My voice went funny at this point. Mal slipped his arms around me and squeezed me. We were close, like two puppies in a box. I was safe in his arms, so I continued.

"It's over now anyway, and I'll never see him again. They found him dead in his bathtub. I know because I overheard Mum telling Nonna on the phone. That's when they gave me the picture of my mum – my birth mum, I mean – and I went a bit wonky for a while because I couldn't remember her and I thought all the pictures of her were gone . . ."

At that point I felt something wet on my face and I thought the rain had got into the tree house, so I looked up to see if there was a leak in the roof, but there wasn't, it was me crying. I was sobbing all of a sudden and I was so embarrassed. But Mal didn't seem to mind and he just held me very tight. I looked up and into his face and I saw he was crying too.

"My Lara," he said. He kissed my forehead and my cheeks and my nose and my lips. "You are so brave. You survived. Not everyone does, my darling Lara. *Not everyone survives.* But you did."

And then he freed me gently from his embrace. He stood up and said, "I'm sorry, I have to go."

There was something in his eyes that terrified me. Something *final*.

"Will I see you tomorrow?"

He shook his head slowly. Tears kept falling from his eyes and it was terrible! I've never seen a boy crying before.

"I'm not sure I can come back," he said, and his voice was like an echo, the wind was so strong. I jumped onto my feet and I felt like I couldn't stand up straight, I was so shocked.

"But why? Is it because of what I said? Is it because now you think I'm weird?"

"No. No. It's because I don't think I can hold on."

"What? What do you mean?"

"I'm sorry, Lara," he said. And then, "My Lara."

236

He turned away and climbed out of the tree house. Maybe it was because of the wind, but I didn't hear him go down the rope ladder. Maybe it was because of my tears, but I didn't see him walking across the grass.

He was gone, like he'd never been there.

It seems impossible it happened just yesterday. I couldn't sleep all night, and then at breakfast I just couldn't take all the questions, with my mum and Nonna fussing over me like I was ill. I wasn't ill, I was just sad. And angry.

Because Mal is nowhere.

I can't believe he's gone like this, without a word. He kissed me and then he went away.

Like everybody does, in my life. Like my real mum.

Everybody goes away.

Mum was going on and on and on about me not eating enough and if I wanted a muffin instead or some cereal or French toast or whatever else, and I snapped. I said something I'd never said to her before, never.

I told her she would be better off without me, and that she wasn't my real mother anyway.

I walked out at once, because I couldn't bear to look into her face after what I'd said. I heard Leo calling for me and I felt like I'd failed everyone. No wonder Mal has gone from me too.

I ran out and walked *everywhere*. I walked round and round the village many times, hoping to spot him, and then to the loch, and up St Colman's Way and to Ramsay Hall, all around the grounds and in the tree house. But no sign of Mal.

This time, I can't just let it happen. I can't let life punch me in the face once again. I have to find him.

I remember every single conversation we had, every word

– I'm sure somewhere in my memories of him there is a clue as to what's happened, to where he's gone. He never mentioned any other places but here. He never mentioned anywhere but Glen Avich . . . and then I remembered.

I go on Ailsa with my boat. I bring some food and a book and spend hours there, reading. Just me, alone with the loch.

Now I know what to do.

37

Liberation

Margherita

I was sitting on the floor, polishing the intricate wooden lace of an armoire, when Torcuil barged into the room, shouting my name. I couldn't believe it when he grabbed my arm and pulled me back onto my feet, and I was ready to protest – but then I saw his face. "What—"

"We need to go. Now. It's Lara," he said, and he just strode off, taking my hand and dragging me along.

"Lara? What's going on?"

"She's on the loch. She's in danger," he simply said as he made his way out of the library and down the hall, into the kitchen and into the garden, with me on his heels.

My legs felt like they were about to give way any moment and I was shaking all over, but I kept going. I had no idea what was going on – all that my mind could make sense of was that Lara was in trouble and I had to go to her. I ran with Torcuil as fast as I could. While I ran, I slipped my phone out of my jeans pocket and called Lara – but it rang out.

"Look," Torcuil whispered. I followed his gaze and saw a flash of sky blue dancing on the steely waters – an abandoned boat. My knees nearly gave way and I felt nausea rising in my throat.

"Did Lara take that boat?" I asked. But how, how could he know the answer? How did Torcuil know what was happening, why had he dragged me over there? He didn't reply and I looked at him – his eyes were closed and it looked like he was listening intently. Listening to something I couldn't hear.

"Ailsa," he said suddenly. "We need to get to Ailsa. Come, I have a boat," he said, and grabbed me by the arm. He led me a few yards down the shore where a little green boat was tied to a pole.

"Maybe you should wait here," he said suddenly, taking me by the shoulders.

"Look. I don't know what's going on, but if my daughter is out there, I'm going," I said, freeing myself from his grasp and stepping into the cold water. He followed me and held my hand; the boat swayed heavily as we climbed on it, and Torcuil freed the paddles at once.

"Lara!" I started calling at the top of my voice, kneeling on the wood and holding onto the boat's sides. "Lara!"

"Lara!" Torcuil echoed me and we called her, over and over again.

"What's going on? Please tell me. Please, Torcuil, tell me!"

"It's hard to explain. Someone told me. Someone told me *Lara is in danger*. He said she'd be on Ailsa."

"Who told you?" I cried, tears streaming down my face.

"It's too complicated to explain now. Just trust me, okay?"

"Okay. Okay."

I kept calling Lara's name in between my tears. The loch was wide and dark in front of me. I recalled Lara's silences, the shadows on her face, and trembled inside. And those terrible words she'd said to me! I fished in my jeans pocket looking for my phone, thinking I was going to call my mum and she'd tell

240

me that Lara was with her, safe. But there was no trace of my phone. I couldn't focus on finding it.

"Look, I know you must think that I'm crazy . . . But please, just trust me," he begged. "Please. Just trust me this once, and I'll explain . . ."

And then my eye caught something blue and crumpled floating beside the boat. I couldn't scream, I couldn't even gasp. I was too horrified. It was Lara's blue hoodie, the one we'd bought when we'd arrived.

"Oh my God, Torcuil! Look!"

I covered my face with my hands for a moment, overwhelmed. Torcuil began calling her name again.

What if I saw her? What if I saw my Lara floating in the water?

It couldn't be.

This couldn't be happening.

When I found the courage to take my hands off my face and look again, the boat had met a little field of reeds. Ailsa was shrouded in mist, the contours of its black trees barely visible.

"Lara!" I called with all my might, over and over again. My throat was sore and my voice was breaking, but I kept calling.

And then a little voice came from the mist.

"Mum! I'm here!"

My daughter was calling me.

My daughter was *alive*.

I had to stop myself from jumping into the water and swimming all the way to Ailsa. Torcuil was rowing as fast as he could, sweat now pouring down his face.

"We're coming! Darling, we're here!"

Finally, Torcuil jumped out of the boat and onto the shore, extending his hand to me in one quick movement. I took

Torcuil's hand, but I jumped out so fast I nearly tripped and hit my face on the ground. Torcuil steadied me and held me up – and before I knew it, Lara was in my arms, drenched and shaking and sort of dazed. I held her close, a million questions crowding my mind but no sound coming out of my mouth except a soft cry of relief.

"Lara. Oh, thank God," Torcuil said, embracing us both.

When Lara raised her face to me, I was shocked at what I saw.

She was pale and looked frightened, but she was *smiling*.

For a moment, a terrible moment, I thought she'd lost her mind.

I took her face in my hands and locked my eyes on hers. "Lara?"

"Mal is really gone, now," she whispered. "But it's okay."

Mal? He was there with her? A lump of terror formed in my mind. "What happened?" I managed to utter, though the words were struggling to come out of my tight throat.

"I wanted to find him. I thought he might be here. I fell into the water and he heard me calling. He saved me."

What had Mal done to her? I searched her face again. "Did he harm you, Lara?"

"No! No way!" she protested. "He saved me! If it wasn't for him I'd be dead now."

"Then where is he?" I said slowly. I could hear my voice trembling. "If he saved you from drowning, where is he now?"

"I told you, he's gone. He had to."

"Gone where?"

"Margherita, enough now. She's freezing," Torcuil interrupted, a protective arm around my shoulders. "Let's get her in the warm. You can ask questions later."

We all piled into the boat and made our way through the silent loch, a million doubts, questions and fears whirling in my mind. Lara was curled up into me, exhausted. I let her be.

An hour later she was sitting at the fire in Torcuil's study wearing an oversized sweatshirt of his and a blanket around her shoulders. We'd decided not to go home at once but to stop at Ramsay Hall first, so as not to alarm Leo, my mum and Michael.

"Lara, your story makes no sense. How did Mal hear you calling? Was he on the island? And then he just left you there soaking and took off?"

"Margherita—" Torcuil began.

"No. Torcuil, no. I need to understand!"

"*I* can help you understand . . ."

"I want Lara to tell me, okay? We can discuss your side of things later," I snapped, thinking of what he'd said to me about someone telling him Lara was in peril. And then a wave of guilt overcame me. He'd led me to my daughter. Without him, I would have had no idea that Lara was there. "Look, I'm sorry. I'm just really confused . . ."

"I understand. Believe me, I understand."

"Mum. It's OK. I'll explain."

"Yes. Yes, Lara, tell me. Tell me what happened," I nearly begged.

"Mal had disappeared for days; I told you, remember?" I nodded. "I wanted to see him. I remembered he told me he loves going to Ailsa, so I thought I'd take the little boat . . . you know, the one that's always tied beside the cottages and nobody uses . . . and I went there." She looked at her hands for a second – her palms were a bit red where she'd

243

held the paddles. "I was about to step onto the island when the boat slipped from under me, and I fell. I thought I was going to die . . ." I shuddered. Oh, how close we'd been to the abyss. "The water was so cold and I was so scared . . . and then somebody pulled me up on the shore. It was Mal. He said he'd heard me calling, that he'd come back for me, but now he had to go. He said not to be sad. That nobody lives forever."

I was horrified. "Oh my God. Do you think he threw himself in the lake? And that's why he wasn't there? We need to call the police—"

"No, Mum. He didn't throw himself in the loch. He disappeared. In front of my eyes. One second he was there, the next he wasn't any more."

"But this is not possible!"

"Margherita—"

"Torcuil, let me speak—"

"Margherita! Let Lara rest and recover herself. Enough questions, for now."

I glared at him. There was something in his eyes, something I couldn't read. Something that silenced me.

"I need to go to the remembrance service now. Well, get changed first, I suppose," he said, looking down at his soaking jeans. "I won't be long, just a couple of hours. Will you be okay?"

"Yes. Honestly," I said, looking at Lara. She smiled a serene smile – it was so strange, that she should be serene, even smiling, with all that had happened. Her hair was soft and feathery on her shoulders, her cheeks red from the warmth of the fire.

"Are you sure?"

"Yes, of course," I repeated. "You worked hard for this moment, it's important."

"What remembrance service?" Lara asked.

"A soldier from Glen Avich who died in the First World War. He was finally returned home three days ago. Look, I'll show you." Torcuil rummaged among a pile of papers on the coffee table until he fished out a copy of the *Glen Avich News*. He opened it at the second page and Lara and I leaned in to see.

There was a black and white picture of a man with black hair and light eyes, sitting solemn in his uniform. He looked so young.

"His family home isn't far from your mum's, Margherita. He didn't die in combat. It was pneumonia. He was eighteen. Malcolm Farquhar . . ." Torcuil continued, but a little, nearly inaudible draw of breath drew my attention.

It was Lara, pale once more, her eyes huge, her hands to her lips. I'll never forget what she said after.

"Mum . . . That's Mal."

I argued with her, of course. I told her it was family resemblance, that her Mal was probably somehow related to the Farquhar family and maybe that was why they even shared the same first name.

But Torcuil was quiet. He just kept looking at Lara like he'd seen her for the first time.

38

Beyond the veil

Lara

Dear Kitty,

He's really gone now. But in a way, he isn't.

He said he'll never go away from me. That he'll always be with me.

He told me on Ailsa, just after he saved my life.

So this is what happened.

I knew how to get to the island, because I'd seen it many times, the little boat swaying on the waters, tied to a pole and left there by someone who never seemed to use it. I walked into the waters up to my knees, climbed inside the boat and then freed it from its mooring. I started rowing on – Ailsa sat in the distance, though I could barely make it out because of the mist. It didn't seem that far, but I was scared. I can't even swim; I can barely float. But I *had* to find him. I know you understand that, because you know me better than anyone and you know what's in my heart.

It took me ages to row the small distance. The paddles were so heavy and I didn't really know how to use them, so it took me a while even to figure out how to row in a straight line. I was worried someone from the shore would see me and stop me, but nobody did.

Finally, Ailsa was so close I could have touched its shore – but I couldn't get the boat any closer to the island edge, there were so many reeds in the water, and it was impossible to see how deep the water was. I stood up and tried to jump, but I swayed with the boat – I landed on the reeds, and I thought it'd be okay, but I sank. I couldn't breathe, everything was black – I tried to keep my head above water, but I was so scared I couldn't control my body. The freezing water got into my mouth, into my lungs, and I thought I would die. All of a sudden everything was silent and calm and I started seeing black.

I thought that the last words I'd said to my mum would be *you're not my real mother*, and it made me so sad.

So sad I should die without telling her it wasn't true.

And then someone held me. Someone dragged me onto the shore without effort, as if I were as light as a feather. I found myself lying on my back, spitting water and shivering. When I opened my eyes, my saviour was leaning over me.

It was Mal.

"I'm sorry," he said. "I'm sorry I had to go. But I had no choice."

"But you came back! You saved me . . ." I managed to say in between short, gurgling breaths.

"I could hear you calling. So I came one last time. But I won't be back."

"Why?"

"Because I can't. It's my time to go. Don't be sad. Nobody lives forever, Lara. We are all on a journey, and this is where my journey ends, at last."

"But I don't want you to go."

"I'll always be with you, Lara. Now listen to me. This is what you need to remember . . ."

He bent towards me and his breath was hot on my ear. He whispered three words. And then right there, in front of my eyes, he dissolved slowly, growing more and more transparent, until he was gone.

And then I saw his photograph on Torcuil's magazine. Although it's impossible, I know.

But it looks like the impossible happened. And it explains everything.

My mum says it's family resemblance. Everybody is related around here; it's not uncommon to see similar features, familiar faces. She says that clearly the Malcolm Farquhar who died is an ancestor of my Mal, which is why they look so alike and they share the same name.

I think it's easier for her to believe that.

But I know it's not true.

I now remember all that Mal said to me, about not seeing anyone, about being cold and alone.

I remember what he said about having to go, about no one living forever.

I remember how fragile, how white he looked as he said goodbye to me. How he disappeared in front of my eyes.

But I also remember that he smiled, that he was at peace.

I have no explanation for what I saw.

I know that Mal saved my life.

I know that Mal gave me my first kiss.

I know he said he loved me, and I'll carry those words with me as long as live.

It doesn't matter if they don't believe me. I wouldn't believe me either, if I were in their shoes.

It doesn't matter one bit what they believe or they don't believe, because I know who Mal was and I know what I saw.

It's a mystery. It's a mystery how this happened, how Mal came to me and why – why I saw him and nobody else did.

It's a mystery I keep in my heart.

It's my secret.

★

Torcuil came to see me up at Nonna's house. He brought me a posy of buttercups he'd picked up at the loch. Everyone was down at La Piazza – I was glad of that, because I wanted to speak to Torcuil alone.

"How was the service?" I asked him.

"It was beautiful. People cried . . ."

"There was no reason to cry, really," I said. "He's at peace. He told me."

Torcuil just nodded, and said nothing. Then he started chatting about other things. We shared tea and some cake, and had a good long conversation about everything and anything. All throughout I had a strange feeling, like he was trying to tell me something and he didn't quite know how.

I had questions too, but I didn't know how to ask them. Mum let slip that Torcuil knew I was in trouble, he knew that I was on the loch, and on Ailsa – then she changed her story, that they were having a walk on the loch shore and Torcuil saw the boat.

I tried to ask him, but I just couldn't find the words. And then it was time for him to go. We said our goodbyes and he was already out on the doorstep; I was about to close the door when he put his hand up and stopped the door from closing.

"Lara."

"Yes?"

"I believe you."

That was all he said: *I believe you.*

39

The moment I looked away

Margherita

"How is she?"

"She's fine. At least, I think so. Oh, Mum," I said miserably. "It's all been a bad idea."

"What has been a bad idea?" My mum smiled, placing a cup of strong coffee in front of me. We were in the kitchen of La Piazza, taking a break as Michael held the fort in the shop front. "Because it looks like things are going pretty well from up here."

"Mum, Lara ended up in the loch!"

"Lara took a boat onto the loch. That is all. She's not the first visitor to Glen Avich who's done that, and won't be the last. Luckily you and Torcuil were out there too . . ." I lowered my eyes. I hadn't told her what had really happened – about how Torcuil, mysteriously, knew that Lara was there, or about the mystery surrounding Mal. ". . . and she was fine. She *is* fine. What happened to Lara is not your fault. She did something silly; what teenager doesn't do something silly at some point?"

"Maybe. But I should have been there."

"She's nearly fifteen. You can't be with her all hours of the day. We're not talking about Leo, here."

"She's been meeting a *boy in the woods*, and I didn't stop her!"

"In the woods?" My mum laughed. "What is it, Little Red Riding Hood? She's been meeting her friend outdoors because there's nowhere around here for teenagers to go and get a bit of privacy. You're bound to meet your gran, your auntie, your teacher and a crowd of assorted relatives every time you step out! This is not London!"

"Still—"

"Okay, now, look at it this way. Tell me what this reminds you of. You're fifteen, you're on holiday with your family, you meet a local boy and you start seeing him every day in secret, behind your parents' backs."

"What should it remind me of?"

She laughed. "Does the name Peter bring up any memories?"

Had I not been so upset, I would have smiled.

"Ah, Peter. Yes." I dried my tears and drank a long, comforting sip of coffee.

"We were at that caravan park in Devon, the one we went to quite a few times—"

"Yes, yes. I remember. But it's different for me. I was . . . Mum, I was a *happy* child. You and dad were always there, I was never . . . never . . ."

"I know. Lara had it so much harder than any of us, so she needs a little bit more watching over. But you can't wrap her in cotton wool anyway. I would have loved to do that to you and your sisters, adopted or not! I would have *loved* to be with you all the time, and know exactly where you were and what you were doing and with whom. I never stopped wanting that, really. Even now, I'd like to keep you and your sisters here, in my kitchen, like when you were small. The three of you, you and Anna and Laura all around me, safe where you belong, even if you're all in your thirties and forties! But mothers have to let their children go, bit by bit, until they stand on their own two feet and can make their choices. Lara is no different. She has to learn her own way; she has to fight her own battles."

"This wasn't a battle. This was a *boy*."

"Margherita, listen," she said, suddenly serious.

I raised my head.

"You have to trust her. You have to believe in her."

"Yes."

"She's strong. Like her mother."

"She said I'm not her mother," I whispered, and my heart trembled. The one thing I could never bear: my children rejecting me. I could never, never bear that.

"It was a moment of anger. Every single time she ever called for her mother, she was calling for *you*. The one who's bringing her up."

"Thank you, Mum . . ."

"It's the truth. Drink your coffee, *tesoro mio*."

I obediently took another sip of my mum's espresso, kissing goodbye to sleep for that night.

"As we are here," my mum continued, "don't think I haven't noticed what went on with Torcuil."

I wasn't surprised, but hearing it mentioned aloud made my hang my head. "I know. I know, and—" I was ready to justify myself, but my mum cut me short.

"I haven't seen you so happy in years, Margherita."

"What?"

"Since you came up here. With Lara relaxing a bit, and with this thing starting with Torcuil, though I have no idea if it's serious—"

"I've only been separated six months."

"But you've been unhappy for years."

I hung my head again. She was right.

"You never said. I mean, you never mentioned this before . . ."

"What was I supposed to say? The whole situation was like a . . . like a dandelion. You know, a blow and it's gone. I didn't want to say anything, I couldn't. I had to leave it with you . . ."

I looked down. "So you don't think I made a mistake? To get involved with Torcuil?"

She took a breath. "I think you need to clear it all up inside your head. Then with Ash. And then with Torcuil. But no, I don't think you made a mistake. I've always known how miserable you've been with Ash, for a long time. Anna filled in the gaps for me, you know, when you weren't telling me things."

"You think I made a mistake marrying Ash, don't you?"

"Oh, Margherita! You keep asking me if you've made *mistakes*. I'm your mother, and I know you probably better than anyone else, but I'm not an oracle! If you hadn't married Ash, you wouldn't have adopted Lara and Leo wouldn't have come along. Who knows what would have happened. But you're apart now, you've been apart for months and it doesn't look like you're getting back together any time soon, does it? Who can say what is a mistake and what isn't, if it takes you where you are meant to be?"

"I suppose you're—"

At that moment I heard a voice that stopped me in my tracks, calling me.

I knew that voice.

"Margherita!"

Ash stepped into the kitchen, trailing mud onto the spotless lino floor, rain dripping from his hair, his jacket, his trousers and forming a little puddle of misery on the floor. He was holding Leo's hand. Leo looked confused and vaguely alarmed.

"I came as fast as I could. Where is she? Where's my daughter?"

40

To mend and to break

Margherita

"It's going to rain and we'll get soaked again," Ash complained as we made our way to St Colman's Well.

"Yes, well, there's nowhere else we can talk in private at the moment, and I need to speak to you before you see Lara."

"This doesn't look very private."

"There'll be nobody there."

The truth was, I couldn't face conducting a heavy conversation indoors, the words weighing over our heads as they were spoken.

"Yes. You're right. We need to talk . . ."

"We certainly do," I said, trying to sound steely, but an edge of vulnerability echoed in my voice. And I hated myself for it.

I sat on one of the benches in St Colman's Gardens. The whole of Glen Avich was at our feet, nestled against the hills. He took his place beside me.

"Margherita. This has been a mistake . . ."

He was echoing my own words to my mum, and it was unsettling.

"*What* has been a mistake?"

"Separating. It makes no sense to be apart. It really doesn't—"

"You seem to not remember all that happened, Ash. You being away all the time. Ignoring the children. Saying we would be better off without them—"

"I was wrong."

"Really? Because it sounded like you meant it."

"I was an idiot. I've missed you all so much."

What? "You haven't even phoned me for *weeks*, Ash!"

"I was angry! I was so angry and disappointed. And we fought all the time, Margherita, I couldn't take any more fighting with you. But when Lara called me and told me what happened I realised how stupid I'd been, how selfish."

That much is true, I thought, but I didn't say.

"Did Lara tell you she fell in the loch?"

"Yes. She did. And I don't blame you for not watching her." *Not watching her?* "I don't blame you for a moment . . ." Then why, when I looked into his eyes I felt three inches tall? ". . . but that just shows you, children need two parents. They need a safe environment."

"This *is* a safe environment! And yes, they do need two parents, and you were never there! You didn't even get involved when Lara got into trouble at school!"

"That is all in the past, I told you. We need a fresh start, you and me. Our family deserves it."

"Ash . . ."

"Please, come back. Come back to London and let me move back in."

My head was spinning. It was all too sudden. I jumped on my feet, and he did the same.

"I—"

"I stopped at my mum's on the way here," he added quickly. "I told her I was driving up to see you and bringing you back.

257

That if she wanted me to choose between them and you, I chose you."

"You said *that*?"

"Yes," he said, nodding his head so strongly that his blond mop bounced up and down.

That was the ultimate Ash gesture. His face looked so . . . familiar. I knew his features, his gestures like I knew the back of my hand.

I felt something in me soften.

"You stood up to your mother?"

"Yes, I did. For you. For us. So that Lara and Leo could have a proper family. Let me move back in. Into our home."

"I don't know, Ash. I don't know."

"We've been married for a long time. We have two children. You'd throw everything away like this? Can't you see, Margherita? Can't you see how our family deserves another chance?"

A wave of guilt hit me so I hard I felt sick. I didn't know what to say.

"Please, Margherita. Please, listen to me. My place is with you, and with the children. I'm so sorry for the way I've been. I want things to change. Give me . . . give *us* another chance. Come home."

"We've been so happy here . . ."

"Here?" he said, as if that was completely unbelievable.

"Yes. Here. We never spoke about staying, but I think it's been in the back of our minds. I mean, mine and Lara's. We both love it here in Glen Avich."

"Margherita—"

"Listen, Ash, I need to think. I need to think about all this. It's all been so hard . . ."

"Of course. Of course. Come back and we'll talk about it at home . . ."

To my intense shame, I burst into tears. Ash wrapped his arms around me, and I smelled his scent, the scent of the man I'd been married to for many years and the father of my children.

And I split into two people.

One was the Margherita of today, with all that Ash had done to her, the neglect of his children, the coldness, the bone-chilling indifference of the last few years.

And the other was the woman I used to be, the twenty-five-year-old who loved Ash so, so much. The girl who had so many dreams for her married life.

The second one won, and I melted in tears against his shoulder for a long, long time.

Ash was triumphant when we walked back to La Piazza. I was full of confusion, my thoughts jumbled up and fighting each other, cutting me inside.

We had agreed we would come back to London, but he couldn't move back in yet. I wasn't ready. None of us were.

"We're going to tell Lara," I said to my mum, wearily. Strange, I thought. We should have been celebrating that the family was getting back together. But my mum and Michael looked grey, and Leo hadn't recovered from the surprise of seeing his father after such a long time, without warning. As for me, I felt numb.

"Coming with us?" Ash said to Leo, offering his hand. But Leo shook his head and hid behind my mum's legs. "He just needs a bit of time," Ash said magnanimously.

And so we went to speak to Lara. I dreaded it. I became more and more apprehensive with every step we took, until

I was in a panic. Before we stepped into my mum's house, I held Ash back by the arm.

"Maybe I should speak to her first . . ."

"Why?"

"To ask her what she thinks. To prepare her . . ."

"But we can't let our daughter make a decision on our marriage." He shrugged.

"It's not just a decision on our marriage. It's about the whole family—"

"It's up to us to make the best decision for them! They are *children*!"

"I know, but . . . it's been an enchanted summer for them. And they won't take well to going back. Lara certainly won't."

"How do you know?"

"Because she told me."

"Well, she told me something along those lines too, but she's only fourteen, she can't—"

"She *told* you that? Did you ask her?"

"No, I didn't ask her. She just told me. Just yesterday, when she phoned me to tell me about the accident. I didn't give it that much weight. I told her I wanted you all to come home. She said she loved it here and she hated her school back home, you know, the usual teenage stuff. I wouldn't make a big deal of it."

"How can I not?"

"Because she's a *child*!"

I looked down.

"Margherita . . ." His hand was on mine. "I thought we had made a decision. You know you *must* come back. You know it in your heart of hearts. Your life is with me. Your home is in London."

"We've had such a difficult time, you and me . . ."

"Yes, and I'm so sorry about that. I told you, I've been a fool. But we're going in circles, here. The question is: do you really want to throw it all away? Our family? Our marriage?"

And then I heard myself replying. Out of my head, not out of my heart.

"All right. Let's tell her."

"It'll be fine," he said, and hugged me again.

But the twenty-five-year-old girl and her dreams and hopes were gone again now, and the weight of responsibilities, the desperate need to make the right choices for my children, was back. And his embrace, those arms that should have been as familiar as my mother's, as my children's, felt strange, alien.

I told myself I'd made the best decision for all involved, and I repeated it to myself again and again, ignoring my heart's protestations.

41

The place we call home

Margherita

"Lara!" Ash called, and made his way into my mother's house.

"Dad?" Lara appeared in the hall. She looked very young and very small in her glasses, lost inside her oversized hoodie.

"Hello, sweetheart!" he said, and opened his arms. Lara walked slowly to him and into his embrace.

"What are you doing here?"

"I came to take you back, darling. After you phoned me, yesterday, I just jumped into the car and—"

"You what?"

"Lara—" I began.

"Mum? Are we going back?" she said in a small voice.

"Yes. Your mum and I will try to work things out. We *will* work things out," Ash said in a reasonable voice. I think he wanted it to sound cheerful, but it came out tense, like he was expecting an attack.

And he got one.

"But I don't want to go back. I don't. I told you I wanted to stay in Glen Avich, Dad! You'd say we'd talk about it . . . You said—"

"And we *are* talking about it!" Ash said. "We're telling you we're going back."

"I want to stay here! I want to stay with Nonna. I'm happy

here. I didn't know what happy even *was*. I want to stay! Mum!"

"Lara . . ." I rested a hand on her shoulder to lead her into the living room, but she shook me off. She was shaking with upset.

"You said we'd talk about it, and now you're just *telling* me—"

"Lara. We're all going back to London." I could hear the edge in Ash's voice and I was ready to jump to Lara's defence.

"Ash, why don't you go for a walk or something, Lara and I can talk it through."

"Now you're sending *me* for a walk? Aren't I meant to be present while our future is discussed?"

"I don't want to go back!" Lara shouted, and I looked at her in sudden fear. Was she going to explode? Would she give in to her rage?

I watched her grab a framed photograph from the mantelpiece, her sweet features scrunched up in pain . . .

"Lara!"

For a second I thought she'd throw the photograph at her dad. And then she put it down, slowly, like it was an enormous effort. She looked at me straight in the eye.

"I'm staying," she said calmly, in spite of the trembling of her body. And then she walked out of the front door.

"Where are you going?" I cried out.

"To Inary's," she snapped, and slammed the door.

"I'll get her back." Ash went to follow her, but I stopped him.

"Let her go."

"What? Let her go where? Back to that bloody lake, so she can fall in again?"

"Don't be silly. She's going to see her friend, that's all!"

"Right. Fine. Fine."

He was trying to keep calm, but I could see he was furious. His cheeks were purple.

We walked back to La Piazza and I caught my mum's eye as Ash and Leo were playing in the children's corner. She had a strange expression on her face. Like she was sorry for me.

"Where's Lara?"

"At Inary's."

"Right." Her tone was clipped. I noticed she was very pale.

"She hasn't taken it so well."

"Margherita—"

"Mum, please. I'm confused enough," I blurted out, rubbing my forehead.

"I just wanted to say . . . don't make rushed decisions . . ."

"I'm keeping my family together. That's all," I interrupted. I didn't want to hear.

"And what about you?"

"What about me?" I snapped. Suddenly, my phone chirped. I jumped, hoping it would be Lara, but it was Torcuil.

Lara is here. Don't worry, I'll speak to her and calm her down, then I'll drive her back.

She wasn't with Inary? Why had she gone to Torcuil?

My heart sank. So now Torcuil knew we were going back. He knew that Ash was here.

What a mess. What a terrible, terrible mess.

I was failing everyone, breaking everyone's heart. And for what?

"Who's texting you?" Ash called from the children's corner.

"My boss," I said, and it was partly true. My mum disappeared into the back, her mouth in a thin line. "Lara is with him."

"With *him*? Who is this guy? What do we know about him?"

What do you know about any of us? I wanted to say. But I held my tongue.

"Don't worry. Lara is safe there," I said.

And so was I.

I used to be safe there, at Ramsay Hall.

I'm sorry, I wrote to Torcuil, but there was no reply.

"So, are you happy Daddy is back?"

"Yes!" Leo shouted at the top of his voice, and hung onto his neck. He'd got over the shock and was now loving his father's attention.

Contrasting emotions tore me apart – so strong were the feelings, they were nearly physical. I had to keep the family together, I had to listen to what Lara wanted, I had to give my husband a chance, I had to keep Leo and his father close, I had to do what was *right* . . . but right for who?

I was so proud of Lara for not exploding in rage. So proud of her for not letting her overwhelming emotions get the best of her. And I felt guilty for wanting to take her away from here, guilty for having broken up the family in the first place, guilty about everything . . . What was I to do? Hot tears pressed at my eyes and I fought to keep them in. And then the phone chirped again.

She's staying here for lunch, if that's okay.

Yes. Thank you. Can I come and see you?

I held my breath as I waited for the reply.

I don't think it's a good idea. I'll drive Lara back. You stay where you should be, with Leo and your husband.

I just sat there miserably. Wondering how come, if I was making the right decision, everything felt so totally and completely wrong.

42

And so you see

Lara

Dear Kitty,

This is terrible. My dad is here, and I was sort of happy to see him, though it was strange. But now he wants to take us back and I don't want to return to London. I can't leave Glen Avich. I can't leave this room where I feel like I'm home. I can't go back to my old school and be the weird girl again.

I am staying.

If Nonna wants me, I am staying.

They can't make me go.

So I saw red and I felt this rage coming over me again, but – wait for it – I controlled it! I controlled myself! I couldn't believe it. I was so proud of myself, but the news we were going back to London was too overwhelming to feel good about it. I ran out because I didn't want to see either of them, Mum or Dad. I meant to go to Inary's house, but instead my feet made their own decision and I went to see Torcuil. Maybe because Torcuil understands about Mal, so he would certainly understand about other things as well, I don't know. I don't know why I went to him, but I did.

I ran along the loch shore, and even just looking at Loch Avich broke my heart. I don't want to leave the loch. I don't want to leave Ailsa and the memories of Mal. Every step I took was a beat of my heart, every heartbeat was a song of love for Glen Avich.

I can't help it, Kitty.

I changed so many houses as a child, and I suppose my mum gave me a home in London – but for some reason, this is the first time I truly feel *at home*.

Torcuil was surprised when I turned up at his door alone and in tears, but he let me in anyway. He made me a cup of tea and took me to his study.

The fire was burning. We don't have a real fire in London. The only time I've seen real flames was at Guy Fawkes, at the big bonfire in the park, from half a mile away. If I go back, there will be no more of this – no more sitting at the fireplace, gazing at the flames. No loch, no real fires, no bridge, no La Piazza, no heathery hills and no changing skies. No Nonna, no Michael, no Inary, no Torcuil.

Everything would be gone.

"So. Tell me what's wrong," he said. When he blinks like that, he reminds me a bit of an owl.

"Well, I . . . Torcuil. Listen. There's this question I've got to ask you." I took a breath. "Who told you I was on the loch? Who told you I was in danger?"

"A spirit. A spirit who lives in this house."

A spirit. Oh.

"Okay. Okay." I had to digest that for a moment. "Had it been only last week, I would have thought you were *mental*. But after Mal . . ."

He shrugged. "I see ghosts. I speak to them. You know it can happen, because it happened to you."

"Yes. That's true."

"You have to promise me never to speak about this with anyone, Lara. Nobody in my family talks about this, unless it's to people they really, really trust."

"Nobody in your family? Do you mean there's other people like you?"

"Yes. Inary is one."

"*Inary?*" Seriously? Kitty, I was *shocked*.

"Yes."

"So it runs in your family. Okay. But it doesn't run in mine. At least, I don't think so. Why did I see him then?"

"I don't know. Maybe you called out to each other."

"Does my mum know? About you?"

"No. I was going to tell her. But she's made her choice, now."

I hung my head.

"It's all crazy. It makes no sense. My mum and dad have barely spoken to each other for years! We never saw him. He was just horrible to her. It makes no sense that she wants to go back."

"Maybe she doesn't want to go back to your dad. Maybe she just wants to go back to London."

"She was miserable there. Yes, she had my *zia* Anna, but apart from that . . . I'd got so used to seeing Mum miserable that I'd forgotten what she used to be like. I only remembered when she came up here and I saw her old self coming back. She started cooking again . . . *with her heart*, you know what I mean? With passion. Even her face has changed. She shouldn't go back. I shouldn't either. I hate my school . . ."

"There are many schools in London. You can change."

"I want to stay here. I want to be near Nonna and Michael. It's so beautiful here, and . . . quiet. Magical. I want us to be riding Stoirin and Sheherazade. I want us to be near you."

"I want you all to be near me too, Lara. But your mum has decided otherwise."

We were silent for a moment. The fire was crackling and dancing and I felt like I was dying inside.

"I said to them I'll stay. If Nonna wants me."

"Oh, Lara. Your nonna can't possibly want you to be away from your mum. You know that. It would break your mum's heart. Your nonna will never agree."

"I thought you were on my side!"

"I am! But it's your parents making the decisions. Not me. Listen, I promised your mum I'd fix you some lunch. What about a sandwich?"

"I'm not hungry."

"But I am. And you can't just sit there and watch me eat."

"All right, then," I said.

Torcuil disappeared into the kitchen and came back with a plate full of sandwiches. I took a bite.

"What is this?"

"Spaghetti hoops sandwich. My mother used to make it for us when we were ill or upset. Real comfort food."

Comfort? I would have used another word. I forced myself to down the spaghetti hoops sandwich, so I wouldn't hurt his feelings.

"You can always come back. Twice a year, or so . . ." he said, and he looked more devastated than me, if that's at all possible.

"I'm not going."

"And whenever you return, you can come here and ride Stoirin."

"I'm not going."

"Lara—"

"I thought she liked you." He looked at me with eyes so sad I could have cried, and then he looked down into his half-eaten sandwich.

"I thought she liked me too."

I felt so, so sorry for him.

"So, the spirit who told you where I was. Where is he now? Is he here?"

"Oh yes. He's sitting just beside you."

A sandwich bite just froze in my throat and refused to go down.

"Is he?"

He nodded.

"For real?"

"Yes, I told you."

"Why can't I see him, but I could see Mal?"

"I have no idea."

"Can he hear me if I speak?"

"Yes."

"I'm not going anywhere, do you hear me? I'm staying. I'm staying in Glen Avich, whatever *they* decide. And . . . and thank you."

I was crossing the kitchen's doorstep and stepping into the garden when the fuchsia plant around the door trembled and shook all of a sudden, even if the air was still. A shower of flowers enveloped me.

Torcuil smiled and said nothing.

We didn't speak on the short drive home. A flower fell from my hair and into my lap, and I cradled it in my hand.

271

43

The ocean is too wide to swim (1)

Margherita

Ash checked into the Green Hat, the local hotel. I couldn't have him at the cottage, of course, and my mum made some excuse about not having any rooms ready. She didn't want him there. I left him at the Green Hat and made my way home as quickly as I could, hoping to catch Torcuil when he took Lara home. I wanted to explain.

I was lucky; they were just driving into the street when I arrived. Lara looked mutinous as she stepped out of the car and strode inside – I wanted to stop her, but Torcuil was about to drive away.

"Torcuil!" I called, and, without waiting for his permission, I slipped inside the car beside him.

"Torcuil, please, let me explain—"

"What is there to say? You're going. That's all there is to it," he said without looking at me.

"You knew I was going back. I never said I would stay . . ."

"No, that's true. I just allowed myself to hope. It was my fault."

"He's the father of my children . . ." I whispered.

A moment. He opened his mouth, but nothing came out.

"I'm sorry."

"Can you see it, now, Margherita? Can you see now I was

right, not to let myself go that night?" The bitterness in his voice was like a blade through my heart.

"I'm sorry," I could only say once more as I bled inside.

"I understand. I really do, Margherita," he said softly, and the sudden kindness made it worse. I felt hot tears running down my face, and I didn't even care about hiding them. "Well, I'll have your outstanding wages sent to you. Safe journey back to London," he said, and he leaned across me to open my car door.

I didn't want to go anywhere.

I wanted to stay into that car with him, and not step out and face everyone. Lara's anger. Mum's disappointment. Ash's shortcomings. Leo's confusion.

But I slipped out of the car and I went inside. I went inside to my family, feeling like I'd departed from my body, like the real Margherita was gone forever and only a shell remained.

"Anna, it's me."

"Hey . . . what's wrong? You sound terrible!"

"Did Mum tell you?" I wrapped my free arm around myself – I was sitting on the cobblestones at the back of our cottage, my knees to my chin; a chilly breeze was blowing and my hands were frozen.

"Tell me what? Are you okay? Is everyone okay? Lara? You're scaring me!"

"Sorry," I said, contrite. "Everyone is okay, don't worry. Just, Ash is here . . ."

"He *is*?"

"Yes. When he heard what happened with Lara he just drove up without warning." Anna knew about Lara's accident, though of course I hadn't mentioned Torcuil's strange premonition.

"Right . . . so he's there. And what did he say? What's happening between you two?"

"He said he wants us back. He said he's sorry. He *does* sound sorry . . ." Was I trying to convince Anna or myself? "Anyway, we decided to give it another try. To come back to London now and just . . . yes, give it another try." I shrugged. The stone wall felt hard and cold behind my back and a sweet scent of peat filled the air, like always on chilly evenings.

"But that's good . . . isn't it? Because you don't sound very happy."

"I . . . I don't know. It seems like the right thing to do."

"And Torcuil?"

"Torcuil . . . he didn't take it well." Dismay filled my stomach and I felt like I was sinking.

"No wonder. Does Ash know about . . . you know, about what's been happening?"

"No, of course not! He would never forgive me. It was a mistake anyway."

"Was it?"

She was echoing my mum's words. And that worried me. Of course it had been a mistake – I didn't want anyone to confuse me about that.

"That doesn't matter! It's Lara I'm worried about. She's distraught. She doesn't want to go back. Remember I told you about the business cards, and all the hints she'd dropped . . . but our lives are in London. We can't stay here."

"Why not?"

"Because . . . because our place is with Ash!"

Silence.

"Anna?"

"Yes, I'm here."

274

"What do you think?"

"I think I'll support you whatever you decide."

"It's like you don't particularly want me to come back!" I said childishly.

"I would love for you to come back. But I'd rather you were far away and happy than here and miserable."

"And who says I would be miserable there?"

"Nothing says you would be miserable in London. But Lara will. And there's a lot of evidence that says it's likely, if not sure you'll be miserable with Ash."

"I need to put the family back together, Anna."

"Like I said, I'll support you whatever you decide."

"Okay."

"Just let me know when you're back; I'm coming home in two days so I'll have some groceries there for you."

An image: bread and milk in my fridge. My kitchen. My house. Empty and silent as we returned, a little mound of post on the kitchen table, left there by Anna. Days and weeks and months of the life I used to have before I came here.

"Thank you. I will," I said, forbidding myself from speaking any further, from thinking any further.

The ocean is too wide to swim (2)

Torcuil

I thought nobody ever could live up to Izzy. Even after my feelings for her turned into the love I'd feel for a sister, nobody could live up to her.

Until Margherita arrived.

I tried not to fall for her. And I failed.

How foolish I was, to take such a risk and love again.

I had made a little nest in my heart for happiness, and dared to hope it would be filled. I let her into my life and into my soul, and her children too. Lara, this wonderful, unique girl, and little Leo.

And now I have a hole in my heart.

I wish I'd never loved.

I wish I'd never hoped.

I wish I'd never met her.

And I'm to pay for the mistake I made, this terrible, terrible mistake I made.

My doorstep is covered in fuchsia flowers.

And only ghosts remain.

Every silence has an end

Margherita

I sat on my bed, looking around me at all the things I would have to pack. Ash had taken Leo for a walk in the village.

This life, this temporary life I'd materialised like a red handkerchief out of a magician's hat, had to be folded back into itself and taken away, taken back where it belonged. Or disappear altogether.

With my mind's eye, I saw how the little cottage would look after we went. I saw it empty, the fairy lights unplugged, the beds unmade and covered so they wouldn't get damp, the curtains drawn.

Our little cottage, our home for the summer, would be hollow again – without Lara's blossoming soul, without Leo's sunniness, without me.

And I thought of our house in London. I tried to picture myself unpacking there, taking ownership of the place again, spilling my energy and my belongings into it once more. I tried to imagine Lara in her room with the flower stickers, and Leo on the wooden floor in the conservatory, playing with the fire engine he'd bought in Peggy's shop. It would be warm at this time of year. We'd be digging our summer clothes out, the proper ones, not the Scottish summer clothes. There would be no wind; the sky would be blue.

I tried to picture all that, and I couldn't. My mind went blank, and all I could see were the hills outside my window, silent and eternal under a cloudy sky.

I stood and walked to the mantelpiece, where the white pebble Torcuil had given me lay on top of the business cards Lara had made for me. I slipped the pebble into my pocket. I never wanted to part from it.

And then I looked at the cards again, their white and blue promise:

Margherita Ward
Catering and Cakes
Italian Recipes and More
c/o La Piazza
Glen Avich

All of a sudden, angry voices reached me from the courtyard. Lara. Mum. I ran out, alarmed.

"I'm staying. If you want me, I'm staying!" she was screaming.

My mum was distraught. "*Tesoro*, please calm down—"

"Do you not want me, Nonna? You don't want me with you?" She was crying.

"Of course I do, but your mum—"

"I don't care! I'm not going back to those stupid people and that stupid school!"

"Lara . . ." An abyss opened in my heart. How could Leo and I ever be away from her? How could the three of us be separated?

"What is going on here?" Ash had walked through the French doors.

"Lara! Don't cry!" Leo held on to her legs.

Lara looked at him with a tear-strewn face. "I'm not coming with you! This is what's going on!"

And then Ash came to our rescue. He saved us all. Lara, me, Torcuil.

He sorted things out for us.

He spoke to Lara.

He said something that made it all clear for me.

"For God's sake, Lara! Since we adopted you you've given us nothing but grief!"

The second the words came out of his mouth, he paled.

The thing with real life is, you can't rewind. You can't delete. When words are out, they are out, and they can never been taken back.

I watched in horror as Lara's face fell, and I felt hatred.

Something I never thought I could feel for anyone, let alone my husband. But I did, I felt pure hatred because he hurt my daughter, my sweet, vulnerable, fragile Lara, who was fighting a battle harder than he or I would ever have to fight. She ran inside the cottage, and I wanted to run to her, but first I had to finish something.

Silence fell upon me as I turned towards Ash, and everything broke into a million little pieces – the earth and the sky and my heart.

What was said couldn't be unsaid.

Ash's white skin was even whiter as he stood in front of me. It looked like he was about to cry.

"I want you to go," I said simply.

"Look, I'm sorry I said that—"

"I want you to go."

There was nothing more eloquent I could say.

From repentant, his face turned wrathful once more. His mouth was in a thin, tight line, his hands in fists at his sides. His voice was icy. "You're coming with me."

And there he was, my husband – no, not my husband. This was the man he'd turned into in the last few years. The same Ash who'd driven us away. The edge to his voice, the coldness in his eyes.

How strange that a memory of starting our life together should come back to me now, after I hadn't thought about it for years. A trip to Lake Garda, right after we got together. A bench in the sunshine, in front of the shimmering waters – my head on his lap – his hands resting on my body comfortably, one on my hair, the other on my stomach, like they just belonged there – the orange light behind my eyes.

His voice vibrating through his body and through mine, before it even got to my ears, my love for him, absolute, complete, beyond all differences, beyond our families' bewilderment at our respective choices, beyond any obstacle we might ever face. What happened to that man and that woman entwined together in the sunshine, convinced it would last forever? Who would have ever thought that twelve years later we would stand in front of each other in the middle of a Scottish village, on a drizzly summer afternoon, and the sun would be nowhere to be seen?

"You're coming with me!" he repeated.

For the first time in the twelve years I'd known him, I realised where I'd seen that coldness before: in his mother's face. I'd always thought he'd been a victim of his mother, and in a way he was, but now, all of a sudden, I could see how similar they were.

He strode towards me, heat and anger seeping out of his body. We were so close, and he looked enraged – he towered over me. But I wasn't intimidated, I wasn't afraid.

"We are not going anywhere with you," I said calmly.

At last. At last I knew my own mind. At last I could see clearly what was best for all of us – my children and myself.

"She said she wants you to go." It was Michael, and my mum was behind him with her mobile in her hands. I realised she'd texted him and he'd run down from La Piazza as fast as he could. "And I want you out of my house too."

"Just go, Ash," my mum said. "You've hurt them enough. My daughter, and *your* daughter."

Lara walked out of the cottage and came beside me, our bodies moulding against each other like the unit we were, our arms around each other. I could smell her fear, her upset – an acrid, pungent scent like a small injured animal. My heart bled, wondering how I could heal the words Ash had said to her, wondering why I'd let him hurt her again. Why I had grown so confused, so torn, when what was right for all of us was now laid in front of me, so clear, so obvious.

"I won't go without my family," Ash declared, gazing at each of us in turn, making a big show of his statement. But his voice was shaking. I could see his conviction ebbing away as he sensed us closing ranks.

As he sensed that a shift had happened inside me, inside Lara.

That things could never be the same again, not this time.

"I am not your family," I said, and I saw the words cutting him, and they cut me too.

And then it happened.

A torrent of threats and insults, pouring out of his mouth

281

into the peace of my mother's house; Michael raising his voice; Lara and I huddled into each other; my mum silent and white-faced while our husbands shouted at each other.

My heart cried for lost love and the broken pieces of a family.

Softly, gently, I untangled myself from Lara. The air was dense with aggression, but I felt removed from it all, like Michael's and Ash's voices were coming from far, far away. In my mind there was silence as I walked into my mother's house, careful not to brush against Ash as I passed him. My eyes met my husband's, and suddenly he was silent. He turned as if led by an invisible force. His eyes never left mine as he followed me and then stepped out onto the street.

We both knew it was the end.

Lara and I were in her room, both drained, both shaken. She stood in front of the window, her arms crossed, her body tense. When she turned around I could see that her eyes were red-rimmed, but dry. She wasn't crying any more.

"I'm sorry, Lara. I'm so sorry for what he said to you . . . He's gone now."

"I don't want to go back to London, with or without Dad."

"No. We are not going. We are not going anywhere, I promise you."

"I want to stay here."

"I know. I know . . ."

"So we are staying?"

"Yes. Yes, we are. Please, don't worry. There's no need to worry any more."

An imperceptible sigh left her lips. I could feel her relaxing; I could feel it on my skin and in my heart.

"Mum, what he said—"

"Just forget about it, forget everything he ever said—"

"How can I forget? He's my dad!"

I took my face in her hands and locked my eyes on hers. "Since you came into my life you have brought me nothing but joy, Lara. Not grief. Joy. This is the truth. Not what Ash said . . ." I couldn't bear to say *your dad*. "That was just a lie. He had no idea what he was talking about."

"Really?"

"Really."

She came into my arms like the little girl she used to be, without any more words. As I hugged her, I noticed that there was something dark pink in her hair. A fuchsia flower. I knew where it came from.

I held her closer, and I prayed, I prayed I could make everything all right again.

46

Voices

Margherita

Ash was gone, with vague threats of lawyers and of making me pay. His words had no weight for me; they were like echoes of what was important once, but now meant nothing. I had my children, a home, and a profession I could go back to. I was unafraid.

It was two in the morning and I couldn't sleep. I looked outside at the cold, black hills, and I longed to just step out and walk, walk, walk all the way to Ramsay Hall, all the way to Torcuil. I was so afraid to tell him we were staying. So afraid that he would not forgive me, that he would send me away even if I'd decided to stay in Glen Avich.

Maybe I deserved it.

The pull of my husband, the emotional blackmail about keeping the family together and doing my duty and sticking to my vows, had been too strong to resist.

But I'd come to my senses. Surely I deserved a second chance?

Or did I, after the way I'd hurt him?

I tiptoed into the bathroom – the only place where my phone worked – to text him, maybe even to whisper a phone call to him. But I changed my mind. I was too frightened of his reply.

I threw a cardigan over my shoulders and walked across to my mum's house to make myself a cup of coffee. Oh, how I would have just loved to go to him, in my nightie and slippers, to say I was sorry, to say I knew what to do now.

To say I would never go away again.

But how could I?

I sat at the kitchen table in the darkness, thoughts whirling in my mind so hard it hurt. Finally, I was so exhausted that I dragged myself back to bed and fell asleep. I woke up with a jolt again an hour later – six in the morning.

I couldn't wait any more.

I threw on a pair of jeans, a T-shirt and my fleece, and I ran through to my mum's house. She was in the kitchen already, making coffee.

"You're up early," she said as she saw me. "Are you okay?" She lifted a hand to touch my face.

"Yes. I'm okay. Only . . . do you mind if I go for a walk? Leo and Lara are still asleep."

If she was thrown, if she suspected something, she didn't say. "Of course. You go, I'll be here when the children wake up."

I ran all the way. As I passed the bridge, the soft drizzle falling from the sky turned into a downpour and soaked me to the bone, but I didn't care. I just wanted to make things right.

Torcuil's eyes were heavy with sleep as he opened the door.

"Hello," I said, and nothing else came out. All the words were frozen in my throat. I just stood there, soaked, gaping, my hair dripping on his doorstep.

"Come in, come out of the rain. You are drenched . . ." he said, and his eyes weren't hard any more, not like yesterday. Just very sad. "Have you forgotten something?"

"I'm not leaving."

"What?"

"Ash is gone. I'm staying. We are staying."

He said nothing.

"I can't go back to him. And Lara doesn't want to leave here. And I don't want to leave here, and I'm so sorry, so sorry . . ."

Torcuil didn't let me say any more. He just wrapped me in his arms, holding me tight.

He wasn't sending me away.

Relief swept through me, and I held on to him with all my strength. Right at that moment, I felt a stir above me, and a warm breeze wrapped itself around me for a moment, tugging at my clothes, playing with my hair.

But we were indoors.

"Torcuil?"

"Mmmm?" he said into my hair.

"What was that?"

"A draught."

"It wasn't a draught."

"No, okay, it wasn't."

"So what was it?"

"I'll tell you after."

"After what?"

"After this."

He took my hand, and led me to his room.

We lay entwined in the morning light, my hair spread across his chest, our breaths in unison. My world had ended and a new one had begun. But I had questions that were still unanswered, and they were tugging at me.

"How did you know?" I whispered. He knew at once what I was talking about.

"I feel things sometimes," he said, and stroked my hair slowly. "I've been like this since I can remember. It runs in the family."

"You *feel* them? Like a ... a psychic?" I couldn't quite believe I was even saying those words. I'd never believed in anything supernatural. Never.

But I recalled all that had happened in the house. Things disappearing, changing place. And the warm breeze embracing me in the kitchen, when we'd reconciled. And, of course, the way he knew about Lara.

"Not really. I see spirits. And they tell me things."

"So when you said there are ghosts in this house—"

"I meant it," he said, and glanced at me warily, waiting for my reaction.

Okay. That was a lot to take in. I sat up, holding the sheet around my body.

"For real?"

"Yes. We call it the Sight."

"You see *spirits*?"

He nodded. "Look, I know it's a lot to wrap your head around—"

"Why?"

"What do you mean why? Why I see them? I don't know why. It's a family thing."

"A family thing? So your parents, and Angus ... and Inary! What about Inary?"

"No, my parents and my brother and sister don't have the Sight."

I studied his face. "But Inary ..."

"It's up to her to tell you."

"She does! She *does*!"

I took a few moments to digest everything. "You think Lara was right. You think it really was Malcolm Far— Farquhar she saw? Not his grandson, or something." I struggled with the Scottish name.

"Yes. Yes I do."

"Why?"

"Another why?" He laughed feebly. But I wasn't laughing. "Why did she see him? I don't know. Maybe she has it in her. Or maybe she was calling to someone and Mal answered. Who knows?"

"Oh my God. This is crazy!"

"Look. How else did I know about Lara being in trouble? And that she was on Ailsa?"

"Torcuil . . ."

"Margherita." He took my face in his hands, and he was deadly serious. "I'm only going to say this once. And I want you to look into my eyes while I do. I'm telling you the truth. I see ghosts, and they speak to me. Lara *did* see Malcolm Farquhar. I believe her. And you have to believe me."

His eyes looked so clear. So honest.

But what he'd said made no sense. It just was impossible.

And still, I believed him.

Yes. I believed him.

"So, what do you say?"

"I say you are crazy, and so am I because I think you're telling the truth," I heard myself saying.

He took a sigh of relief and held me tight. His skin against

288

my skin was warm and infinitely soft. "I was so worried about telling you."

"And Inary is the same? She has the . . . Sight too?"

"Yes. Have you read her first book?"

"*The Choice?* Yes."

"Well, she didn't make that story up. Mary told her."

"Mary, the protagonist, who'd died long before we were born."

"Right."

"Oh, God. Does anyone else know about your Sight? I mean, apart from Inary and me."

"My mother, my siblings, and one more person."

"Isabel?"

"No. Lara," he said decisively.

"Lara? As in, my daughter Lara?"

"Yes. I told her yesterday when she came to me after you'd told her you were going back to London."

"And she believed you?" As I asked the question, I gave myself the answer: of course she would! Lara was forever looking for magic in the world around her; she was the one whose imagination coloured everything.

"Yes. I mean, she'd just seen one herself."

"Oh my God," I said, and took my face in my hands. Maybe my daughter was like them. How would I know? I never met her biological family. Maybe they were all like that. Or maybe it was a one-off.

Oh, let it be a one-off.

"Don't worry. It might not happen again. Or she might have a very interesting time ahead of her . . . Anyway, there's something else I need to tell you." He fixed his eyes on mine and we felt closer than ever.

"What else, now? There's a monster in the loch?"

"I don't know. Maybe there is. But what I had to tell you is that I'm in love with you."

Later, much later, we stood on the doorstep of Ramsay Hall. I was about to walk back to my mum's house and to my children. I was so happy that the bliss turned to fear around its edges. Maybe now I knew what Lara meant when she said she was afraid of happiness.

And still, there I was, and my heart was alive like it hadn't been in years.

"So when did you say you were going to move in with me?"

"What? Not today anyway," I said with a smile.

"No, that's right. It's too soon. Next week?"

I laughed, and my laughter resounded through the grounds of Ramsay Hall in a sudden silence and a strange echo. It was like the whole house breathed, an immense, all-encompassing breath of relief.

Thank you, I whispered silently, though I wasn't sure who exactly I was thanking.

Days of the dancing

Margherita

When I walked from the purple dusk into the light and music, the ballroom was glimmering and twirling with dancers and lights. It seemed impossible that Ramsay Hall had begun to emerge from its decay and that this ball was just the beginning. There was a long way to go before we could open properly to the public, and it would take time – but it would happen. Finally, Torcuil had started to believe in Ramsay Hall and its potential again, and he had contacted the National Trust for Scotland for support; with their help, we were on our way. A representative from the Trust was there tonight, Anne – she was standing beside Torcuil with a glass in her hand and a smile on her face. She had fallen for Ramsay Hall's charm and she would help us bring it back to life. I felt so proud that all my hard work had contributed to making this happen – that I had been a part of this.

Our eyes met, and she lifted the glass in my direction; I smiled back, and then my eyes went to Torcuil beside her, as if in spite of all that light, everything was dim to my eyes but his face. He glanced at me from across the floor; then he turned to Anne and murmured something, and walked towards me, his eyes never leaving mine, like we were drawn towards each other by an invisible ribbon tied to our wrists.

"Come," he whispered into my ear and led me away, through the busy hall and outside, back into the summer twilight. I knew that more than a few people would notice we'd made our way out, but neither of us cared.

Torcuil took me across the garden and onto the grass, wet with the evening dew, and, finally, under the trees and away from curious glances. We stopped and wrapped our arms around each other seamlessly, as if of one mind, and for a moment the whole situation seemed so surreal, so thoroughly impossible, that I felt disconnected from myself. It was like I was watching myself from above, this woman who made changes and took brave decisions and followed her heart. Two months ago I had been standing in my bedroom in a London suburb, wondering how my life could have tumbled away from me the way it had, and turned into something I didn't recognise and didn't feel mine. And now I was somewhere in Scotland, in the arms of a man who wasn't my husband and still seemed to know me and understand me so much better than Ash ever had.

I remembered what Torcuil had said to me only a few weeks ago – a lifetime ago, it seems – about life being like a film or a novel, minus the happy ending. But our happy ending was just there, ready for us to grab and make it ours.

"You set me free," he whispered in my hair.

I pulled back just a bit to look into his face. I was going to say, "You set me free too." But it didn't sound right.

Because it wasn't true.

He hadn't set me free – I'd set *myself* free.

So I didn't say anything. I just kissed him, and in that kiss there was something I hadn't felt in a long time. The possibility of more love in my life, and a different one from that of my children. The chance to love again – to let this feeling bloom and grow in my heart. The chance that everything might be well.

His hand pressed the small of my back and his kiss was tender and slow – from Ramsay Hall came the distant sound of music – the fresh, pine-scented breeze blew in my hair and on my bare shoulders – everything came together in my heart like a symphony of happiness.

Yes, I'd set myself free, and there was a new life in store for me.

We slipped inside, my cheeks tingly from the evening chill. From the windows in the ballroom I could see night slowly falling after an endless summer evening. The music was in full swing and the girls and women looked like dancing roses in their evening gowns: and there she was, my daughter, chatting with Inary. She wore the dress we'd chosen together, shimmery and off-the-shoulder and showing off her long legs. Her hair fell in rich, golden waves and her skin glowed – her young beauty was a joy to behold – but what made me so happy was what emanated from her, a sense of joy, of confidence that I'd never seen in her before. Our eyes met across the room and she smiled at me, a smile that was a woman's and a child's at the same time – blooming with promise, but also somehow innocent, enchanted.

My Lara.

A small crowd of people surrounded her all of a sudden. Two boys and two girls, dressed in kilts and evening gowns. One of the girls had braces and the boys looked awkward, both of them tomato-red as they approached Lara. Inary made her excuses and left Lara with her new friends – our eyes met across the hall, and she nodded slightly, smiling.

My mum was at my side – she saw me watching Lara, and she took my arm to attract my attention. "That's Madison . . . oh, and Rebecca Paterson. I know their parents. The boys are Davy and Calum Munro. They all go to Kinnear High School. They will be in the same class as Lara."

The schools had already reopened in Scotland, but Lara would only be a week late and the head teacher of Kinnear High had reassured me that it wasn't going to be a problem.

I watched Madison and Rebecca smile and chat to Lara, with the boys grinning and looking on, and my heart warmed. After a while, Lara made her way to me. Her cheeks were rosy and her eyes were shining.

"I'm going to hang out with them next weekend," she said.

"That's great."

"I have a good feeling about my new school."

"Yes. I have a good feeling too," I said as the band, with Angus among them, jumped into a joyful, crazy reel. The music made my heart sing. It wasn't long before Torcuil made his way back to me and wrapped an arm around my waist, without caring who saw.

My butterfly summer had drawn to an end, and my whole life had changed. The days of looking at myself in the mirror and not recognising the woman I saw were over, as my head and my heart aligned again, and I felt I was where I was meant to be, with the people I loved.

I recalled something I'd thought when I first arrived in Glen Avich: that I was hoping for a new Margherita to come to life. But now I realised that what I'd been looking for wasn't a new me, it was the *real* me.

All I had to do now was live my life.